# WINTER OF FAITH
# COLLECTION

RACHEL STOLTZFUS

Note: This book was previously released in 2014. The updated edition has been revised and edited with additional content added.

ISBN: 1530142261
ISBN-13: 978-1530142262

# TABLE OF CONTENTS

# ACKNOWLEDGMENTS

I have to thank God first and foremost for the gift of my life and the life of my family. I also have to thank my family for putting up with my crazy hours and how stressed out I can get as I approach a deadline. In addition, I must thank the ladies at Global Grafx Press for working with me to help make my books the best they can be. And last, I thank you, for taking the time to read this book. God Bless!

# WINTER STORMS

## CHAPTER ONE

Miriam Beiler shivered as she trotted towards the barn to help her *daed* with feeding the livestock and milking their cows. As she walked swiftly towards her goal, she buttoned her coat more securely around her pulling it up around her neck and cheeks until she entered the barn. She could see her breath in white, cloudy patches as she walked, and her hands ached slightly in spite of being covered. While she liked winter with all of its beauty and starkness, the cold against her face and the wind a bit chill, she didn't care for it when it got this cold.

"Good, daughter, you're here. It's cold, isn't it?" Miriam's father looked up smiling. Joseph Beiler had seen many winters in his day, each unique and different in many ways while in other ways exactly the same. The frigid air and unrelenting chill was one thing that he was very accustomed to, although as he aged parts of him withstood it without some pain and creaking. He didn't mind, though. The simple lifestyle he led was enough for him, and his satisfaction with the health and well-being of his family always bolstered his faith in how God handled things correctly.

"*Ya, daed*, it is. And it's getting colder, and the wind is blowing harder, too," Miriam said glancing outside as she grabbed a bucket for milking.

"*Ya*, this winter will be a hard one. I can feel it in my arm," Joseph said, massaging his left arm which he had hurt several years earlier in a carpentry accident. While the accident was long in the past, the pain and arthritis it wrought stayed with him still. He grimaced when he moved it.

"*Daed,* ask *mamm* for something to wipe on your arm," Miriam said. "You're rubbing it again, so the cold and wind are really something fierce."

"*Ya, denki,* daughter. I will. Let's get this work done so we can get into a warm house faster."

Miriam snuggled her cheek against the cow's warm side and, after washing her bag of milk and teats, began pulling, coaxing the warm, foamy milk out. After they had milked all twelve of their cows, they fed and watered them, then began mucking out the stalls for their two horses. After feeding and watering them, Joseph closed the barn's doors securely, keeping the warmth inside. Placing one hand on Miriam's shoulder, he walked swiftly with her to the house. As they walked, Joseph looked around. Seeing a dark bank of clouds off in the distance, he stopped Miriam.

"Miriam, look . . . to the north and east. See that dark line of clouds? We are in for a winter storm. A bad one," he said, absently rubbing his arm again.

"*Daed*, I'm worried. Tomorrow's meeting day. What if it starts storming while everyone's here?" Her father sometimes called her a worry-wart, and in some ways she agreed. So much had happened to her in her short life that she sometimes fought anxiety. Her *daed* said to pray for peace of mind, and many times those quiet reflections worked. But, not all the time. She looked at her father raising her eyebrows, tightening her mouth slightly giving her face a taut, rigid appearance.

"All we can do is all we can do. That, and put our faith in the Lord. *Ach*, this wind is stiff, isn't it? Let's go . . . inside, where it's warm and your *mamm* has a hot supper ready." Still, he paused, disregarding his own words, silently measuring the falling temperature, the stiff wind and the clouds in the far-off distance.

She had seen that look on his face before, right before a large storm came through. It seemed as though he could feel it coming even before it became a reality. Something in his bones told him, he would sometimes say. But most times he was silent, looking into the distance as if he could see and grasp the storm somehow. "It will be what it will be." That was usually the end of what he would say about his weather feelings.

\*\*\*

At the Fisher farm, Samuel and John Fisher felt the same sharp cold and stiff winds as they finished their work day. Both men pulled their jackets closer around their bodies as they worked to feed their livestock.

"Get the milk into the machine so we can get inside," Samuel grunted against the cold. His stout frame had seen many a winter, but even with experience the cold was the cold. He pulled his hat down and pushed his scarf up raising his collar and burying his beard in the warm spot it created. His cheeks and nose were red,

"*Daed*, it's gotten colder just since we came out here a few minutes ago. This won't be a good winter, will it?" John usually wanted some kind prediction of things to come, and he always thought his father could provide it.

"*Nee*, John, it won't. It will be a very hard winter . . . very hard. Plan to do a lot of work inside here or inside the house – more than usual," Samuel smiled at him. He was better at predicting coming weather than his son, but it was something he learned over time. Not to be in any way prideful; it was just an experience of things and the aches and pains that went with it.

"*Ya*. It will be bad. Worse than last winter . . ." Plain living was the best kind of lifestyle around; it was not always easy, but it was pure. Weather changes like these simply tested your resolve, built character and made you strong. Even though the wind was biting it was also bracing, refreshing and clear. As things got colder, the warmth of the house and all of the hot foods served tasted even better. John loved the cold weather and the challenges it brought with it. Anyone could be inspired to work in the spring when the fields were alive and the breezes warm. It was in the winter months when things were harsher, that character was built and bodies were made strong against the elements.

"Don't forget, son, last winter, and the two before that were all mild for this area. We got snow, but the winds and cold didn't start this early. It's barely November," Samuel interrupted his reverie. John marveled at his father's strength; he had endured the winters for years like they were nothing to withstand. He had grown up, grown rock-solid and stood tall against the weather. John wished himself as strong when he reached his father's age.

***

Joseph and Miriam continued talking as they trotted toward the warmth of the Beiler kitchen. "I just hope the storm holds off until services are over and everyone has returned home". Miriam's father took in the site of the other men unloading frowning slightly. He changed course heading towards the men working. "*Ach,* tell your *mamm* that the men are here to help unload the benches and arrange them. Start supper without me, and I'll be inside before too long,"

"I will. *Denki*," Miriam said, hurrying past him and inside their house. She stopped, waved and smiled after her father's disappearing form. She knew he was tired and that his arm was sore, but he would never shirk his duty to work, not even when the weather was cold or if his joints were aching. She would make sure that *mamm* had that rub ready when he came in so that he could relieve the soreness in his arm and sit down to a nice hot meal and a bit of relaxation.

Joseph returned to the barn to help three other men begin removing the long, wooden benches from the back of the wagon. "Wait. It's getting much too cold. Let's arrange these in the house. We have the space. No sense in having service outside if it's going to be this cold."

They reloaded what had been unloaded and moved the wagon to the front of the house. They removed the benches and took them inside, positioning them in several rooms inside the sprawling Beiler home. By the time they finished, benches filled the living room, quilting room and the length of the long hallway.

"Miriam told me it's getting pretty cold out there. I'm glad we rearranged furniture when we cleaned," Sarah Beiler gestured towards the table inviting them to sit and eat.. "Sit down while the food's still hot. Come on, there's enough for everyone," My mother generally cooked enough should company come, and her meals were well known for being some of the best in our community. As a result, it didn't take much convincing to get the men to sit down to eat.

When they were done, Miriam busied herself cleaning up while her father bid the others a good night. *"Denki,* for your help. We will see you bright and early tomorrow!" Everyone left smiling, pulling their jackets close together for the long, cold trip home. They lowered their hats against the wind, smiling as they left.

***

Early the following day, Miriam arranged her light-brown hair neatly, pinning it into a bun at the back of her head. Smoothing strands of hair back, she set her black prayer *kapp* on her head. Looking down at her dress and snowy-white apron, she made sure she was neat and presentable. Satisfied, she ran downstairs to help her *mamm* with a hot breakfast. After they had eaten and washed dishes, she and Sarah rearranged the large countertop and refrigerator. Sarah turned the gas oven on so the hot foods could stay warm as families brought them inside.

Miriam, hearing knocks at the front door, ran to start welcoming families inside, directing the wives and girls to put their lunch contributions in the kitchen.

In the kitchen, Sarah was doing the same. She paused as she saw 14-year-old Hannah Miller walk slowly into the house – Hannah's cheeks were flushed with more than the cold outside, and her eyes were glassy. Sarah shot a sharp look at Hannah's mother, Mary.

"Is Hannah ill?" she asked Mary.

"*Ya*, but it's only a cold. She told me she feels well enough to be here," Mary responded, taking her long scarf from around her neck.

"I hope you're right – that looks like more than just a cold," Sarah replied quietly.

As the two women talked, Hannah sat listlessly on a bench in the hallway. Sarah glanced at her, noting her drooped head and slumped posture. Her eyes sharpened when she saw Hannah jump from the bench and run to the bathroom.

*This is more than a cold. I hope it's not the flu.*

By the time Hannah returned to the bench, Bishop Stolzfus had begun the service delivering the day's lesson in a sing-song High German dialect.

Sarah, hearing Hannah's dry cough, sighed. "Hannah, sit here. You don't want to make anyone else ill." She directed the girl to a kitchen chair she turned around. Hannah seemed grateful for the chair with a back, and she sank into it gratefully. Sarah got her some tea with honey and sat down next to her. Hannah had always been a sunny, happy child; now, she seemed almost a ghost, a waif who didn't speak. Her only sounds were the hacking cough muffled by her hand covering her mouth. The light and sparkle in her gaze was gone, and she looked at Sarah with blank, staring eyes that seemed almost out-of-focus.

"Is everything all right at your home." Sarah placed a reassuring hand on the girl's knee. "Can I do something for you?" The girl's eyes widened, her eyebrows going up in surprise, and if Sarah wasn't mistaken, fear. Her eyes drifted into the gathering area where her husband was sitting, eyes locking on and staring at him. She opened her mouth as if she was about to speak, then closed them shaking her head quickly back and forth in the negative. She lowered her head taking another sip of tea.

"If you need anything at all, just let me know. I will always be here for you." Sarah didn't know why she said that to the girl, but she felt compelled to say it.

"Denki." Sarah barely heard her reply; it was so soft.

# CHAPTER TWO

Rachel Zook, hearing Sarah's quiet words, looked at Hannah, then at her son, Adam. Worry filled her eyes. Adam had been diagnosed with asthma two years earlier and she had been told to keep him from others who were sick with colds and flu, which could be worse for him. Seeking and finding her husband on the men's benches, she kept looking at him until he felt her gaze. When he turned around, she silently motioned that she was sending Adam to sit with him. Michael quickly spotted the reason for Rachel's look of worry. He nodded and motioned Adam to sit with him.

After the day's message had been given, along with several announcements, the meeting finally ended. Several men rearranged the benches, creating picnic benches with long tables that had been set in the kitchen entryway.

The women glanced at each other, talking about the coming storm. They were glancing outside, seeing the dark-gray clouds, heavy with snow as they raced to cover the pale-blue sky.

"Let's hurry and serve everyone – it wouldn't do to have anyone outside when this storm hits," Sarah said briskly.

The women arranged themselves so they could move platters to the long tables. The first shift, composed of the oldest members of the community and the men, sat down, dishing up their plates. When they were done, girls collected dirty plates, glasses, cups and silver, setting out clean ones. Children sat down next.

Sarah looked outside and her heart stilled – it was snowing heavily. Looking for Joseph, she motioned to the kitchen window with her eyes. He saw what she was telling him.

Finally, the women were able to sit down. Eating quickly, they moved as one into the kitchen so they could wash platters, serving dishes and dishes. Sarah glanced outside once more – this was no good. The storm was even heavier now, and the wind was picking up. Squinting, she tried to spot the carpentry shop – all she could see was a faint outline of one corner. She stopped breathing momentarily as a sharp gust of wind took the snowflakes, moving them horizontally.

"Sarah, Bishop Stoltzfus wants to talk to us," Joseph said quietly into Sarah's ear.

Sarah motioned to Miriam to take her place then followed Joseph into the cold entryway.

"Mr. and Mrs. Beiler, I am worried about allowing anyone

to drive home in this storm. It's too dangerous. Horses could go snow-blind and go off the road," said the bishop.

"Bishop, we can put everyone up here," Joseph offered. "We have enough room – we might need blankets, though, but if we double families, with women and children upstairs and men downstairs, we could do it."

"*Ya*, we would need more blankets. We have seven bedrooms," Sarah said.

"That's settled, then. *Denki*. There is no sense, allowing families to travel in this blizzard. I will tell everyone," the bishop said.

# CHAPTER THREE

Sarah turned her head sharply, seeing Hannah bolt up from her chair once again. Following her to the downstairs bathroom, she grimaced as she heard the sounds of Hannah's vomiting behind the locked door. She decided to wait until Hannah emerged.

"*Mamm*? Is that Hannah Miller in there? She didn't look good at all this morning. The only time she perked up was when she saw Joshua Lapp walk in with his family," Miriam said.

"Daughter, I'm worried that she has the flu. Her *mamm* says it's just a cold, but you don't throw up with 'just a cold,'" Sarah said drily.

"Oh, no. What are you going to do? We have so many families here . . . it's bound to be contagious, and we're going to have several sick people here until this storm ends," Miriam said with worry lining her voice.

"Trust in the Lord, my daughter. He will protect us. In the meantime, we can do a little protection of our own. Hannah and her mother will get the back bedroom upstairs to themselves. Everyone else will have to double up. Oh. Make sure that Adam and Rachel Zook are put in the room farthest from Hannah. No need to put him in any danger," Sarah instructed. "Please bring Mary Miller here. I'm not happy that she and Hannah put the entire community at risk of the flu, particularly now that we're forced to wait this blizzard out."

"*Ya.* I'll find her and bring her here," Miriam said.

Sarah, still waiting for Hannah to come out of the bathroom, shifted her feet impatiently. Seeing Miriam and Mary approaching, she fixed the other woman with a sharp look.

"Mary, this is much more than 'just a cold.' Hannah has vomited twice already. That doesn't happen with a cold. *Ach,* here she is! Hannah, are you feeling better?" Sarah asked.

"*Nee.* Worse. My body hurts. My head aches and I feel exhausted," Hannah said quietly. Tears trembled at the corners of her eyes as she tried to keep them from falling.

"Sarah, she only has a . . ." Mary started to say.

"Mary! I worked as a vocational nurse before marrying Joseph. She has vomited twice already. The symptoms she's spoken of match those of flu."

"Oh . . . I was sure that it was only . . . " Mary began.

16

"*Nee. Nee, nee, nee.* Are you aware that Adam Zook was diagnosed with asthma two years ago? That, if he gets this flu, he could become very sick? Deathly ill? Hannah. Why would you risk coming out in such bad weather, feeling as bad as you do? And don't tell me that you 'didn't feel that bad' this morning. When you get the flu, you know it. It hits very hard, very fast," Sarah said, breathing hard and trying to contain her temper.

Miriam, watching the interchange at a distance, was surprised to see Hannah's cherry-red cheeks becoming even redder.

"I . . . I wanted to see Joshua Lapp. I had to . . ." Hannah whispered miserably, looking down at the smooth wooden floor.

"Sarah, I wanted to keep her home . . . I tried, but she insisted she was well enough to come to service . . ."

"Hannah, why would you come out when it's this bad and you're so sick? I've had the flu. *Mamm* is right – it kicks like a mule. One minute you're sniffling, the next, you're feverish and can barely move," Miriam said. She had scooted back, away from Hannah when Sarah diagnosed Hannah's symptoms as flu.

"But . . . it . . . I didn't think it would . . ." Hannah whispered, her chin trembling.

"*Nee.* No. You didn't think. Instead, you put the health of some fifty people, including a small asthmatic boy, at risk – just so you could make eyes at a young man. We can't send people home in this blizzard. It's too dangerous. Mr. Beiler, Bishop Stoltzfus and I decided that we're putting everyone up here until the storm blows itself out. I am putting you in the upstairs room at the end of the hall. By yourselves. You've done quite enough damage by being here at all. All I can do is hope and pray that nobody else gets sick. I'll bring blankets and pillows along. Now, go," Sarah said sharply, motioning the two upstairs. She followed them to make sure they found the right bedroom.

Miriam, released from the tension, raced from closet to closet, then to benches and chests, rounding up as many pillows and blankets as she could. Passing them out to families, she reserved blankets and two pillows for the Miller women.

\*\*\*

Bishop Stolzfus and Joseph were directing the men to retrieve as many blankets from their buggies as they could."Men will bunk out downstairs while women and children will stay upstairs. Now, let's get these tables and benches onto the wagon. Buggies and horses will need to be put into the barn as well."

All the men and older boys trooped outside to finish the task as quickly as they could. The horses and livestock were fed and watered. Several men milked the cows, fed and watered them as well.

"Samuel," Joseph said, looking at Samuel Fisher. "We should tie a guide rope going from the barn to the house. I don't know how long this storm will last, but no sense in losing anyone because they got disoriented." He held up a long, sturdy length of rope in one hand.

"*Ya.* Let's close the barn against the wind, then we can tie this to something," Samuel said.

Joseph led the way back to the entryway off the kitchen. As he did so, he fed out more and more of the rope. As he reached the bottom of the porch steps, he and Samuel tied the rope securely to the bottom of the porch.

Stamping their feet heavily, all the men and boys removed the thick snow from their boots before walking into the house. Each man carried several blankets, which would become makeshift sleeping bags.

Miriam and Sarah stayed busy for the next several minutes, assigning women and their children to the remaining empty bedrooms.

"Families will need to double up. Men will sleep downstairs. Now, Hannah Miller has come down with flu. She and her mother will be the only ones to be in a room by themselves – we don't want to expose anyone needlessly. We have board games for the children. Once you have made up beds and sleeping areas, come downstairs where it's warmer," Sarah instructed.

She and Joseph went into their storeroom to check on their food supplies.

"Fortunately, we have stocked up more than enough. We have frozen meat and the fruits and vegetables you canned at the end of the summer," Joseph commented. "Do you have sufficient flour for baking?"

"*Ya*. We bought almost 100 pounds and I believe we still have most of the first bag that I opened. We can make enough bread and biscuits to feed everyone. Desserts . . . yes. And, in the meantime, I am going to make some chicken soup for Hannah, Mary and Adam. The more they get into themselves, the better. I want to keep Adam healthy."

"Flu? She's sick with the *flu*? Why? Why did she come to meeting so sick?" Joseph asked in confusion.

"She hid the severity of her symptoms from Mary. Mary should have realized that she was sick with more than a cold. And it was all so Hannah could lay her eyes on a boy," Sarah said with exasperation.

"Sarah. Look at me. I know how passionate you are about good health. She did wrong . . . but it's done. All we can do is protect Adam from getting sick and keep others healthy," Joseph said.

\*\*\*

The next morning, the storm still howled. Snow fell heavily, sometimes coming straight down and, at other times, blown so it appeared to be falling horizontally. The men went out as a group to tend to the livestock. Coming in, they reported that the snow that had not drifted was now knee-high. Drifts were as high as the bottoms of the windows of the house.

Mary Miller tried to come downstairs so she could help. Sarah, seeing her in the kitchen doorway, set her bowl down sharply and motioned with her hands for Mary to get back upstairs.

"Mary! *Nee.* You have been exposed to flu. Go upstairs and tend to Hannah. We will bring food and drink to you when it's done. Go!" Sarah said, more sharply than she had intended.

Mary, surprised at the sharpness in Sarah's voice, turned immediately and went back upstairs.

"Sarah, are you sure you weren't too harsh with Mary?" asked another wife.

"*Nee*, Barbara. She was not too harsh." This came from Emily Fisher. "She saw that Hannah was feverish. She could have stayed at home with her."

"But . . . they would be alone . . ."

" . . . In this blizzard. *Ya.* But Mary has taken care of her older children, and younger, when they have fallen ill. She knows how to care for them. Now, everyone in our community has been exposed to flu. Adam Zook has asthma. If *he* gets sick, he is at even higher risk of serious illness," Emily finished.

"Oh. I will pray that he stays healthy," said Barbara.

By the end of that day, it was clear that Adam had the flu.

Sarah and Emily, talking quietly in the hallway, decided to tag-team each other.

"I'll take this first shift and watch over him," Emily offered. "First, though, I'll move him and Rachel into another isolation room and we'll clean this room completely. The family in the room next to the Millers will have to double up in here . . ." She found the family occupying the room that would now become the Zook's room and told them they would be moved. Moving Adam and Rachel into that room, she and Emily donned face masks and cleaned the room thoroughly, disinfecting all hard surfaces.

"Tell us if you start to suddenly feel bad," she told the other family. "Meantime, I'm making up a large pot of chicken soup. Everyone is getting that for supper." After washing up, she and several other wives chopped up vegetables, boiled water and added several whole, frozen chickens to the water. Sarah bustled back upstairs with glasses and a bottle of fever reducer. Putting a face mask on, she checked on Adam and gave him a tablet with water, which he immediately threw up. After trying several times to get water and a pill into Adam, she decided he needed a suppository. She limited Adam to tiny sips of cool water, waiting until she knew he could hold these down before giving him more.

"I have to go downstairs to check on dinner, Rachel. Keep giving him tiny sips. You have to keep him hydrated. I will be back upstairs in a while with a bowl of chicken soup for you. We'll see if he can tolerate the broth then. Let me know if you need me," Sarah said quietly.

# CHAPTER FOUR

The next morning, Rachel had fallen asleep curled around the limp form, and Sarah took over Adam's nursing care.

"He seems to be getting better. His fever's down and his breathing is a little easier," Emily observed. "I want him to use his inhaler to keep his airways open. Oh, and Hannah seems to be getting a bit better as well," she said.

But by midafternoon, Adam had taken a turn for the worse. He was lethargic and difficult to rouse.

Rachel was awake. She looked up at Sarah with a helpless gaze. "His fever is back up to 103," she said. "And he's not breathing well. I've given him the inhaler, but it's not – I think it's running low."

Sarah nodded. "It's all going to be okay," she said, doing her best to comfort Adam's frantic *mamm*, but she was worried. "Give him a bit more water, if you can," she said. "I'll talk to the men downstairs."

"He needs a hospital," Rachel said.

Sarah nodded. But how would they get him to a hospital? Outside the window was a sheet of white. "The men just came in from caring for the livestock. It looks like the storm might be letting up."

And maybe it was, a little. "Let me speak with the men."

Joseph confirmed that the blizzard appeared to be easing off, at least somewhat. "We can almost see the sun and the wind isn't as strong as it was yesterday. But, the snow is thigh-deep, even if it's not falling quite as fast."

"We have to get Adam to a hospital, somehow," Sarah explained. "Unless we can get him to breathe more easily on his own. But his inhaler is almost empty. And even if it wasn't, he looks bad. I'm worried that he might need a nebulizer treatment to open his airways properly."

It would have been better to take Adam that moment, but she doubted the roads near their farm had been cleared and Sarah despaired at how they might carry Adam through thigh-deep snow. Even if one of them made it to one of the emergency phone booths, how would the Englischers get a rescue vehicle through the blizzard?

That night, Sarah and Rachel prayed over the child until they both fell into a fitful, exhausted sleep at Adam's side. The next morning, Adam's condition had grown even worse. He was having even more trouble breathing and he was beyond lethargic – he was barely conscious. After using a damp cloth to moisten his lips and hopefully get some fluid into him, Sarah washed her hands and ran downstairs to report the latest developments to Joseph and the Bishop.

"We can't wait any longer to get Adam to a hospital! He's much worse and I'm afraid his body is starved for oxygen!"

"I was praying that he would improve overnight. The snow has let up a lot." Joseph said. "We'll send a some of the young men to one of the phones to call for help. The roads should be cleared somewhat by now. If we can get one of the buggies through, we'll be able to meet with an ambulance."

Sarah nodded and ran back up to Adam's bedside. His lips had a decided tint of blue. Sarah lifted him up in the bed of pillows so that he could breathe more easily. He moaned something incoherently.

Rachel had fallen back asleep again, and Sarah was reluctant to wake her. As much as the virus was ravaging her son's body, it was also taking its toll on Rachel. The woman had a blistering fever and had taken multiple trips to the toilet through the morning.

'Dear God, help us please,' Sarah prayed. The door creaked behind her, and Joseph's heavy footfalls sounded over the wooden floor. He placed a cold hand on Sarah's shoulder. "Should we wake her?" he whispered.

"Not yet," Sarah whispered and stood.

When they were in the hallway, Joseph asked, "How is Adam?"

"He can't breathe and his lips are nearly blue," Sarah said. She clenched her lips against frustration and sudden tears of worry.

Joseph sighed against his own wave of frustration. As he did so, he absently rubbed his left arm, trying to ease the dull ache inside. "The Bishop's sent two of the Stoltzfus boys to make their way to the phone. If we have the rest of the healthy men shovel a path though, we might be able to get the buggy through to one of the roads. With God's grace, they've been plowed by now. It will have to be enough."

Sarah was caught between terrors. Couldn't they send a rescue vehicle here? If they couldn't, Adam was unlikely to last another night. His rescue inhaler was empty, and without it, the virus was making it almost impossible for him to breathe. At the same time, a treacherous buggy ride through the tail end of a blizzard to a road that might not even be plowed – that sounded just as dangerous.

"Joseph? What do you think? Should we try to take him to the road?"

"*Ya*. Now, while the sun is still high. You and Samuel Fisher and Adam's *daed*. I don't know if Rachel is strong enough--"

"She won't let her son go without her."

"All of you go. Leave now before he gets any worse," said

Joseph. "We really don't have another choice."

Sarah ran upstairs and, putting her face mask back on, she went into the Zook's room.

"Rachel, please put your coat, gloves, hat and scarf on. Bundle Adam up. We're taking him to the hospital right now. He needs more care than Emily and I can give him," she said.

Rachel paled. She had known this, but hearing it made the precariousness of their situation real. Obeying Sarah, she bundled Adam's limp form in his coat, scarf and mittens.

Emily, wearing her own coat and face mask, helped them get Adam into the Zook's buggy. Seeing Adam breathing more easily, she looked at the Zooks, her husband and Joseph Beiler.

"This is temporary. The cold air shocked his airways into opening up, but they'll swell up again. He has to be hospitalized. Go. Now!" Stepping back, she prayed quietly that they would get to the hospital in enough time – Adam was rapidly approaching respiratory failure.

*** 

The buggy trip was slow – they stopped and started as the young men worked to clear the snow well enough so the buggy could pass. It was slow, exhausting work with the raspy wheeze of Adam providing a horrifying reminder of what was at risk if they failed. As they approached the final stretch to the road, Sarah caught glimpse of the flash of red lights. An ambulance! Thank the Lord!

Three EMTs dressed in bulky winter gear stood at the side of the road with a stretcher. One of the young men shouted, and the trio started trudging through the snow towards them. One, a young woman, carried an oxygen tank. Sarah was immediately relieved. Though the stretcher was too bulky to make the snow, it seemed the EMTs had decided to carry Adam in their arms.

When they reached the buggy, one of the EMTs, a woman wearing a prayer kapp, put the mask over Adam's mouth and nose. She shocked Sarah by speaking in Pennsylvania German. "My name is Judith and we're going to make sure that your son makes it to the hospital safely."

"You're – are you Amish?" Rachel asked.

Sarah remembered, hadn't there been something in the Amish paper about a young Amish woman on Rumspringe performing CPR on a man last year? She didn't live close to Sarah, by buggy at least.

Judith said, "*Ya.* I'm still in training, but they're letting me assist today because of the blizzard. We need to get your son to the ER."

Rachel nodded, and she and her husband followed Judith and the other EMTs to the ambulance. Sarah breathed a sigh of relief, knowing that the family was safe and in good hands.

Dear God, thank you, Sarah said in a mumbled prayer.

Then, stepping out of the buggy, she waved the exhausted young men back toward the buggy. "They're on their way. Let's get back to the house as quickly as we can in case this snow starts up again."

***

At the hospital's emergency department, Adam was seen immediately.

"Mr. and Mrs. Zook, your son has to be admitted. His flu aggravated his asthma. He has pneumonia, which is making his breathing even more difficult. We need to rehydrate him and give him antibiotics intravenously. He'll also need a breathing treatment," said the doctor on duty.

Rachel trembled as she heard the tired doctor's words.

"*Ya*, doctor, admit him, please. He's our only child. Please help him!" Michael said, trying not to cry.

"Don't you Amish people usually have lots of kids?" the doctor asked in confusion.

"*Ya*, normally, we do, but Rachel can't have more children . . . it would . . . it would kill her," Michael said. "He is our only child."

"Ah. I see. Okay, then, we're starting treatment on him now. What short-acting bronchodilator do you have for him?"

Rachel pulled the small inhaler out, showing it to the doctor.

"It's empty. We had to use it overnight and –" she sobbed.

"It's fine. You did you best. Just dispose of that. We'll give him a fresh one here, plus several nebulizer treatments," the doctor said.

# CHAPTER FIVE

By the next morning, Hannah Miller began showing signs of improvement. While Sarah breathed a silent sigh of relief that one of her patients was on the mend, she still struggled with anger at the girl for giving in to her desire to see a boy when she was sick. Sarah also felt anger at the girl's mother for not asserting her parental authority and making her stay at home when she was obviously ill.

Sarah felt herself growing more and more angry at the duo, especially when she and Emily found it necessary to shuffle families among their bedrooms yet again – three other families were now showing signs of flu. Even worse, a stomach bug, showing that it would be virulent, began racing through the families held captive by the stubborn blizzard inside the Beiler home.

"Emily, you've been up all night, taking care of sick families. Go, lie down so you don't get sick yourself. I'll take over," whispered Sarah to her friend and nursing counterpart.

"*Denki*, Sarah. It's been a busy night. I am very tired. Let me know if you need any help and I'll get up," Emily said.

"*Nee*, don't worry. Miriam will help me. Sleep is more important for you. Now, go!" Sarah ordered with a smile.

Sarah and Miriam bustled from room to room upstairs, both wearing face masks as they took care of their patients. Sarah gave Miriam instructions on taking care of the patients, then ran downstairs to give instructions to two healthy women who had volunteered to make soup and heavier fare for dinner and supper. Seeing Joseph coming back in with several of the men, she sent him a silent question: *What is the weather like outside?*

Joseph motioned with his head to the downstairs hallway.

"It's slowing down considerably. The wind has almost completely died down, but it's still snowing. We are praying that this will end sometime tonight or tomorrow," he told Sarah.

"Good. Three more families have the flu – and now, we have stomach flu making the rounds. I just sent Emily Fisher to bed and Miriam is helping me out. How are you and the men feeling?"

"I feel fine. I did notice that one of the men was sniffling and coughing, so I sent him inside – Aaron Lapp, Joshua's father. You might want to check on him," Joseph said.

"*Ach*, no. Not another one! *Denki*, Joseph. I will check him out and give him something for fever. Two women are making more chicken soup in the kitchen. I'll have them separate out more broth for those who can't handle solid food," Sarah mused.

After checking Aaron Lapp, she concluded that he was, indeed, coming down with flu. She gave him cool water and a painkiller for the fever and body aches, and then sent him to lie down in a corner of the quilting room.

That night, Emily had just come downstairs from her day of sleep. The healthy men came back inside after taking care of the livestock, reporting that the storm's intensity seemed to have worn itself out.

Sarah and Emily smiled at each other – maybe this nightmare would end soon!

\*\*\*

The next morning, Emily and Sarah looked to the back door as the men stomped snow off their boots and tramped into the house.

"Well? Is it cloudy, snowing or has the storm moved on?" Sarah asked, holding her breath. Inside, she was saying a fervent prayer that God would have mercy on them and send the storm elsewhere.

"Sunny, Sarah. We saw the sunlight as we looked – the storm is over!" Joseph said with a broad grin showing through his beard and mustache.

"Do you think it's safe sending everyone home? We still have several sick families here. This flu won't end until it has no victims living in such close quarters."

"Let us talk to Bishop Stolzfus and see what he advises," said Joseph.

"Okay. Breakfast will be ready in less than ten minutes," Sarah said.

"*Denki.*"

Joseph and Samuel, the self-appointed leaders of the storm-isolated group, sought out the bishop.

"Bishop, it's clear now. My wife tells me that this flu won't stop until we're no longer isolated in one large bunch. Do you think it advisable to send everyone home, sick or healthy?" asked Joseph.

"Let's go back outside and talk," said the bishop. Once outdoors, he made sure his coat was snug around his neck and torso. Standing in the snow-filled yard, he gazed around, turning a full 360 degrees so he could assess the horizon surrounding Ephrata.

"*Ach,* look to the east – do you see that far-off bank of clouds? Another storm is coming in, but, if we make good time, eat breakfast and help the Beilers clean up, then hitch the horses to our buggies and get home before noon, we should all get home before the next storm hits. *Ya,* we need to do this. Tell the women so they can get the families ready. Follow

Sarah's and Emily's instructions on bundling up the sick ones so they don't get worse by being outdoors, if possible. Let's tell them," he instructed, with a new spring in his step.

While the women were serving breakfast to those healthy enough to eat, the bishop, Joseph and Samuel broke the good news to Sarah and Emily.

"We're sending everyone home today. It has to be today, because we saw a new bank of storm clouds in the distance. If you have any suggestions for sick families to get home without getting any sicker, we need them," Joseph said.

"Thank you, Lord! First, feed everyone, even those who are sick. If they can only handle chicken broth and dry toast, so be it. They must be bundled up, with their mouths covered up so the cold air doesn't irritate their airways. As soon as they get home, they must remove coats, hoods, gloves and scarves so their fevers don't go too high. We'll start spreading the word. All of you, sit down and eat, now," Emily said with a grin on her tired, plump face.

Three hours later, everyone had eaten. Healthy community members helped straighten the mess inside the Beiler home – furniture was put back into place, sheets and blankets were stripped from beds and pillows and windows were opened upstairs so the fresh air could sweep out the germs. Emily, Samuel and Joseph volunteered to stay and help wipe down the house and all hard surfaces.

"*Nee*, don't worry!" Sarah said. "You don't want to get

caught in the next storm!"

"Sarah, more hands make lighter work. We will finish in plenty of time to get home before the storm hits. We are staying," Emily said firmly. "Now, let's eat breakfast before it's all gone."

"I will be having a little talk with the Millers about exposing everyone to this kind of illness. Adam Zook could have died if we hadn't been able to get him to the hospital!" Sarah said. After breakfast and making the announcement that the weather was clear enough for everyone to leave, Sarah carried out her promise. Spotting Hannah and Mary, she motioned with a finger to a quiet spot in the full house.

"Hannah, I know what it is to like a boy. However, you knew you were sick – and you still chose to come to service, exposing everyone to your 'cold.' We had to assign families to rooms and bed the men and older boys downstairs, because it was too dangerous to go home. As a result, the flu took its opportunity to move from victim to victim – and it very nearly killed Adam Zook. I don't think you know this, so please accept it as educational only. Flu can kill people with lung conditions. We thank God that we could get him to the hospital for treatment, but by then, he already had pneumonia. If he had gone without specialized medical treatment for much longer – he would have died. Now, this is where I want you to think of the good of the community and selflessness. Was seeing Joshua Lapp worth that?"

Hannah's eyes welled with tears as she shook her head.

"*Nee*, Mrs. Beiler. I am so sorry! I promise you, the next time I feel so bad, I will let *mamm* know, and I will stay at home."

"*Denki*. And you, Mary – you are the *mamm*, not your daughter's best friend. It is up to you to be the parent and guide her when you know she is doing wrong or making a mistake. Had Emily and I not been blessed with nursing training, little Adam would have died. I know just how bad a 'simple illness' like flu can get. It is nothing to discount. I trust you will remember this the next time one of your children falls ill?" Sarah asked pointedly.

" . . . *Ya*, Sarah. Thank you. I did suspect that she was more seriously ill than she was admitting to," Mary said softly.

Two hours later, the house was blessedly empty. As promised, the Fishers stayed to help clean the house and barn. Sarah, Emily and Miriam tackled the house while Joseph, Samuel and John handled the barn. Sarah sent the Fishers home with extra chicken soup and fresh-baked bread, as thanks for all their help.

After the house was finally empty, Miriam collapsed onto the sofa in the living room.

"Ahh! It is heaven not to be tripping over children, blankets, legs and feet! Not to be cleaning up illness or taking temperatures . . . not to have to wear a face mask!" she said.

"Yes, it is! Now, help me freeze all that extra food. I sent some home with every one, but we still have so much left!" Sarah said.

"Gladly." Miriam helped Sarah finish getting the large house straightened, cleaned and sanitized.

"Now, I can't say we killed every flu germ in here, but we've given it our best," Sarah mused, rubbing her hands over her arms.

"*Mamm*, can we close windows yet? It is cold!"

"Give the cold temperatures a little more time to kill the bugs in here," Sarah instructed. "Cover yourself with a heavy shawl."

Finally, Sarah was satisfied with the cleaning and disinfection efforts she, Miriam and Emily had made. She and Miriam went from room to room, closing and locking windows against the cold air.

# CHAPTER SIX

The next day, the ominous clouds had edged closer to the community. Temperatures dropped once again as the wind picked up.

Inside the community schoolhouse, Rebecca Yoder glanced outside several times, seeing the clouds moving closer and closer. Picking up some wood, she stoked the fire inside the stove, encouraging warmth to move to the farthest corners of the room.

"Okay, everyone, let's move to . . . Wait here. Open your language books to the unit on parts of language and I'll be right back," she instructed. Wrapping her shawl more closely around her torso, she walked to the front door, where Bishop Stoltzfus waited.

"Bishop? Is something wrong?"

"*Ya,* there is. I'm sure you feel the cold and hear the wind. We have alerted the families to come pick up their children before lunch. Another storm is coming and it would be too dangerous to keep them here until the usual dismissal time," said the bishop.

"*Denki*! Yes, I saw the storm coming up and I began worrying about getting the children home," Rebecca said.

"Do you mind?" the bishop asked, gesturing to the head of the classroom.

"*Nee*, go right ahead," said Rebecca.

"*Denki*. Scholars, please listen to me! We are sending your parents to pick you up now. Another blizzard is coming and it would be safer to release you now rather than try to wait until this afternoon. Allow Miss Yoder to set your assignments for the next few days. Listen close, now! Your parents will be here – good, I see some riding up already," the bishop said, trying to speak cheerfully.

"Scholars, read the parts of language assignment. I am writing everything down. Please write these assignments down and have them ready to give to me once we come back to school in a few days. You will have language, math, Bible, science and history. Now, your parents are waiting. Bundle up, take your books home and don't make them wait! I will see you when it's safe to have class," Rebecca said over the sudden bustle of children putting their jackets on and finding their books.

"And, do you have a way home?" asked the bishop.

"*Ya*. My horse and buggy are inside the barn," she said.

"I will follow you home – it is on my way, so don't worry about putting me out. I am responsible for you, since the school board president is home sick with flu," said the bishop.

"*Denki*. I'm ready – I just want to get inside, where it's warm!"

Outside, Rebecca gasped as she saw the heaviness of the glowering clouds. Even though they were filled with snow, they appeared to hold something much more substantial. Hitching her horse the the buggy quickly, she tossed her belongings in and got into the buggy with the help of the bishop. She followed him, trying to keep the wheels of her buggy in the tracks created by his buggy. The trip was slow, and she squinted against the cold, stiff wind. Finally, she saw her *daed's* and *mamm's* farm. Dimly, she saw the bishop turn and give her a vigorous wave. Waving back, she turned into the driveway and urged her horse to the barn.

\*\*\*

Joseph and Sarah Beiler decided to take the opportunity to stock up on their depleted stores of food. As fast as they tried to go, they realized they were in a race with the storm, which was now almost on top of them.

"Sarah, let's hurry! If we move quickly, we can beat this storm!" Joseph shouted over the shriek of the wind. He signaled to the horses to move fast – as fast as they could without going off the road. Breathing a sigh of relief, Joseph brought the horses and buggy into the barn. As they were unhitching the buggy, he looked up, seeing snow falling heavily, blown about by the stiff winds.

"We'll both have to carry as much as we can . . . Miriam, here! Take some of the food! Let's try to get everything into the house in one trip. Thank God I left the guide rope up!" Joseph kneeled, handing several bags to Sarah and Miriam. Grabbing what was left, he managed to close and secure the barn door, walking as fast as he could to the kitchen door.

"*Mamm*, I'm working on dinner. Do you want me to help put the food away?" she asked Sarah.

"*Nee*, daughter. Keep working on dinner. I will put things away while your father brushes Brownie and Red down. Joseph, hurry before this gets any worse," she told her husband.

That evening, the storm was still blowing strong. With Miriam's help, he fed and watered the stock, then they milked the cows, pouring the fresh milk into the milk machine. Looking up, he saw a large tree branch swaying wildly in the wind. Hearing a sharp *krak,* he grabbed Miriam's shoulder, pushing her out of the way. Both father and daughter landed on their sides in a deep, freezing snowdrift.

"Come on! Now!" Joseph yelled. As he did, he grabbed Miriam's gloved hand and pulled her along the rope.

This second storm was a repeat of the first, with heavy snow, howling winds and bitterly cold temperatures. Miriam, closed inside the house, peered restlessly out the windows, wishing the winter weather would ease. The first day wore slowly into the second. Miriam, working on her quilt, stopped sewing as she felt a sudden, dull headache, body aches and a heavy exhaustion slam into her. Rubbing her throat, she coughed against a soreness there.

"*Mamm*! I think I'm sick with the flu. It just hit me and I feel bad," Miriam said.

"Come here. *Ya*, this is bad. You have a temperature. Upstairs, into your nightgown and I will bring some chicken broth to you. Go," Sarah said with a sigh.

Miriam struggled to climb the stairs as the exhaustion and body aches conspired to push her to the ground. As she was putting on her long-sleeved nightgown, she clutched her stomach against nausea. Running to the bathroom, she lost her dinner. Coming out several minutes later, she swabbed sticky sweat from her face.

"Come on, sweetheart. To bed with you. I'll give you small sips so you can stay hydrated," murmured Sarah.

Miriam huddled under her covers, alternately freezing and roasting. She obediently took small sips of the tasty broth, shaking her head at her *mamm* when her stomach began to rebel. She dozed off after several minutes, sleeping restlessly, visited by fever dreams. After several hours she woke up, with her mouth feeling as dry as a withered stalk of corn. Wincing against her body's soreness, she got up and went downstairs slowly, needing cool water.

"Miriam? Go back upstairs and I'll bring what you need. The only place for you right now is under your covers," Sarah commented.

"But, *mamm*, I am thirsty. And hot!" Miriam complained.

"And you'll be freezing cold again too soon. Upstairs, now. I'll bring water and some more broth to you," said Sarah, bustling into the kitchen.

"Okay," Miriam said, realizing the truth of her *mamm's* words. She hunched over, folding her arms over her torso, feeling a sudden chill moving from the center of her body. "I'll be upstairs."

Upstairs, she slowly sipped water, allowing it to moisten the dry tissues in her mouth. Sarah held a small bowl of chicken broth with potatoes out toward Miriam. As she did, she spooned up some of the broth, offering it to Miriam.

"Ohh, so good! *Denki, mamm*." Miriam said as her voice cracked.

"I'll give you a little broth. You need nutrition, but not to be sick at your stomach again. I'm also leaving some water up here – just promise me that you'll only take sips, you won't try to guzzle it," Sarah said in warning.

"Ugh, after this afternoon, I don't want to try to guzzle,

*mamm*. I promise you, I will be very careful. That's enough. I feel full, anyway," she said waving the spoon away.

"Good. Depending on how you do tonight, let's see if we can add hot tea, more vegetables and a slice of bread to tomorrow's menu," Sarah suggested.

"M-maybe," Miriam said, feeling her stomach roll at the suggestion.

"Take this for your fever. It'll help you sleep more restfully as well – something you need," Sarah said, holding out an ibuprofen tablet.

Miriam took it, then rested her head against her pillow.

"*Denki, mamm*. I think I'll be able to sleep now," Miriam said, feeling exhaustion roll over her again. Her long, brown eyelashes fluttered down against her flushed cheeks as she drifted off to sleep.

***

The next morning, Miriam was still asleep as Joseph and Sarah struggled to the barn against the strong, frigid wind. Sarah bent her head, trying to avoid the stinging pellets of snow. In the barn, she and Joseph tended to the livestock and fed the cows.

"I hope this storm won't last for long," she told Joseph.

"*Ach*, Sarah, I told Miriam that we are in for a very hard

winter. I felt it the day before the first blizzard struck."

# CHAPTER SEVEN

Rachel and Michael Zook sat up attentively as the doctor strode into Adam's room.

"Well, how are you this stormy morning?" asked the doctor.

"Worried, doctor. When Adam is better, we still need to be able to get home – we can't do that when it's storming like this," Michael said, peering through the window.

"Rest easy, Mr. Zook. Adam has definitely gotten better, but he still needs more nebulizer treatments and I want to make sure his flu and pneumonia have really ended before discharging him. God willing, we'll be able to discharge him on a clear day soon."

"*Ya*, God willing. So, he is getting better?" Michael said. His worry made his German accent sharper.

"Yes, he is. He's been fever-free now for about 16 hours. I'm going to send him to X-ray today to see how his lungs look.

At this rate, I'm guessing it will be another two days – three at most – then we can discharge him. So, Adam, how are you feeling, sport?"

"Better, *denki*. I can breathe now without coughing so much," Adam said quietly.

"Well, you just keep doing what your nurses say, and we'll have you at home in a few days. All right?"

"*Ya, denki*." Adam said with a wide smile.

"One question, Mr. and Mrs. Zook . . . Adam will need continued nebulizer treatments. I don't want to subject him to a long, cold trip here every day to take those. I know you don't have electricity at home. Do you have any other way you can hook up an electric compressor to an energy source so he can get the medication he needs?" asked the doctor.

"*Ya*, we do. I have a diesel-powered generator and I can connect that to the nebulizer. We don't want to take him out in this any more than you want us to. In fact, the more he can stay inside, the better," said Michael.

\*\*\*

The second day of the storm continued with heavy snowfall and howling winds. Michael and Rachel Zook alternated standing by the thick plate glass window of Adam's hospital room, staring outside. Rachel measured the storm's ferocity by how clearly she could see a small diner across the street –

currently, the diner was completely invisible. Rachel sighed, wanting the blizzard to miraculously melt away.

"Rachel? Are you okay?" asked Michael.

"*Ya*, husband. Just wanting this storm to end. I want to go home! With you and Adam," Rachel said. Inside, she felt the storm-enforced confinement weighing her down. "I need fresh air. Will you stay here with Adam? I'm just going to stand by the doors so I can smell the air. I'll be back in a few minutes. I promise."

"*Ya*, okay. Don't be too long," Michael said. *I know how she feels. We're both from the country and we are used to being outside for several hours a day. When she comes back, I'll go stick my nose outside as well.*

Ten minutes later, Rachel came back. She looked happier, even if her nose was reddened by the cold, harsh wind blowing outside.

"Okay. I feel more normal now. If you want to get some fresh air, I'll stay here with Adam," she told Michael.

"*Mamm*, when can we get get fresh air?" Adam asked, with a plaintive note in his voice.

"Son, I'm sorry, but I don't want to take any chances. I'll ask your doctor. I just want you well so we can go home and sleep in our own beds," Rachel said.

"*Mamm*, I miss home."

"We do too, Adam. We'll get home soon. The doctor said it would be two or three days, once this storm blows itself out," said Rachel.

Two days later, Rachel woke in Adam's room, wondering what she was hearing. Focusing more strongly, she realized she didn't hear the wail of the wind. Throwing the hospital blanket back, she smoothed her hair away from her face and went to peek through the blinds. She looked out on a bright winter wonderland. The sun shone on the snow, seeming to pick out individual snowflakes to bounce off of. Running back to Michael, she shook his shoulder.

"Michael! It's stopped! Listen!" she whispered.

Michael roused, rubbing his eyes and cocking his head.

"Where's the wind?" he asked.

"Go! Look!" Rachel said with a broad grin. She felt as if she was giving him a precious gift.

Adam stretched, working the kinks out of his muscular back as he walked to the window.

"Hah! We're probably going home today!" he turned with a wide grin to Rachel.

"*Daed*? You look happy," Adam said.

"Come here, son. Look outside," Michael said as he twirled the wand to open the blinds.

"No storm! Are we going home?"

"Adam, if you're doing as well as you did yesterday, you're going home!" said the young doctor, standing in the doorway.

Forty-five minutes later, after examining Adam and reading the latest X-rays, he nodded in satisfaction.

"Well, Adam, it looks like God and our medicine beat that old flu germ. I'm going to give that machine to your mom and dad and you'll be going home. Do you need a ride, Mr. Zook?"

"Yes, we do. Do you have a list of drivers we can call?"

"At the desk. I'll have a nurse call someone for you. Someone with an SUV and very good snow-driving skills. Now, about this nebulizer . . ." Several minutes later, Rachel was confident she could give daily breathing treatments to Adam.

"Hi! I'm Al and I'll be driving you home. We'll go slowly because the roads are pretty snow-packed," said the driver.

One hour later, Adam and his parents were back home.

"Take a nap, son. You need to get your strength back," Rachel said.

# CHAPTER EIGHT

The flu and stomach virus that had felled so many families in the Beiler home was still racing through the Amish community. Every day, families learned of others who had fallen ill with one illness – or both. In addition, the weather stubbornly continued with days of high winds and deep snowfalls. Families were unable to get out of their homes to take their children to school; and, if they did, they were frequently unsure whether weather conditions would permit them to pick their children up at the end of the school day. Every family in Ephrata learned to scan the horizon, looking for the telltale clouds that preceded another blizzard. What made the situation even more stressful was the short time period in between storms – often, no more than two days at any one time.

With this in mind, Bishop Stoltzfus visited the community's school teacher, along with the community's remaining healthy deacon.

"Miss Yoder, we're going to have to postpone school until these illnesses wear themselves out here in Ephrata," said the bishop. "In addition, this harsh weather we're having makes it too dangerous for families to send their children to school. We are in a temporary lull – for at least the next day or two. You know where your scholars are in their learning. If you'll give the deacons and me assignments for several weeks more, we will visit each family here in Ephrata and give them to all of your scholars."

"Bishop, that is excellent! *Denki*! I have been worried about this long lull – my scholars learn best when they work on books, math problems, reading and language questions on a regular basis. If you'll give me a few minutes, I can have something written up for you," Rebecca said.

"Good. Write it out two times so we can both take something for each family to write down. Once this weather and illness come to an end, your scholars will be back in the school house with you," promised the bishop.

Twenty minutes later, Rebecca had written out several pages of assignments, handing one copy to both the deacon and bishop. Outside the house, they decided how to divide the district up.

"And hurry . . . we'll be hit with another storm by nightfall tonight," predicted the bishop.

Before Bishop Stoltzfus directed his horse in the direction of home, he decided to stop at the Beiler and Fisher homes to discuss the progression of the flu and stomach bugs chewing their way through the community.

"Bishop, I am sure Sarah Beiler told you the same thing, but we need to see several days without another person coming down with one of these illnesses. I have spoken to several of the wives, and they tell me that the stomach bug, in particular, is very bad. If I had access to a library, I would study the symptoms. This is just a guess, understand, but I believe what we're dealing with is called norovirus. It's highly contagious and hits everyone hard, especially the youngest and oldest. Because of how contagious it is, Sarah and I both recommend that families not get together with each other. Not until we know it has played itself out. The same goes for the flu. I would hate to see anyone vulnerable – like Adam Zook – come down sick. I'm glad you've decided to keep the scholars home. *Denki.*"

"What do you think about our church meetings?"

"*Ach*, Bishop! The same thing! We can all read our Bibles and worship as families – at home. You saw what happened when just one person with flu came to a meeting! Imagine if four or five came to meeting sick! Someone who is coming down sick, but still not showing symptoms is just as contagious as someone who's obviously ill – and it's more dangerous because he won't know he's sick until it hits him. *Nee*! We cannot advise allowing families to gather right now," Emily said forcefully.

"Not to mention the threat of blizzards. Well, *denki*, Mrs. Fisher. Until the threat of both blizzards and illness has dropped, we will all stay at home. Once the threats are over, we will resume school and our bi-weekly meetings," concluded the bishop. "I had better go – those clouds are moving in faster than I am comfortable with."

"The wind has picked up, too. Travel safely, please bishop," Sarah said.

Outside, Bishop Stoltzfus flipped his coat collar up around his scarf, then unwrapped the scarf and positioned his collar closest to his neck, wrapping his scarf snugly around his neck once again.

"Go, Patch! Get us home. This storm will be here fast," the bishop said, looking at the heavy clouds. His heart fell as he saw hard pellets of snow beginning to fall.

In response to the bishop's voice, Patch began trotting, wanting to be inside his barn. Despite their best efforts to travel quickly, the bishop and Patch pulled into the Stoltzfus yard as the snowfall became heavy. Patch trotted as fast as he dared for the barn. Inside the barn, the bishop quickly brushed down Patch, giving him extra feed and making sure he had sufficient water. Once inside, the bishop went outside only when it was necessary to care for his livestock.

Other families in the district respected the fierceness of this storm, which was particularly bad. Still, two families lost husbands and fathers as the combination of the howling wind, frigid temperatures and thick snow made being outdoors dangerous. One man was killed when a tree branch fell, hitting his head and neck. The second man was killed when he grew disoriented and got lost trying to return to his home from his barn.

The storm blew for five days. When the winds ended, families went outside to take stock of the damage. The families who had lost husbands and fathers mourned when they found their bodies. Bishop Stoltzfus prayed with these families and urged them to hold private memorial services.

"We cannot bury him now. The ground is frozen hard. For now, bury him under snow so he won't decompose. In the spring, I will be back to help you with a funeral service and a respectful burial," he instructed the bereaved families

***

January quickly passed into February. Because of the unpredictable weather and illness ravaging the community, no youth get-togethers were planned or held, and the next meeting was canceled to keep illness from spreading further.

John Fisher, sitting in the gentle light of a kerosene lamp in the living room, thought about Miriam Beiler. Before the weather had turned so ugly, he had approached her and her parents, letting them know he wanted to court Miriam. Her parents had agreed to allow Miriam to make the decision for herself – Miriam, knowing of John's love for God, agreed to begin courting.

John thought of Miriam's gentle, light-hazel eyes and her ever-present smile. He had heard that she had been hit with the flu. *Lord, let her be healthy, now. She is a strong, beautiful woman and I want to get to know her better. Much, much better.*

He looked up, scanning the horizon – a practice that had quickly become habit for all families in the area. Spotting a dark bank of clouds far away, he grabbed his scarf and jacket, telling his parents he wanted to visit Miriam.

"Just be back before nightfall, especially if those clouds get any closer," instructed Samuel.

"*Ya*, I'll be keeping a close eye on them. *Denki, daed.* I will see you before nightfall," promised John.

"John, take this plate of cookies over, please. I'm sure Miriam would appreciate them now that she's better," Emily said.

"*Denki, mamm*," said John. In the barn, he quickly hitched the horse to the buggy and drove to the Beiler farm. As he did, he glanced occasionally toward the far-off bank of clouds – thankfully, they were still staying away, but he had learned this was no guarantee for the next few days.

# CHAPTER NINE

At the Beiler farm, Miriam welcomed John into the house. They talked, munched on cookies and drank coffee. Talking and laughing, they whiled away the afternoon, unaware that the winds had, once again, picked up. The light quickly dimmed inside the house.

John was only alerted when he heard the wind beginning to shriek around the corners of the large home. Jumping up quickly, he peered through the snowy-white window sheers.

"*Ach*, no! Miriam, look! I should have left a long time ago. Now, it's too late," John said.

"John, there is no way you can go home safely. Stay here and you can use a spare bedroom," Sarah said.

"*Denki*, Mrs. Beiler. I am so sorry! I should have been keeping an eye on the weather," said John soberly.

"John, it is hard to know how fast these storms will hit. My only concern is for your parents to know you are safe. I will call your father in the barn when we go out to take care of the livestock. Do you know what time he'll be in your barn?" asked Joseph.

"Not very long. He likes to milk, feed and water before it's full dark."

"Let's go, then. It'll take a few minutes for us to get to the barn."

Both men put their outer wear on and struggled to make it to the barn. While this storm didn't appear to be as severe as the five-day storm that had hit the week previously, the winds were still harsh and cold.

"Go ahead and call. Hopefully, he'll be in your barn as well," instructed Joseph.

"*Denki.*" Picking up the phone, he dialed the number for the Fisher barn.

"Hello?" Samuel answered, slightly out of breath.

"*Daed*! I'm okay – the storm hit before I realized it. I am sorry. Mr. and Mrs. Beiler offered a spare room to me until the weather calms down," John said.

Samuel let out an exasperated sigh. "Son, I told you to watch the weather! Just make sure you help Mr. Beiler out. As soon as the weather allows, come home. And thank you for calling."

"*Ya, daed*, I am sorry. I . . . just got involved in talking with

Miriam.

"*Ya*, I know about young love. Next time. You be more watchful, do you understand me?"

"*Ya, daed.* I am sorry. I should have been more aware of the change. I will help out. *Denki.*"

Back in the house, Miriam and Sarah set four places at the long, wooden kitchen table. Miriam carried hot casserole dishes, setting them on the table. She turned around as she heard the men stamping their feet on the entry-way floor.

"Just in time! Supper's hot and it's good, so sit down so we can say the blessing and eat," she said.

Sarah dished up steaming, fragrant meatloaf, mashed potatoes and both vegetables.

"Miriam, take what you think you can handle, although you lost weight you didn't need to lose," she said. "So, Joseph, do you think this storm will be as bad as the latest one?"

"*Nee.* Still, even more snow on top of what we've already gotten – spring should be very interesting because of the threat of flooding," Joseph said.

After giving the blessing, Joseph picked up his fork and began eating.

After supper was over, Miriam and Sarah cleaned up the kitchen, then joined Joseph and John in the living room, where they read the Bible and talked until bedtime.

In the spare room, John paced, struggling against his desire to visit Miriam in her room.

*No, it is not right! We are only just beginning to court. But she is so beautiful! And her parents would rightfully be upset if you violated their rules.*

John continued to pace, even after pulling his long-sleeved blue shirt off and draping it over the hook in the wall.

In her own room, Miriam closed her eyes and prayed fervently with the sudden temptation to walk into John's room.

*Nee! I don't want to ruin my reputation within the community.*

Keeping this thought firmly in mind, she took a long drink of cool water and pulled her Bible out. Opening it, she found a chapter to read and focus on. After several minutes, she felt better. Giving a long, quiet sigh, she blew out the lamp in her room and got under the covers.

The next day, Joseph was grateful for John's help. While Miriam was over her attack of the flu, Sarah didn't want her outside in the bitter cold and deep snow, which left Joseph to tend the livestock with Sarah's assistance.

"*Denki* for the help, John," said Joseph. "With Miriam still getting over the worst of her flu, it has been difficult getting things done before another storm hits."

John laughed. "*Ya*, hasn't it? My *mamm* will help my *daed* while I'm here. Still, the more hands there are, the faster we can finish and get inside. Is there anything you need help with, that you can do inside?"

"Hmmm. I do need to select the wood for my next order. An *Englischer* family wants me to make a chest of drawers and a headboard, using this pattern." Joseph pulled a piece of paper with a colored design printed on it, showing it to John.

"This is beautiful! *Ya*, I will be happy to help you – do you have heat in the shop?"

Joseph let out a large, pealing laugh, throwing his head back.

"*Ya*, I do, John! I bought a wood-burning stove a few years ago, when it became obvious that working through the winter would be necessary if I was going to keep up with all my orders. Besides . . ." he paused, rubbing his left forearm.

"Your injury. It hurts on days like today?"

"*Ya*. My . . . assistant back then wasn't so handy. He neglected to check the condition of one of my power saws and I was injured. Needless to say, as soon as I got home from the hospital, I told him never to return. I paid him for his work through that day. To this day, cold, humid and wet weather causes pain. I'm grateful I can still work," Joseph said with a smile.

That night, the storm still blew hard, with snow coming down heavily. After the family went upstairs for the night, both Miriam and John struggled with their twin desires to visit each other in their rooms. Miriam put her robe on over her nightgown, wanting to go downstairs for some cool water. Hearing steps on the other side of the door, she paused.

*What if it's John? I can't allow him to see me in my night things. I'd best wait until I hear him pass by on his way to his room.* She walked around her room, thinking and listening for John's steps to return in the opposite direction. Once she heard him walk past, she waited for another minute until she heard the catch of his door catch in place. Opening her door, she checked the hallway in both directions, then sped downstairs to fill a tall glass with cool water. Back upstairs, she took a long gulp of water, continuing to struggle with her desire to go see John.

The third day of the storm dawned with the wind continuing to shriek angrily around the house. John and Joseph squinted their eyes against the cold, snow pellets and wind, seeing the snow being blown horizontally when a sharp gust of wind blew by. As with the previous day, they stayed in the carpentry shop, warmed by the wood-burning stove as they worked on the chest of drawers and headboard.

In the house, Miriam and Sarah cleaned the house, then began working on their individual crafting projects.

"Miriam? It is dark in here. Do you have an extra lamp?" asked Sarah.

"*Nee,* I don't. I'm working on some delicate stitching, so this helps. *Denki,*" said Miriam.

Sarah lit the kerosene lamp, adding to the gentle glow in the room. She opened the curtains, allowing the dim daylight to enter in. It was enough for Miriam to continue working, although she had to admit that she had done this so many times that she probably could do it in the dark. It was something she loved doing; calming, peaceful and a time for reflection. As her hands worked, she could pray her mind unencumbered by realistic things.

"I'm lighting fireplaces so we can keep the house warm. We will have potato soup and homemade bread for dinner." Sarah went back to what she loved – cooking. Although her daughter was a good cook, Sarah loved the craft. It allowed her to be creative while keeping with traditions. Her soups and breads always had a little twist, something different that was nuanced in the presentation. It was these subtle additions she loved; she hummed softly as she went about her business.

"*Mamm*, that sounds delicious! Do you need help?" Miriam called from her quilting area. She didn't want her mother to be left to do everything, but she also knew of her mother's love of cooking.

*Nee*, daughter. It is done. All I need to do is combine the ingredients and allow them to boil. The bread is rising now. We will have a hearty, healthy dinner soon. You keep working. When is that due to your customer?"

"Thankfully, not for another month. Getting sick didn't help me. I may work after supper to get some more done tonight,"

Miriam said.

"So, right after Christmas?"

"*Ya*, it is a birthday gift for someone," Miriam said. After her mother moved to the opposite side of the long room, they both began concentrating on their quilting and cross stitching.

As she had mentioned, Miriam returned to the quilting room so she could get more done and catch up on the time she had lost while she was in bed with the flu. By the time she finished, she was yawning and sleepy.

"It looks like someone needs to sleep!" John said with a tender smile. He caught Miriam's hands in his own, drawing her into the kitchen. "Your *mamm* made some hot chocolate. Drink some with us."

"Delicious! On a cold night like tonight, it will warm me up. And I know I will sleep," Miriam said, stifling another yawn.

"You worked very hard today, Miriam. You shouldn't overdo – you just got over being sick," John said. It was his way of intimating the conversation. He worried about her, and she liked that cared for feeling. He was such a strong man, and as she'd gotten to know him better, she realized he was also very caring. Kindness would be a virtue with anyone, but he smiled at her in that special way and his worry was personal, deep and just between the two of them.

Is this what her *mamm* meant when she said a man could be good, strong and honorable, but a man who loves you shows a softness that the rest of the world never sees. There is a special bond between people in love that transcends the normal constraints and is expressed in the simplest of statements.

"*Ya,* I know, but I fell behind on the quilt. It's due to my customer right after Christmas. It's a birthday gift, so it must be done on time. As it is, I will barely make it."

"I will help your father for as long as I am here, Miriam. You concentrate on the quilt, but don't work so hard you get sick again."

"*Denki,* John. I will be careful. And you – you be careful," Miriam murmured.

John, knowing that Joseph and Sarah had already gone upstairs. Gently pulling Miriam closer to him, he wrapped one arm around Miriam's waist and kissed her lips softly.

It was Miriam's first kiss.

Feeling his lips on her own caused her heart to skip and then beat rapidly. Stepping back, she looked at John with new eyes. As she looked at him, taking in the man she knew she would spend the rest of her life with, she struggled to bring her breathing back under control.

"Goodnight, John. I will see you in the morning," she said softly. She wanted to dance, although it would be frowned upon by the elders. She wanted to sing; ditto on the elders. But the smile in her heart made its way to her lips and she couldn't stop smiling. Yes, it was silly, and the smile felt goofy, but it was still there plastered on her face.

"Goodnight. I think we should both go to our rooms – I want to respect you," John said, feeling breathless after his kiss.

When he had left, Miriam allowed herself a brief twirl of happiness. What the elders didn't see wouldn't hurt them.

\*\*\*

The next morning dawned more bright as the storm seemed to be blowing itself out. As they walked to the barn and carpentry shop, John and Joseph peered to the sky.

"It looks like the clouds are thinning out, Mr. Beiler. Look, to the west over there," John said, pointing.

"Yes, you're right! The wind has stopped and the snow has almost ended. Until the next storm blows in," Joseph said.

After helping Joseph with the livestock and eating a hearty breakfast, John returned home. Aside from the gently falling snow, there was no reason for him to continue staying, so he thanked the Beilers for their hospitality and, holding Miriam's hands, said he would return when the weather permitted.

Miriam smiled. "Yes! Weather permitting, we will see each other soon."

"John, please tell your *mamm* and *daed* that, if another storm blows up while you are visiting Miriam, you will have a place to stay here until it's safe to go home. That way, they won't worry needlessly," Joseph said.

"I will, sir, thank you!" John said, smiling gratefully.

\*\*\*

The next week, another storm came. This development sparked much conversation around dinner tables and in barns as Ephrata families began to hope that the string of harsh winter storms would be ending soon.

Bishop Stoltzfus used the time to visit the families in the district. His message for each was the same – they would continue to wait until the threat of storms was gone before gathering for services. He reminded families that illness still raged through the community. As families heard this, they decided that it was better to wait.

Families used the sunny lull between storms to shovel the high snow drifts, wash and dry clothing, chop wood and replenish wood piles and go grocery shopping to stock their pantries. Farmers and carpenters repaired damage to barns and homes caused by the high winds.

Because school was still canceled, children did their lessons at home as their mothers instructed them. And, for those families still dealing with illness, the solitude helped them to focus on treating sick children and parents, as well as getting better.

John took advantage of the calm, visiting Miriam as often as he could. He watched the sky carefully, peering through the windows of the Beiler home while he was there. One visit, he saw a bank of clouds far away as he arrived at the Beiler farm.

"Miriam, I'll really have to keep an eye on the sky today – we have another storm coming in," John said as he shrugged out of his coat.

"*Ya*, it is getting colder, isn't it?" Miriam observed, rubbing her arms briskly.

"I'll stay for only a few hours, then I'll go home so I can beat the storm," John promised.

In fact, he was halfway home when the winds suddenly picked up. John, feeling the icy cold like a sharp knife as it cut through the thick fabric of his coat. Pulling the coat closer around him, he slapped the reins on the horse's back, urging her to trot more quickly.

'Go, go on! Let's get home!" He shouted against the rising wail of the wind. The horse needed no more urging. She stretched full-out, wanting to be inside the warm barn. John steered her so she and the buggy went straight into the open door.

John jumped out of the buggy, unhitching it from the horse. Brushing the horse, he put a blanket over her, fed and watered her. Shutting the barn door securely, he gripped the icy rope and struggled against the stiff wind and gusts into the house. The door slammed, pushed by a particularly stiff gust of wind.

"*Ach!*" Emily screamed, dropping an empty casserole dish.

"*Mamm,* I'm sorry! I left the Beiler house an hour ago and the storm hit just as I got home," John said, panting.

"Oh, John, I don't care about the dish! You're home, safe from the storm. That's all that counts," she said, rushing to John, hugging him and thanking God for bringing him home.

***

"*Mamm,* will we can have anybody over to celebrate my birthday with us?" Miriam asked as she quilted.

"*Nee,* daughter. Too many people are still sick – these viruses are still epidemic here. Also, we don't know if a storm will hit or not. Bishop Stoltzfus wants families to worship and celebrate in their own homes. We will still be able to celebrate, but your brothers and sisters won't be coming over," said Sarah.

"That's what I was thinking about. I'll miss them. It won't feel the same with them gone, but at least we have each other."

"*Ya.* Don't worry. It will still be a happy and blessed day. And I am making your favorite cake. Who knows? If the weather is calm and John stays healthy, maybe he'll come to see you." Miriam's *mamm* gave her a knowing look.

"Maybe he will," Miriam said hopefully.

"He is a good, young man. Strong in his faith."

"Yes, he is, *mamm*. He's very strong in his love for the Lord."

Miriam's birthday was a quiet one, but the weather stayed calm – it had stayed so for the previous few days. Thus, nobody in the Beiler home was surprised to hear a knock at the door.

"John! Come in," Joseph said with a wide smile beaming through his long beard.

"Miriam, Happy Birthday," John said with a warm smile.

"Thank you. I'm very happy to see you."

"*Ya.*"

"Why don't the two of you warm up in the kitchen, and John, you can have a slice of Miriam's birthday cake."

"Denki," John said, his face flushed. While Miriam knew that her parents tacitly blessed the courtship between her and John, it was warming to hear them express it so plainly.

As they stood at the counter, eating twin slices of cinnamon apple cake, John said, "It is so good to see you, Miriam."

"*Ya.*"

"I'm just hopeful the storm holds out until tomorrow."

"Storm?"

"Didn't you see the clouds to the northwest? We're going to have another storm soon."

Miriam sighed. She didn't want to complain, but when was this going to end?

"*Denki*, John. We'll keep an eye out in that direction. We're supposed to be going to the *grossmudderhaus* to see if Miriam's grandfather is feeling better tomorrow morning. Maybe it would be better to go today," Miriam said without enthusiasm.

"Before you have to go," John said, reaching into the pocket of his trousers. "I wanted to give you something. For your birthday."

"You didn't have to—"

"I wanted to. It's not much, but I think it represents who you are," John said, handing Miriam a small box.

Opening the box, Miriam gasped as she saw a small, wooden box made of a light-colored wood. John had sanded the wood so that it gleamed. Lifting the box out of the box, Miriam opened it, finding several Bible verses and psalms nestled on small sheets of paper inside.

"Oh, John, *denki*! This is beautiful! I can store more Bible verses inside," Miriam said, feeling breathless.

"*Ya*. I thought of you as I made the box and looked for the best verses. Each one describes a quality I see in you – as you read them, you'll see what I mean," John said with a gentle smile.

Miriam blushed.

John leaned down and brushed Miriam's lips softly with his own. The contact tingled through him, and he struggled to breathe normally when they parted.

Miriam reacted in the same way to John's soft kiss. Inhaling deeply, she looked out the side window of the living room – and saw heavy clouds.

"Oh, John, look," she said sadly.

"*Nee*!" John said as he jumped up and jogged to the window. As he reached it, Joseph and Sarah came in, removing their coats and unwrapping their scarves.

"John, it looks like we're about to have another storm. We'd love to have you stay . . ."

"*Denki*, Mr. Beiler. But *daed* is just over his own flu. I have to go help him with the livestock. I'd better go now so I can beat the storm home," John said, pushing his arms into his coat. He wrapped his dark scarf snugly around his neck and set his hat firmly on his head. "Miriam, I hope you'll enjoy your gift. I know I'll enjoy mine. It is perfect – thank you! Goodbye, everyone!" John stepped outside, feeling his breath sucked out of his lungs by the strong, bitterly cold wind. Running to the barn, he quickly hitched the horse to the buggy. Slapping the reins, he told the horse, "Home! Now!" The horse needed no more urging.

John made it home and was able to get the horse unhitched

and brushed down before the storm hit in its fury. As he was jogging to the kitchen door, the snow began coming down, blown in all directions by the stiff wind.

This latest storm wasn't as strong as previous storms had been – but it was one of the longest, lasting six days. Amish families all over Ephrata were ready for the severe winter to end. Illness continued to take its toll on individuals and families. One infant came down with the vicious norovirus and, despite her parents' best efforts, she died after becoming severely dehydrated. Bishop Stoltzfus and the deacons heard of this tragedy, as well as the news that several families had found it necessary to take family members to the hospital to receive medical treatment for the stomach virus or flu.

After the storm ended, the bishop decided it was high time he visited individual families to pray with them.

"I want to make sure they are holding up emotionally and spiritually through this hard winter," he told his worried wife. "I will be fine. No clouds are in the distance – the sky is clear in all directions. It is only very cold."

"But husband, you will expose yourself to illness!" objected his wife.

"*Nee*. If any family members are still sick, I will not go into the house. I will pray with healthy family members only. Do not worry – God will protect me," he told his wife. "This harsh winter and season of sickness must end soon. I need to give families hope that this period will end. I will be back before nightfall." With that, the bishop climbed up into the buggy and left.

At the end of a long day of visits and prayer, he returned. Inside his house, he reported what he had learned.

"We have to pray for the Lapp family – their daughter's baby is the one who died of the stomach virus. She became extremely dehydrated after she couldn't keep anything in her stomach. Several families are still dealing with illness and they are understandably tired of not being able to leave their homes. *Ach*, this will be a very quiet, sober New Year's Eve," he sighed.

"Here, eat. I made roast beef with potatoes and plenty of vegetables. You need to eat right – your responsibilities take a lot out of you," his wife commented.

"*Ya*, they do. But I would have it no differently. Our community is very precious to me. The Lord willing, we will soon see an end to everything ravaging our families," he said, digging tiredly into his roast.

\*\*\*

Two weeks later, Miriam, warmly wrapped against the bitter cold, lugged a heavy basket full of wet laundry outside. As she set it down, she belatedly realized that it wasn't as bitterly cold as it had been for most of the winter. She cautiously loosened her scarf so she wouldn't overheat. After she had hung out the clothing, sheets and towels, she held the laundry basket out away from her so the mud caked to the bottom wouldn't get on her coat. Sitting on the bench in the entry way, she took her shoes off so she could clean them of the mud more easily.

"*Mamm*, good news! It's not as cold outside as it's been! I have to scrape mud from the bottoms of my shoes," she said, laughing happily.

"Thank God! Give me your shoes after you get the worst of the mud off. I'll clean them for you. Put your slippers on so you don't get cold," Sarah instructed.

Handing her shoes to her *mamm*, Miriam had a thought.

"How long has it been since the last blizzard?"

Sarah paused, thinking.

"Two weeks? Not quite two weeks? That's a good question. It makes me think that, finally, this hard winter is going to be over – especially if I can't remember when we had our last storm," Sara commented.

Both women turned toward the door as they heard Joseph stamping hard on the wood porch.

"Mud! I don't like it, but it's a good sign! Miriam, after the laundry has been brought in and we have cared for the livestock tonight, you and I will have to sweep the porch clean. It will look very messy, otherwise."

"Joseph, give me your boots. I'm cleaning Miriam's shoes. There's no need to bring mud into a clean house," Sarah said, vigorously cleaning Miriam's shoes with an old towel she had dampened.

Indeed, Amish families all over Ephrata soon realized that the heavy-handed grip winter had been exerting seemed to be loosening. Families began to ask when the children would be able to return to school.

Then . . .

"Sarah, there's a new bank of clouds outside! Still at a distance, but you might want to bring the laundry in. I checked it. It feels cold but dry," Joseph said.

Sarah, peeling potatoes and carrots for supper, looked up at Joseph in alarm.

"*Nee*! Not another storm!" She dropped the peeler, wiping her hands as she hurried to a window to check outside. "The wind is picking up. Oh, Joseph, this doesn't look good. Miriam – oh, good, you have your coat on. *Denki,*" she said as she pulled her own coat on. She and Miriam hurried outside, where they brought clean, albeit slightly damp laundry inside.

Late that evening, after the wind had continued to blow and gust, Miriam looked up curiously from her latest quilting order pattern.

"*Daed*? Is that . . . rain?" she asked.

"*Ya*, it is," he said, peering outside. "I can't tell if it's just rain or rain mixed with snow. We will have to wait until daylight to see what happened. I just hope we will be able to avoid any more blizzards – we are still in winter," Joseph mused.

"*Ya*. That worries me, too. Farmers are having to try and plan their crops for this spring, not knowing what will happen between now and planting time," said Miriam.

"That's why we trust in the Lord, hope for the best and prepare for the worst," said Sarah briskly as she walked into the kitchen. "Hot tea, Miriam?"

"Yes, please! I still need to finish this quilting pattern so I can start on this order," said Miriam.

"Well, I am going to rejoice in the sound of rain, not wind," said Joseph.

Waking the next morning, Miriam made a beeline to her bedroom window. Peeking outside, she was disappointed to see that snow had fallen – but the snow had ended overnight. Dressing, combing her hair and setting her prayer *kapp* neatly on her head, she bounded downstairs.

"Well, *guder mariye*, daughter! We got snow, but not a blizzard last night. I'd call that progress, wouldn't you?" Sarah said as she beat eggs for breakfast.

"*Ya*, I would! I'm going to help *daed*, unless you need me in here?" Miriam asked.

"*Nee*. Go help him. When you get back to the house, take

your shoes off and I'll clean them for you."

In the barn, Miriam milked cows and helped Joseph muck out stalls. Once that was done they fed and watered all the horses and cows.

"Inside. It is still very cold out here," Joseph said. As he spoke, great clouds of steam blew out of his mouth.

***

All across the district, families rejoiced that the previous night's snow had not become a full-blown blizzard. In the Zook home, Michael and Rachel began talking about the school house reopening.

"Adam needs to get back to school. He's doing well here, but Miss Yoder is an excellent teacher," Rachel said.

"I expect we'll hear some news before very long, Rachel. When I was at the store yesterday, the talk was that fewer and fewer people are coming down with flu or that stomach virus. If the weather actually calms down, it's possible the school board will see fit to send the scholars back," said Michael as he sipped his coffee.

"Adam, are you ready to go back to school?" asked Rachel.

"*Ya, mamm,* but are you tired of teaching me?" Adam asked with a worried frown.

"Oh, *nee,* son, *nee!* I just feel that Miss Yoder is more

qualified to be teaching you language and math," Rachel said with a wry grin. "And it is time for me to start supper."

Bishop Stoltzfus met with the three deacons.

"Sickness is getting less and less every week. It's still winter, but as long as we have some idea when a storm is brewing, I believe we might be able to resume church meetings. I'd like to hear from each of you," he said.

"I agree . . . to a point. I'd like to keep an eye on both situations for two weeks more. If we have more mild weather and no violent blizzards, and if the flu and stomach bug are truly going down, I support resuming services two weeks from this Sunday," said Paul King.

"I agree. The situation looks good now, but families could start getting sick again," commented Isaac Kurtz. "Or the weather could turn again."

"I would like to wait a little longer, said Abram Kuhns. "The Lapp family is still mourning the loss of their daughter and granddaughter, after she died from the stomach bug. We must be cautious."

"Why is that?" asked the bishop.

"Because I don't want to see other families bereaved. Waiting for a month won't hurt us. The flu season won't truly end until after spring begins."

"Let's talk. Then we'll vote," decided Bishop.

After some spirited discussion about the pros and cons of resuming church services sooner rather than later, the group finally decided on a tentative start two Sundays later, provided no new outbreaks of illness were reported.

"We can handle the weather. Illness, not so much. Abram, if it appears that people are beginning to get sick again, I'll postpone the church services for an additional two weeks," said the bishop.

"*Ya*. Okay, that is good. *Denki* for listening," said Abram.

"It's calm today. Let's divide the district into four parts and spread the news of our decision. Now, about school . . ."

At the end of their meeting, the deacons and bishop had decided to resume school the next week, provided no new outbreaks of flu were reported.

"Now, the last meeting when we had our first blizzard and the flu started was at the Beiler farm. Samuel and Emily Fisher are next on the list. I will visit them and the families near them. I'll let the Fishers know of our decision so they can get things ready," Bishop Stoltzfus said.

Families were happy when they knew that the isolation imposed upon them had a foreseeable ending date. Scholars were happy, knowing they'd be learning – and visiting – with each other soon. All across Ephrata, families sent up fervent prayers that the illnesses ravaging the area were truly on the decrease. Farmers and carpenters prayed that they would get the moisture their crops needed, and that the wild blizzards were truly coming to an end.

For the families forced to stay at home, the next two weeks passed excruciatingly slowly. Children, teens, young adults and parents all looked forward to the meeting scheduled at the Fisher farm. That day dawned clear and cold. Most farmers had retained the habit of scanning the horizon, looking for clouds. Seeing only a light gray grouping of clouds far in the distance, families happily boarded buggies, loading their lunch contributions.

"Husband, I pray those clouds hold only rain," said Mary Miller.

"It's not as cold as it was when we were getting the blizzards. We have little wind. These clouds hold rain, not snow," said Mr. Miller.

However, the air temperature took a sudden, sharp drop while families were eating lunch. Feeling the sudden bite to the air, the wives and girls serving lunch sped up their serving and cleaning so families could get home before the storm hit.

Samuel, Emily and John Fisher all breathed a sigh of relief as families boarded their buggies for home.

"I pray they all get home – the families who live farthest out will need to move fast," said Emily.

"I believe they will," Samuel said. "John, let's take care of the livestock before the snow starts."

# CHAPTER TEN

Most families made it home safely before the snow began falling. Three families were still en route for home when the snow started falling. Two families, very close to their farms, managed to find the entrances to their yards. They got their buggies and horses into their barns, then stumbled into their homes. The third family –the Millers – wasn't as fortunate. Their horse became confused as the road seemed to vanish in a sudden heavy snowfall. He went off the road before reaching the yard. Both horse and buggy foundered in the deep snow, piled on top of roadside foliage.

"We're not that far from home! Just a few yards more. Bundle up and everyone hold hands!" shouted Mr. Miller. He led, breaking the deep snow with his boots and shins. Feeling for their wood fence, he became snow-blind and confused. The extreme cold, wind and snow all conspired to make him get lost. After several minutes more, his youngest children were overcome by the cold, developing the beginnings of hypothermia. He, Mary and Hannah soon began experiencing hypothermia as well.

"Come here . . . sit . . . with me. Stay . . . warm," he mumbled, not thinking clearly. He and Mary gathered their three children into a close group, huddling to share what body heat they had. As the storm blew and raged, the family's hypothermia became severe, leading to extreme tiredness and confusion. The two youngest girls went first, then Hannah. Finally, believing the children had only dozed off, Mary and her husband fell asleep, not realizing they would never wake up again.

This latest blizzard lasted until early Wednesday morning. Bishop Stoltzfus, worried about the members of his community, went from farm to farm, reassuring himself that everyone was safe and healthy. As he drove past the Miller's farm, he saw their buggy some distance from the gate, lying canted at an odd angle in a snowbank.

"No, no! Please, Lord, let them be inside and safe!" he muttered. As he stumbled through the deep snow, he fell to his knees – the horse was still hitched to the buggy, frozen stiff. The bishop stood, fearing the worst. He scanned the countryside, looking – for what?

His eyes stopped on an odd formation of snow. Slowly walking to it and not wanting to see what might be buried underneath, he began brushing at the powdery cover.

Eventually, he uncovered a dark-green hood, then a maroon-colored hood and scarf.

"*Nee*, Lord, no! In your mercy, why?" he asked. He continued to brush at the snow, uncovering five bodies. As soon as he confirmed that the Millers had not made it safely inside, he drove to the next farm to break the sad news.

"We need to get all the bodies inside – or bury them under snow so they won't decompose too quickly," the bishop said sadly. The weather had outsmarted him and his deacons.

Back at the Miller farm, he, the farmer and his two oldest sons extricated the Millers from their snowy bank, lifting them tenderly onto the wagon. Once every body had been uncovered, the bishop, farmer and farmer's sons sadly buried the bodies under several feet of snow.

"Once it begins to warm, we will bury them. *Ach*, how sad to lose an entire family to weather! *Denki*. Get inside, where it is warm. We will let you know about school for your scholars," said Bishop Stoltzfus.

"*Denki*. If they had only gone a few yards further . . ." said the farmer.

"No. I think the horse was blinded by the snow and wind. He couldn't have taken them even one foot farther," the bishop disagreed. "If you will start spreading this sad news, I'll start letting families know. We will have another funeral to attend when it warms."

Regardless of the recent blizzard, school resumed only a few days off schedule. Families sent their children to school on the following Monday, five days after the blizzard ended. Children trooped eagerly into the school room, greeting friends and classmates with excitement.

"It is good to have all of my scholars back!" said a beaming Rebecca Yoder. "We will be watching out for the weather. About illness – we believe the flu and stomach bug have ended, but if you do not feel well, tell me right away. I will get word to your parents so they can pick you up. Do you understand?"

"Yes, Miss Yoder," chorused her scholars.

"We have been out of school since before Thanksgiving. I trust you did the work I sent home with Bishop Stoltzfus?" At her scholars' confirming nods, Rebecca smiled with approval. "Good. I will be testing all of you to see how far you got with your learning. It isn't Easter yet, but I have to set the dates for our final examinations! We will have much work to do between now and then, so let's get busy . . ."

***

All across Ephrata, Amish farmers and carpenters began preparing to plant their spring crops or buy wood to make furniture for their *Englischer* customers. At farm after farm, men and older sons were out, plowing the earth with mules and plows. Sons and older daughters followed behind, sprinkling seed behind the slow-moving plow. In carpenter's shops, like

Joseph Beiler's shop, carpenter after carpenter gazed at their customers' orders and drew out plans. Once they knew what they needed to do, they began sawing the wood preparatory to making the furniture under order.

The sad aftermath of the harsh winter still overshadowed the Amish community. Bishop Stoltzfus met with his deacons to plan the funerals for the community members who had not survived illness or weather.

"We need to bury them before it starts to get too warm. We will visit each family and schedule funeral services. Once these are scheduled, we will let the community know so everyone can be present to help the families," the bishop said.

# CHAPTER ELEVEN

As February moved into March, the Amish residents of Ephrata were grateful to see an end to the wild storms that had pummeled them. Miss Yoder began helping her scholars prepare for their final examinations, giving them review work.

On one long, hard day, John Fisher helped his *daed* with the spring planting. Coming back to the barn, he wiped sweat and dirt from his face and neck, then unhitched the mule from the plow.

"Let's feed and water the cows, horses and mule, John, then go inside. It's been a long, very hard day and I'm grateful for your help," Samuel said, exhaustion in his voice.

"*Denki, daed.* I'm just glad that we planted the last of the crops today," John replied. "If the weather holds, I plan to visit Miriam later this week."

"*Ya*, that's fine. Just let us know first," John said.

"*Daed*, I am thinking of asking Mr. Beiler for Miriam's hand in marriage. She is a very wonderful girl, strong in her love for God," John said, feeling nervous.

"Oh! So, it's that way, is it? I agree – she is a very good girl, but I wouldn't be surprised if her parents ask you to wait for a year or so before proposing marriage. She is only seventeen, you know."

"I know. I just want to let them know how I feel about her. I have fallen in love with her and I want to spend the rest of my life with her."

By now, the two men had finished feeding and watering their livestock and had begun milking their herd of cows. They continued talking about John's plans to propose to Miriam.

"There is also the matter of her baptism into the community. She needs to make a firm decision that she is going to learn and follow the *Ordnung* before she takes her Kneeling Vow, John," said Samuel, reminding his son of the lifelong commitment that the Amish made.

"*Denki, daed, ya.* I am positive she will decide to make that commitment. She has never shown any discomfort with the *Ordnung*. Plus, her parents are strong in the faith and they can help her understand just how serious this kind of commitment truly is."

"Good. Yes, I agree, Joseph and Sarah are very good teachers. They've helped their older children understand just how important it is to understand the importance of baptism to our community. Also . . . on the topic of children, you should know this. We are very protective of our community, beliefs and faith for a very good reason. We want to keep our beliefs and protect ourselves from the intrusion of *Englischer* beliefs and practices. A part of that has been our practice of intermarrying. Third and fourth cousins – and even second cousins – have married in past years. This practice has caused some health issues to become more . . . what is the word? Pronounced. Thankfully, there is no blood connection between our family and the Beilers. Any children that you and Miriam have should be strong and healthy," Samuel said. Seeing John's bright-red face, he chuckled.

"I am sorry to embarrass you, but I thought you needed to know this piece of information."

"*Denki* . . . I think. *Ya*, it is important for us to know that we will have healthy children in time. I just . . . this topic is a bit . . ." John said, unable to continue.

"Embarrassing, I know. When you are innocent, discussing it is never easy. But discuss it you must. I know of too many other Amish who disregarded the danger in the practice of interfamily marriage. Now, they regret it, with their children suffering from heart defects, other conditions and even mental conditions. If you had come to me, telling me you wanted to marry your cousin Rebekah, I would have told you to reconsider. *Ya*, I know we don't have formal education past the eighth grade, but as long as we take our book-learning and use it for the better of our community, we can try to prevent something that can hurt us as a people. Do you see what I'm saying, Son?" Samuel asked, looking deep into his son's dark-brown eyes.

"When you put it that way, it's easier, *daed*. *Ya*. I do see why it's important. It's just that . . . well, when I had to stay at their farm, when that blizzard hit . . . it was . . . difficult, staying out of her room at night." John's red face had become even more red as he made this admission.

"And?"

"I stayed in my room and prayed. I went downstairs for a glass of water. *Daed*, I don't want to disgrace her or ruin her reputation. That's the only thing that kept me from knocking on her door."

"Good. I know you love her and it was a huge temptation. I am glad you resisted it, with God's help. You are learning how difficult it is to truly love a woman, John. It won't be easy, this next couple of years before you marry. I'm warning you of that right now. While you are courting Miriam, it is highly important that you keep her reputation as an honest woman in mind. Don't put yourself or her into situations where her virtue could be doubted. If she does plan to take the Kneeling Vow, she must become very familiar with the *Ordnung* and she must protect her reputation. You and her parents can help her with that. It is harder for a young Amish woman than it is for a young man. In the end, you both have the serious responsibility of staying true to Amish beliefs and rules – and I believe you are very capable of that." Samuel, giving John a serious look, clapped his hand on John's shoulder.

"*Denki.* Thank you for believing in me. I will do everything I can to protect her reputation," John promised.

\*\*\*

The next evening, John drove the family buggy to the Beiler farm so he could visit with Miriam. Because the evenings were still cool, they visited inside the house, talking, laughing, sharing jokes and drinking lemonade. John had chosen to wear the dark-green shirt Miriam had given him for Christmas.

Miriam, seeing that he was wearing her gift, smiled softly at him.

"It looks . . . very good on you, John. Turn around and show me," she said. As he slowly turned in front of her, Miriam's eyes roved over his muscular, but lean torso. Feeling her heart pounding, she nodded. "It fits you beautifully. I will be finished with this next quilt earlier than I thought, so I would like to make another shirt for you – one you can wear as you work in the fields," she promised.

"*Denki!*" John smiled. "Miriam, I have been wondering something . . ."

"*Ya?* What is it?" Miriam asked.

"Do you plan to take the Kneeling Vow? Do you want to

learn and follow the *Ordnung*?"

"Well, *ya*, of course! I have never thought of not being baptized into our faith – it's too important to me . . . why? Are you thinking of not . . ."

"Oh, *nee*, Miriam! Like you, our faith has carried me through some very difficult times. I am planning to take my own Kneeling Vow . . . I just wanted to see if you were going to do the same thing, that's all," John said.

"Oh . . ." Miriam said. She now understood more than she had before John had brought up his question. "Oh!"

"I will see you in the next few days, *ya*? It will be getting dark soon, so I have to leave," said John, taking Miriam's hand in his and caressing it gently.

"*Ya*, we will see each other soon," Miriam promised.

Before he left to go home, he sought out Miriam's *daed* and *mamm*.

"I . . . would like to speak with you for just a few minutes . . . " John said, trying to keep his breathing regular.

"Certainly. Let's go outside . . . I take it this is between the three of us for now?" Joseph asked.

"*Ya*, sir, it is," John nodded, glancing quickly toward the quilting room, where Miriam had just gone.

Outside, the three sat on the long bench just outside the barn.

"Mr. and Mrs. Beiler, I have been courting Miriam for the last several months. We have grown close and I have developed . . . strong feelings for her. We talked this evening about our Kneeling Vows. I wanted to see what she had thought of and whether she'd made a decision. She told me she's going to be baptized . . . and so am I. Mr. and Mrs. Beiler, our faith is very important to both of us. It's gotten us through some very painful times," John said.

"And you want . . .?" Joseph asked.

"I want to marry her. I'm asking for your permission to propose to her," John said, feeling a distinct quaver in his voice.

Joseph and Sarah looked at each other, surprise in their eyes.

Sarah thought about her youngest child, now nearly an adult. She had seen six older children meet, fall in love with and marry young Amish men and women. Her home would be empty, probably within the next two or three years. Knowing this, her heart gave a twinge.

Joseph realized Miriam was now old enough to contemplate becoming a married woman and, eventually, a *mamm* of children of her own.

"I am glad – *we* – are glad to hear that. Yes, our faith is very important to us," Joseph said slowly. He looked at Sarah, who gave a tiny nod. "We have no objection. In fact, we are very happy that you want to spend your life with her, but we would ask you one thing. She is still young and she must finish her *rumspringe*. You have our permission to ask her, but would you wait for another year or two? You must be baptized into the church before marrying, as well."

"*Denki! Denki! Ya,* I will wait, but I do want to let her know of my intentions, if you don't mind," John said, trying to catch his breath.

"Good. Yes, that is fine. We will urge her to speak to Bishop Stoltzfus about her baptism into the church as well," Sarah promised.

Inside the quilting room, Miriam peered outside. Seeing the Fisher's buggy still parked outside, her brow creased in confusion, then her jaw dropped.

*Oh! He's talking to mamm and daed! That's why he asked me about whether I'm going to be baptized.* Miriam's hand covered her heart, now pounding strong and hard. Looking to the empty doorway, she scuttled to her comfortable chair – it wouldn't do for her *mamm* to see her peeking out the window at John's buggy. She picked up the almost-finished quilt with shaky hands, and then set it down again. Closing her eyes, she said a silent prayer for calm – it wouldn't do for her shaky hands to cause her to make a mistake on a very expensive Amish Wedding quilt.

At home, John sat down with his *mamm* and *daed*.

"I spoke with Miriam and she plans to take her Kneeling

Vow. She's still on her *rumspringe*, but I don't think she'll change her mind about being baptized. She told me that her faith is just too important to her." John let out a huge, shaky sigh. "Then, I spoke to her parents and asked them for permission to ask Miriam to marry me. They gave me permission, but asked me to wait for a year or two, until she's a little older."

"*Ach*, good! You will make each other a good husband and wife!" Emily exulted, clasping her hands together.

"It's as I thought, John. She is young and I had a good idea that they would want her to wait until she is a little older. Are you disappointed?"

"*Nee, daed.* How can I be? I have permission to propose in a couple years, but I will be telling Miriam what my intentions are. I want her to know that I am falling in love with her. Besides, it gives us more time to get to know each other," John said firmly.

"John . . . just remember to respect her. Don't put her into situations where her character or virtue could be questioned," Sarah said.

John colored. "*Mamm*, I talked about that with *daed*. She – Miriam – has nothing to worry about from me. I want to protect her good reputation as much as you want to. Don't worry . . . I will do nothing to hurt her. She is too precious to me," he said.

Sarah gave a quick nod. "Good. Just keep your love for her

in mind when you go courting her."

\*\*\*

Miriam woke early in the morning a few weeks later. Listening, she realized she was hearing the pitter-patter of rain as it hit the house's roof. Stretching luxuriously, she threw her blankets back and got up. Dressing and coming her hair, she made sure she was presentable. Downstairs, while she and Sarah made breakfast, someone knocked at the door.

"You keep working on the eggs and I'll get that," Sarah said. Wiping her hands on a towel, she answered the door.

"Emily! What is it? Come in. Coffee?"

"*Denki*. Sarah, we are needed at a difficult birth. The mother is young and it's her first child . . ."

"Say no more. Eat before we go, because we don't know how long it will be before that baby is born," Sarah directed. As Joseph walked in from the barn, she began filling plates with scrambled eggs, hash brown and bacon. "Joseph, Emily and I are needed at a birth. We'll leave as soon as we've eaten."

"Oh, what about Miriam?"

"*Daed*, I'll stay here. I can get dinner ready. Besides, I need to finish a quilt. *Mamm*, don't worry. Take as long as you need. I know what you plan to make, so it is no problem," Miriam said.

"Good," Sarah said. She and Emily began eating quickly. Miriam was right – they didn't know what they would find when they arrived at the Hofstetter farm and they might be there, helping the new *mamm* for several hours.

Grabbing her cloak and purse, Sarah waved goodbye to Joseph and Miriam, then hurried out with Emily.

"Well, it looks like Mrs. Fisher and your *mamm* are still in high demand, doesn't it?" Joseph asked.

Miriam chuckled. "*Ya.* It's good though – they are using their nursing knowledge to help others. I think I'll get the vegetables and meat ready for our dinner, then work on my quilt. Then, I'll cook dinner and we can eat. I don't think she'll be back by dinnertime."

"I doubt it. You may also have to prepare supper. Do you know what your *mamm* had planned?"

"I think she was going to bake some chicken and make potatoes and vegetables," Miriam said. "I'm ahead on my quilt, anyway. I'll make dinner if *mamm* is still gone."

"Okay, just as long as you know she might be gone for some hours," Joseph said. Standing, he took his plate to the sink and ran hot water over it. "I have several orders to work on, so I'll be in the shop. Let me know if you need me," said Joseph.

"I will. Be careful in the shop!" Miriam stood and gathered the plates, cups and silverware. After washing the dishes and cleaning the stove, she prepared the vegetables and made sure the meatloaf was ready to bake.

*\*\*\**

Sarah and Emily heard the screaming even before they got inside the house; the screaming of someone very young and extremely desperate. There was a ragged quality to the voice as if the owner had been screaming for a long time. It was a girl's scream, punctuated by intermittent cries for her mamm. As they walked across the porch and knocked on the door, they prepared for the worst. It was going to be a long, horrible day.

The door opened inward revealing a man in his early thirties.

"Jacob," Sarah began, her lips pressed tightly together in a fine line. Her eyebrows were furrowed as she stepped into the kitchen. "Where is the child." Screams gave her an answer, and she quickly headed towards the bedroom, followed by Emily. In the bed was a girl, hair plastered against her forehead, a reddening quilt covering her. She was thin, pale and shaking. Her eyes were opened wide, sweat running down her forehead.

"Please help me," she sobbed. "I want my *mamm*. It hurts so much." Another wave of pain came upon her and her words dissolved into howls as she grabbed at Sarah's arm.

Jacob stood by the door, shifting silently from foot to foot. Sarah placed her hand on the girl's distended belly, feeling her, then placed her other hand between her legs under the quilt.

"Water's broken and there's a lot of blood. The baby isn't turned completely around, but at least it's not completely breached."

Emily shooed Jacob out of the room as the pain passed and the girl quieted. She hurried into the kitchen, put a big pot of water on. "I'm going to need a lot of towels, and you should call a driver."

"Why?" Jacob grumbled. "Is the girl going to die?"

Emily stopped for a moment looking at him. "I don't know." She replied finally, but we may need to take her to the hospital if we can't deliver the baby." He turned and went for towels as Emily shook her head silently, returning to the bedroom. Sarah wiped the girl's forehead with a warm cloth.

"Where are her parents? Her mamm should be here/" Sarah made soothing sounds to the girl who seemed more confused than anything.

"I want my mamm," the girl cried. "Please. I thought I could do this, but I can't. I don't want to have a baby anymore. Can you make it stop?"

"Elizabeth, I need you to listen to me," Sarah held the girl's hand even though it hurt her because the girl was holding on so tightly. "I want you to think of the sea. As the pains come I want you to breathe in with it. Think of the ocean waves as they come to shore. As the pain ebbs and starts to go away, think of the sea waves going out. Match your breathing on a count of four. Count with me – one, two, three, four…."

Emily turned back to Jacob who was standing in the kitchen holding towels. Taking them from him, she said again, "You need to get her mamm here. I don't understand why she isn't here. The girl needs her mother at a time like this."

Jacob shrugged his shoulders, turned and put on his coat and hat and went out the door. It closed behind him, Emily watching him go. She went back into the bedroom and spoke softly into Sarah's ear, "Why did he marry a child." Sarah shook her head and continued to coach the girl and dry her forehead.

"And why isn't her mother here." Sarah shook her head sadly. "Let's just work to get this baby born, and if necessary, get her to the hospital if things go more wrong than they already have."

"He is an idiot. When her labor started, he should have sent for her mother." Emily squinted and handed Sarah towels. I'll get the hot water, and let's get her off this filthy sheet and quilt."

"It will help if you try to stand," Sarah gently helped the girl to a standing position. "I know it hurts, but it's something we've done for centuries. You'll be fine." Emily hurried around the bed pulling the bloody sheets and quilts off of it, laying down plastic, then towels and finally a fresh sheet. Sarah helped the girl to sit on the edge of the bed. "We've sent for your mamm."

# CHAPTER TWELVE

Glancing at her watch, Miriam made a mental note to come back to the kitchen shortly after eleven so she could start dinner. Hurrying to the quilting room, she got busy right away. Two hours later, she stood and stretched her neck and back, then glanced at her watch. Seeing that it was nearly time to start dinner, she shut her sewing machine off and hurried into the kitchen. Forty-five minutes later, she removed a bubbling, fragrant meatloaf from the oven, taking it to the table with the rest of the food.

Joseph walked in, sniffing appreciatively. "That smells *wunderbar*!" Washing his hands at the kitchen sink, he returned to the table. "If your *mamm* is not back by mid-afternoon, you might want to get started with supper," he said after swallowing.

"*Ya*. I have the chicken ready to go into the oven and I've picked out vegetables we can eat – I hope you won't mind if they're ones that *mamm* and I canned last summer," Miriam said.

"*Nee*, it is no problem! Whatever you feel like making will taste *wunderbar*, Miriam . . . ah, and there is your mother!"

Sarah walked in quietly, her shoulders slumped slightly.

"*Mamm*? What happened?" Miriam asked, fearing her mother's answer.

"No matter what we tried, the baby died. He was born too soon. He could not live outside his *mamm's* womb. Emily and I tried everything to stop her labor, but it was too far advanced. *Ach*, why her parents let her marry this young, I do not know! She was bleeding, so we forced them to take her to the hospital." Sarah slumped in exhaustion on a kitchen chair, forcing tears back.

"Oh, no! Was it Elizabeth Hoffstetter?" Miriam asked, shocked. *She's only fifteen!* "*Mamm*, how old is her husband?" Miriam was half-afraid to hear the answer.

"Ugh, Miriam, it is bad. He is past thirty. Why he could not choose an older wife, one who is more-capable of bearing a child, I do not know."

Miriam lost her appetite. Pushing her still-full plate back with her thumb, she frowned.

"Isn't that unnatural for a man his age to want to marry someone who's still almost a child?" she asked.

"*Ya*, it is, daughter. Jacob Hoffstetter has always been . . . odd. I think this time, that his . . . *preferences* are going to get him much unwanted scrutiny from the state. Thankfully, the bishop registered his objections to their marriage. What worries me is that her parents didn't seem too worried," Sarah said.

Joseph set his fork down and pushed his own plate back as well.

"I'm not hungry, either. *Ya*, the state will investigate. If Bishop Stoltzfus kept a record of his conversation with Jacob and with Elizabeth's parents, we – the Amish community – will not be blamed. The scrutiny will fall exactly where it should. On Jacob Hoffstetter. I've always thought he was too attracted to underage girls. Do you remember when he started to follow Miriam home from school?"

"*Ya*! I do! I talked to the bishop about it . . ." Sarah said.

"He scared me when he was trying to get my attention. That's why I asked for permission for rides home with Katy. Her father never allowed Jacob to come around us. Never. *Mamm*, you go rest. I'll clean up and put the food away. I think we've all lost our appetites anyway,"

"*Denki*, daughter. I am tired and very sad. I will come downstairs after a nap and make supper." Running her hand over Miriam's hair and *kapp*, Sarah walked slowly upstairs.

After hearing the sad news, Miriam found she had to force

herself to focus on finishing the Wedding quilt.

John came to the house that night. The mood in the Beiler home was still somber.

"So, you heard about what happened to Elizabeth Hoffstetter, too?" he asked.

"*Ya. Mamm* thinks the state is going to be looking very closely at Jacob," Miriam said quietly.

"And they should. He has always had an . . . odd . . . attraction to teenagers. *Mamm* and I talked after she had a good, hard cry . . . Mrs. Beiler, how are you feeling?"

"Angry. I agree with you. Pennsylvania should look hard at Jacob Hoffstetter. I know that some of our families intermarry and this makes some health problems worse. But, for a grown man to have such an interest in a girl who has barely left her own childhood behind – there's a word for it, Miriam. I believe he's a pedophile – someone who has an unnatural interest in children," Sarah said, frowning in distaste.

Miriam, who was innocent of all sexual matters, began to blush.

"You mean . . . there are men who are interested in . . ." she clamped her mouth shut against the bad taste at the thought and idea of a man touching her when she was young. Looking at John, she saw he was experiencing the same distaste.

"Okay. Enough of bereavement and sadness. You two focus

on yourselves. Let the community and state deal with Jacob Hoffstetter. Go, now," Sarah said, shooing John and Miriam to the living room.

Miriam and John sat in the living room talking. It took Miriam a few minutes to pull herself out of what she had been learning about Jacob Hoffstetter. John seemed to have a hard time coming back to the present, as well.

"Would you like to go for a buggy ride?" he asked.

"*Ya.* Let me tell my parents and get a sweater," she said, hurrying to the kitchen. Coming back, she said, "It's fine as long as I'm back before nightfall."

"Let's go. I want to allow nature to get those ugly thoughts out of our heads," John said grimacing.

Driving the buggy down the road, John went to a large tree by the river. Jumping down, he took Miriam's hand and helped her come down. Keeping her hand in his, he walked to a large rock sitting under the tree.

Miriam sat down next to John, letting out a huge sigh. *God, allow Your beauty to drive away that ugly knowledge I now have about Jacob Hoffstetter! I want to thank You for sending others to protect me from him. If I had not had them around, I could have been the one giving birth.*

"Why so quiet?" John asked. He took Miriam's hand in his, holding it securely.

Miriam enjoyed the soft touch of his hand enveloping hers.

"I am just grateful to God for protecting me from Jacob when I was fourteen and getting ready to graduate from school. Having my friend and her *daed* there to help me get home from school safely means that, today, I don't have to worry about being married to him or having to deal with . . . with . . . whatever his sickness is. It could have been me giving birth and not Elizabeth."

"It is a sickness. I thank God that He intervened and protected you." John fell silent, gazing around that the cool spring evening. Seeing the light-green buds coming out on the tree, he sighed deeply. Raising her hand still caught in his, John kissed the back of it as he gazed at Miriam.

"Miriam . . . I brought you out here for a very specific reason. We have been seeing each other since last fall and I have begun to fall in love with you. We are both going to be baptized into our community. I know you're still on your *rumspringe*. I spoke to your *daed* and *mamm* a few weeks ago, and I asked them for permission to propose to you."

"Oh! Oh. Really?"

"Yes, really," John said laughing.

"And? What did they say?"

"Yes . . . but . . ."

"'But?' But . . . what?" Miriam was tense, waiting to hear.

"'But' they want us to wait a year or two until you are older. Until you've been baptized in the Kneeling Vow. And, of course, I still need to do the same . . . so . . . will you marry me in a few years?"

"Yes! Yes, I will!" Miriam said, laughing. Her previous sadness had been blown away with her excitement over John's proposal. "And, I agree – this time before we get married gives us time to get to know each other much better."

John swept Miriam into his arms, rejoicing. Lowering his head, he kissed her.

THE END.

# TEST OF FAITH

## CHAPTER ONE

Several weeks after Miriam Beiler had agreed to marry John Fisher, she was returning home from the weekly Amish market where she had just finished talking to a wealthy *Englischer* couple about quilts they wanted to order for their grown children and grandchildren. They wanted a Wedding quilt for their youngest daughter, who would be marrying her fiancée in about nine months. The couple also wanted quilts for their three young grandchildren.

"If you can make these four quilts, we are prepared to pay you well for your work and materials. We've been looking at quilts for some time now, and yours stand out as the best-made. We also love your use of color," said the *Englischer* woman. "So, can you do it?"

"*Ya*, I can. *Denki* for your trust in me! Now, we need to talk about what colors you want for each quilt. For the *kinner*, I can make smaller quilts that will easily fit their beds," Miriam said, holding a pencil over a writing pad.

"Well, Robyn's wedding colors are gold and purple – can you make a Wedding quilt using white, gold and purple? For the . . . *kinner?* . . . Andrew loves the primary colors, Becky goes nuts for pink and lavender and Ashley enjoys shades of the same color. I'm thinking for her, two or three shades of green would go well in her room. Can you do all this?" asked the woman.

"I can, but I need to look through my supply of fabrics to see what I already have. I believe I have the green, but it's a darker green, like my dress. How old is Ashley?"

"She's seven, going to be eight this year. If you could, maybe lighter and brighter greens?"

"*Ya*, I can do that. I will buy the fabric and get started. This will take me to the end of the year – probably between Thanksgiving and Christmas – before I finish. If you would be so kind as to write your phone number down, I will call when all four quilts are done," Miriam promised.

"Excellent! We will be telling friends and family about your work - that's how you advertise, right?" asked the *Englischer* man.

"Yes, it is. Let your family and friends know that, when I'm done with your order, I will be happy to meet with them to discuss anything they might want me to do," Miriam asked.

"Will do! You have a wonderful day!"

"*Denki*!" Miriam said.

As she walked out with Anna, Miriam told her about her big order.

"So, why are you so worried? You are the best quilt-maker in Ephrata, if not Lancaster County! You learned from your *grossmudder*. Is your machine oiled and working well?" Anna asked.

"It is, but I don't want it stopping mid-stitch. Can your *daed* check it for me today?

"*Ya*, I will send him over today. Now, why don't we go shopping for our supplies tomorrow? I have a big order of my own!" Anna said with a twinkling smile.

"Yes? How big?"

"I have two large cross stitch projects to make for the *Englischer* woman that always stops here. She finally decided what she wants and asked me to do the work!"

Both girls looked at each other with big grins.

"Anna, things are finally starting to pay off! My customers said they would tell their friends and family about my work!"

The two friends parted after promising to meet after dinner the next day. Miriam, caught up in the excitement of her huge order, was thinking about that rather than paying full attention to what was going on as she drove home. She came to reality when the horse reared, giving a frightened whinny.

Miriam looked in horror at the shiny, late model black truck that had almost run her over. Her temper flared. She opened up the door to the buggy and shouted at the driver, "Be careful!"

"Whoa, miss, I'm sorry!" the driver said. He jumped out of the truck, babbling, "I'm lost . . . and I missed seeing the stop sign." His tone was flustered, but his eyes seemed strangely cool.

Miriam took a breath, reminding herself that allowing herself to let her temper get out of hand was not what God would want for her. "Well, vehicles like yours can do a lot of damage to our livestock," Miriam explained. "I would appreciate it if you would pay attention to the road."

"Do you know where the high school is?" the man asked. "All I know is that it's north of Ephrata. With no street signs, it's pretty . . . pretty easy to get lost..."

Miriam let out a sigh. Of course, now that she wasn't yelling at him, he wanted to be her best friend. All she wanted was to get home.

'Phillipians 2:4,' Miriam reminded herself, 'Let each of you look not only to his own interests, but also to the interests of others.'

She forced a smile and said, "Turn right onto this road. Look for a two-story house with black shutters and a white fence surrounding the yard. Turn right onto the road just past that house. When you come to a four-way intersection, turn left and the *Englischer* high school should be down the road a ways."

"Say, what's your name?" the man asked, giving her an appraising look.

Miriam felt distinctly uncomfortable. "I have a lot of work to do and I need to get started right away," she said, raising the reins to flick the horse's back and start moving again.

"Please. I like to know the names of those who help me out, so I can thank them appropriately," said the man with an grin.

"A simple 'thank you' will do. Now, if you don't mind . . ."

"Please? Your name? Miss . . ."

What was wrong with this man? "Miriam," she said. It was a common enough name. "Now, I really must go." She flicked the reins, and the horse, picking up on her nerves, trotted away, carrying her home to safety.

Behind, her, the man stared. His icy-blue eyes held a cold, appraising look. "Miriam. Lovely Miriam. You won't be racing off again very soon. I can guarantee that," he said. He waited a bit longer before getting back into his truck. Better not to be too obvious about things. When he got back into his truck, he drove in the direction Miriam had indicated, hoping he could spot her and find out where she lived.

\*\*\*

After brushing down the horse and feeding him, Miriam raced into the house, shouting for Sarah.

"*Mamm! Mamm!* I have a huge order from an *Englischer* customer! I am so scared!"

"Calm down, daughter! Calm down! You've made quilts before and you'll do well on this quilt . . ."

"'Quilts,' *mamm*. In the plural. I have a Wedding quilt and three children's quilts to make! Oh, and Anna and I are going to buy the fabric tomorrow. Her *daed* might be stopping by today to service my sewing machine."

"Four! This is your biggest order! It's good you thought about the sewing machine –do you have the fabric and thread you need?"

"*Nee*. That is why we are going to town tomorrow. I have to buy fabric for every quilt, even the shades of green one."

"You have a bolt of green fabric," Sarah said, opening the large armoire that held all of Miriam's fabrics.

"Too dark. This is for a child, so they want me to find light and bright green fabric," Miriam said, rustling through several pages of notes.

"Let me see . . . White, gold and purple. That will be a colorful wedding! One child's quilt in primary colors, one in the shades of green and one in pink and lavender. Lovely! Did they give you an idea of what patterns they want?"

"*Ya*, these here, Miriam pointed, showing Sarah the different patterns.

"*Ach!* Well, your sister will be here after dinner, so you work on the quilting. She will help me with supper and the housework today. How much are they paying you?"

"Three thousand dollars, *mamm*! I have half of that now, so I can buy the fabrics and threads. I will pay Mr. King for servicing my machine, too. Will the *kinner* be here?" Miriam said.

"*Nee*, they won't. Their *grossmudder* is taking care of them for the afternoon. Okay, let's eat dinner, then you can get started on your work. Very good, Miriam!"

"Oh, and they said they would tell their family and friends about me, so I might have more orders coming in!" Miriam said, following Sarah to the kitchen.

"What's this I hear about a big order?" Joseph said with a big grin, washing his hands.

"*Ya, daed*, I have a huge quilting order and I have to have all four quilts done before Christmas!" Miriam said.

"Thank God they gave you the time to do the work! Do you have anyone looking at your machine first?"

"*Ya*, Mr. King is coming later on this afternoon," Miriam said. As the family sat down, she had completely forgotten about the unsettling encounter with the insolent *Englischer* man on her way home.

After dinner, Miriam settled in the quilting room, opening the drapes and sheers wide for sunlight. Adjusting the drafting table to a comfortable angle, she began expertly drawing out the patterns, using the colors her customers had requested. As she worked, she heard the familiar sounds of her sister and *mamm* conversing as they worked. Noticing that the room was becoming dim, she looked up and realized how late it was.

Looking at the work she still had left to do, she lit a kerosene lamp and set it on a sturdy table, then finished the last of the pattern-drawing. As she looked at her work, she nodded, satisfied with her effort. Standing up, she blew out the flame of the lamp, then stretched her kinked back muscles.

After supper, John came by. The couple went for a buggy ride, talking as the horse clopped along. John aimed the buggy for a large, spreading tree near the river. After parking the buggy and pulling the brake, he looked at Miriam.

"Cold? Come here," he murmured, wrapping one arm around Miriam's slender waist.

Miriam scooted closer, nudging her shoulder under John's arm. She allowed her head to rest on his shoulder.

"*Denki.* This is good. It is a little bit cool, so this feels . . . oh!"

John had hooked a finger under Miriam's chin so he could give Miriam a few soft kisses. Miriam closed her eyes, safe and warm in his embrace, a tingle of passion running through her from where their lips met.

***

In the distance, a black truck was parked. Its lone occupant, a tall, blonde man with ice-blue eyes spied on the young couple. His name was Lance Newman, and he was in love.

"Sure, you're kissing someone else, for now," he murmured. "But you'll be kissing me – and much more – before too long."

He continued to spy on John and Miriam until he saw John release the buggy's brake. Not wanting them to know he'd been spying on them, he started his truck and drove off, the tires of his truck kicking up a plume of dust behind him.

"I'd better get you home. It will be dark before long – and *daed* and I have a long day ahead of us," John said. He cocked his head and pointed towards where they'd just heard the sound of a car engine. "I wonder who just took off? Look at that dust!"

Miriam, still wrapped in the warm haze of John's kisses, glanced up at the dust plume. "Hmmm, it could be kids... No, it's too much dust, and the Englischer teens don't drive their cars off the road in places like this." She shrugged. "I don't know."

"Doesn't matter. I'll get you home."

They kissed again, and then John drove Miriam home.

When they crossed back onto the paved road, the steady clip-clop of the horse's hooves sounded on the asphalt. Occasionally, an Englischer car would pass. Miriam and John paid it no mind. Nor did they notice the black truck in the driveway of the next house they passed, not even when it pulled out and followed them slowly from some distance behind.

The truck kept pace with them until John turned up the dirt driveway towards Miriam's family farm.

# CHAPTER TWO

The next day was a Saturday, and Anna came for Miriam after dinner.

"Be home before it gets dark!" Joseph said.

"*Ya*, we will, *daed*," promised Miriam. As they drove off in Anna's father's buggy, they talked about what they had done to prepare for their large orders.

"I checked my supply of embroidery flosses. I have to buy several to make sure I don't run out. How did your *mamm* like the size of your order?" Anna asked.

"She was shocked how big it is! She thought it was just one quilt, then when I told her it was four, she was just as excited as I was – well, I'm still excited. I drew out the patterns yesterday, so now I'm ready to cut the pieces out and start sewing them together. I will spend over one hundred dollars easily today. I need to buy thread, too. I'm going to need quilting batting as well. I want to have everything ready so that, when I need it, I won't have to stop working," said Miriam.

"*Ya*, I am the same way. I need cross stitching fabric as well. *Mamm* told me to get extra-big hoops so I can put them on the frame. As busy as I will be, I think I'll need the quilting frame to get everything done," Anna said.

At the store, the two friends loaded their carts with the items they needed. As the *Englischer* clerk saw the number of fabric bolts Miriam had loaded in her cart, her eyes rounded.

"Will you be buying every bolt you have in your cart?" she asked.

Miriam looked at the girl's name tag.

"Yes, Kelsey. I have a huge quilt order to work on and I'd rather have the fabric on hand so I don't get stopped by not having what I need," she said.

"Smart girl! Okay, have you had . . . you do use sewing machines, right?"

"Yes, we do. I had it serviced yesterday, so it should work just fine on this order," said Miriam.

"Well, right on the ball there, aren't you? Okay, your order total comes to . . . two hundred-sixty-six dollars. You're lucky you came in today. We've got a sale going on the fabric . . . and your friend will be lucky as well. Our crafting items are also on sale," said the tall, friendly girl.

Miriam counted out the money, handing it over. After Anna

had paid for her items, they stashed their purchases in the back of Anna's buggy. On the way home, they talked about their beaus.

"We are doing well. John is happy that I want to be baptized," Miriam said.

"You're still on your *rumspringe*!"

"Well, *ya*, but I can make that decision early," Miriam said. As she and Anna talked, something was niggling at her, but she couldn't figure out what it was. Passing the spot where the stranger had nearly hit her horse, she remembered.

"Oh!" She told Anna what had happened the previous day.

"And he knows your *name*? Miriam, that is not good! You are the only Miriam living here – he can find you, if he wants to, you know! And John won't like that," Anna said, censure in her voice.

"Anna! I tried to get away without telling him my name – he wouldn't let the horse pass. Besides, he said something about liking to know the names of those who help him."

"Pah! My *bruder* spent time with *Englischers*, working with them. He would tell you that this stranger did this so he could find you – and try to start spending time with you. Not good!"

Miriam looked at Anna, dismayed. "No . . . he wouldn't . . . I'm courting!"

"Do you think he'll care about that? *Nee*, he won't! Miriam,

*Englischer* men don't care about the *Ordnung*. All they want is to get . . . close . . . to us, if you know what I mean," Anna said significantly.

At that dark pronouncement, Miriam blushed, wanting to sink into the earth.

"No!" she moaned.

"You'd better be on the lookout for this man. What kind of vehicle does he drive?"

"A . . . a black truck. Shiny. It looks new. He had something to do at the *Englischer* high school yesterday."

"Hmm, I'll ask Joshua what he tells me and I'll let you know. Just . . . Miriam, you had better be very careful. You don't want to lose John! He is a *wunderbaar* man, and he loves you!"

"*Ya*, and I love him just as much. Anna, why didn't I know this before?" Miriam said sadly.

"Because you're the baby of your family. They – your *bruders* – are too protective. Mine told me . . . well, as much as they could . . . without taking away my own innocence," Anna said. "I know that some men are out only for themselves and what they can get from women. Those are the men to stay away from. I don't know who this man is, but . . . he might be one to stay away from. We're at your house. Let's get your fabric inside so we can both get busy," Anna suggested.

Joseph and Sarah came outside so all four of them could get everything Miriam had bought into the house.

"I will see you tomorrow at meeting, Miriam! Tell John I said 'hello!'"

"I will! Thank you for going with me!" Miriam said. She tried to smile, not wanting her parents to know just how upset she really was.

"I'd better get this all sorted out and put away. I'm going to start with the Wedding quilt so it's done first. It will take me the longest," Miriam told Sarah.

Are your patterns drawn and colored?" Sarah asked.

"*Ya.* I'm ready to pin on the pieces and cut them out. I'm eager to get started!" she told Sarah, rubbing her hands together.

"Let me know if you need any help!"

"I will, *denki!*"

Miriam spent the rest of that Saturday, pinning pattern pieces to the fabrics and cutting them out. Once they had been cut out, she separated them into different piles and began hemming them on her machine. By the time supper was ready, she had just about finished hemming every quilt piece she needed for the Amish Wedding quilt. Turning off her machine, she sighed in satisfaction, knowing she'd made a good start on the quilt.

\*\*\*

After services ended the following day, Miriam motioned to Anna that she needed to meet with Bishop Stoltzfus for a few minutes, then scurried off with her parents.

"Miss Beiler, I understand you've made a decision to be baptized into the Amish faith, am I correct?" asked the bishop.

"*Ya.* I would like to start receiving instruction and following the *Ordnung*," Miriam said nervously.

"Good! This makes me very happy, especially as your beau has also made the same decision," said the bishop. "Now . . . are you *quite sure* that you are ready and willing to follow the *Ordnung*?"

Miriam, knowing the significance of her decision, nodded slowly, with no smile on her gentle face.

"I am very sure. I'm still on my *rumspringe*, but this is my home – my faith," Miriam said, knowing her decision was the right one – and knowing that the blonde *Englischer* stranger scared her, for some reason.

The adults and younger children all left after lunch, leaving the Amish youth to participate in the singing scheduled for that day. Gathering under a tall tree with wide, spreading limbs, they sat on the grass and sang hymns of praise. Miriam and John sat next to each other, enjoying their time together. Other friends and couples joined them, sang with them for a short time, then moved on to other friends. By early evening, Miriam was pleasantly tired and ready to go home.

"I am so happy you spoke to Bishop Stoltzfus today," John said, a wide grin on his face.

Miriam, looking at him realized how much she loved his honest, open expression – in comparison, she sensed secrets and an ulterior motive in the face of the *Englischer* stranger. Knowing what Anna had told her, she shivered slightly.

"Are you cold? Come here," said John, edging slightly closer.

"*Denki*," Miriam said, not wanting – or knowing how to bring up how the stranger had nearly collided with her.

# CHAPTER THREE

After finishing the day's work on the crops, John and Samuel Fisher sat on the fence, talking about the prospects for the harvest.

"We have all that extra moisture from the blizzards this past winter. Unless something very unusual – like a drought or a very wet season – comes up between now and harvest, we should have a lot of corn to sell," Samuel predicted.

"Of course, the Lord will decide what happens," John said.

"*Ya*, he will," Samuel agreed. He broke off his conversation as he saw a black, late-model truck ease up and stop by the fence. "May I help you?" he asked.

Lance gave a crooked smile to Samuel as he sized up John.

"Hey, man, I'm lost. I'm looking for the young woman who makes the Amish quilts," he said.

John felt a quiver of warning and gave the other man a very

sharp look.

"How did you learn if this young woman's quilts?"

"I got her business card. As it turns out, I'm glad I have it – my grandmother knows I live in Philadelphia and asked me to order a quilt. I told her that I knew of someone who could make one for her," Lance said artlessly.

"Well, that's odd, because we Amish don't use *Englischer* methods of advertising. That is, we don't use business cards, billboards, the television or radio or newspapers. Instead, we rely on word-of-mouth only."

"Oh . . . why don't you use those methods? You'd get a lot more business, you know," Lance said, trying to draw the young man away from his lie.

John would not be distracted. Instead, he answered the question and came back to questioning him.

"We don't call attention to ourselves. In living a Plain lifestyle, we give all the glory to God. Now, why did you try to lie to me? I know this woman of whom you speak. She's a Plain woman and she follows our rules. She doesn't have business cards. Her customers tell their families and friends about her work. That's how she gets new business."

"Yeah, I lied. What of it?" Lance asked. All humor had left his face and his eyes grew glacier-cold.

"Miriam is my intended. We will be getting married. I want

you to leave her alone," John said.

Lance realized he wasn't going to comply with John's request. Instead, he fully intended to continue pursuing Miriam – fiancé or no.

"Hey, man – no harm? I . . . I didn't know that she was engaged. I'll leave her alone, now that I know," promised Lance.

"What is your intent in trying to find her? Her reputation is valuable. If even the hint of misbehavior is attached to her name, she will be ruined in our community. She is not like that."

"I . . hey, man, I just wanted to get to know her better."

"You should not be trying to get to know an engaged woman better. Just leave her be and stop coming here. If you truly need someone to make a quilt for you, I know of several Amish artisans who can fill your order," said John. As he spoke, all friendliness was gone from his face and voice, but he still spoke politely.

After Lance drove off, Samuel looked at John.

"That's a serious matter there. Did Miriam tell you how she met this man?"

"*Nee*, but I am sure that she has a good explanation. I'm going to go see her tonight, *daed*. I'll find out what happened."

"See that you do, son. I am sure she has an innocent

explanation, but you are right. If this man manages to get to her, it could be bad for her good name," said Samuel.

***

As he drove to the Beiler farm, John's mind went from one possible explanation to another. *She just got a very big order and that has been taking up much of her time. She just spoke to the Bishop about being baptized. I'm sure there's a good explanation. Just talk to her and see what she says.*

In the Beiler living room, John took Miriam's hand.

"Miriam, a blonde stranger stopped by the farm today . . ." John paused, feeling Miriam's startled response. "Is . . . is everything OK?"

"*Nee*. That stranger – was he driving a black truck?"

"Yes – he was. So you have met him?"

"Not in the way you mean! No! He nearly ran me down after the Amish market on Friday. I was thinking of my order and he scared me. He said he was lost, looking for some *Englischer* high school. I gave him the instructions and tried to leave, but he wouldn't let me go. He asked me for my name. I refused. He said something about . . . about wanting to know the name of someone who'd helped him so he could thank them. I gave him just my first name, then I left as fast as I could . . . I don't even know who he is!'"

"Well, he knows who you are. I don't think he knows where

you live, but I wouldn't count on that. Miriam, I'm worried. He knows your name and he knows you quilt. He seems to be driving through Ephrata, looking for you."

"Oh, no! Not now! I'm about to begin instruction for baptism. He could ruin everything for me! I know my actions must be above reproach and he could make it look like I'm doing . . . well, wrong," Miriam said, trying not to cry.

At this point, Miriam's parents came into the living room.

"What's wrong?" Joseph asked.

John told the Beilers everything that had happened.

Joseph and Sarah became very concerned.

"John, I think I am going to take a buggy drive. Sarah, I would like you to go with me. John, you and Miriam will need to take a ride as well, so you aren't alone in the house together. Let's see if we can find this Lance character," suggested Joseph.

Sarah nodded, feeling fear for Miriam.

"If we find him, do you want me to watch him and see what I learn?"

"*Ya.* I do. Let's go," Joseph ordered.

After hitching the horse to the buggy, he and Sarah left the yard first with John and Miriam following at a short distance. After riding for several minutes, Joseph's acute eyes spotted a black truck idling on a side road. Stopping, he motioned John to pull up next to him.

"Is that his truck?"

"*Ya*, it is." Both John and Miriam nodded.

"Okay. I am going to pull up to him. You stay behind me. I don't want him to know who I am just yet," Joseph said. Driving slowly, Joseph pulled up to the truck.

"Do you need anything, sir?" he asked Lance.

Lance simply shrugged, unable to come up with anything. He was not aware that John and Miriam were at a distance behind him. "I'm just taking in this beautiful countryside."

Joseph waved to John with his far hand.

John, responding, drove up so he was across the road and abreast of Joseph.

Lance, seeing his Amish "competition," ground his teeth.

Joseph, seeing Lance's frustration and working jaw muscles, spoke, "John, here, is courting my daughter. For the sake of her good reputation, I would appreciate it if you would stop trying to pursue her,"

Lance laughed, "'Courting?' You still use that archaic term? Yeah, OK, man, whatever. I get your drift. She's taken."

Miriam, hearing Lance's anger, realized Anna was right – Lance had an ulterior motive. Feeling embarrassed and angry, she leaned down so she could look directly at Lance. Never one to shy away from standing up for herself, she spoke up. "Just leave me alone. I have no interest in you. I want nothing at all to do with you. John, please take me home."

John, complied, pulling the buggy up and around, taking Miriam back to the farm.

"She told you exactly what she wants – for you to leave her alone. I advise you to listen to her," Joseph said. "She is very angry." Flicking the reins, he signaled the horse to turn. Giving Lance a significant look, he drove off.

At the farm, all four sat down to talk. "Miriam, I don't think it's safe for you to drive anywhere by yourself. We told him to leave you alone, but I don't think he will," Sarah said.

"*Nee*, he won't," Joseph said. "When you need to go anywhere, get your *mamm* or your sisters. If I can take the time to drive you, I will. Tell Anna what's happening and get her to go around with you. Just . . . don't try to drive around by yourself. That Lance character is up to no good. Did you see his reaction when I told him that you and John are courting and engaged?"

"*Ya*. I did. He was . . . he was mad. He spoke disrespectfully to you," Miriam said.

"He was quite a different person this afternoon," John said. "Friendly, smiling and looking for help to find you. I had the feeling he was up to no good, though, and, when he lied about how he learned about your quilting, I knew I was right."

"What did he say about my quilting?" Miriam asked, feeling apprehensive.

"He said he learned of your quilting – through your business card," said John.

"'*Business card*?' I don't use them! I rely only on word-of-mouth!" Miriam said angrily.

"We know," said Sarah soothingly. "We are here to help you, protect you from him. He is up to no good. I am only grateful that we found out now, instead of after him trying something."

"*Mamm, daed*, I'm sorry I forgot to tell you about nearly being hit by him. I was so excited about my big order that I forgot," Miriam said apologetically.

"We wish you had remembered to say anything. We understand your excitement, so don't worry," said Joseph. "We know now, so we are doing all we can to make sure you stay safe."

# CHAPTER FOUR

The next Sunday was not a meeting day. Miriam and her parents stayed at home, reading their Bibles and reflecting on the messages they got. Miriam was still upset after the events of the day before. Setting her Bible down, she wandered to the back porch to get some sun.

Thinking, she allowed her eyes to roam over the countryside immediately surrounding her parents' farm. The back porch was not visible from the road. Thinking about this, she was grateful, fearful that Lance would still try to seek her out, in defiance of her father's and John's warnings.

That evening, John came by to visit with Miriam. As he drove the buggy to the farm, he saw the now-familiar black truck poking around first one road, then the next. John decided to take a different route to the Beiler's farm – one that would not put him in the pathway of Lance's truck.

Arriving at the Beiler farm, he suggested that they take their snacks to the front porch. He was quiet as he did so – Miriam, getting the snack, picked up on his mood.

As they drank the tart lemonade and munched on cookies, their moods improved. After several minutes, Miriam spotted Lance's truck, nosing down the main road. Grabbing the lemonade, she ran into the house. John followed closely behind, holding the plate of cookies.

Joseph, reading his Bible, looked at John with a quizzical expression on his bearded face.

"He is out there again. If he knocks on the door, please tell him Miriam's not available to speak to him," John asked.

Joseph nodded, returning to his reading.

A few minutes later, he stood, hearing a knock at the door. Gazing into the kitchen, he motioned John and Miriam to hide themselves a little better. Opening the door when he was satisfied that the couple was completely hidden, he gazed at Lance.

"Uh, hi. Is your daughter here? I'd like to see her," Lance looked nervous.

"*Nee.* She is not coming to the living room. It is up to me to make sure she is not exposed to any situations – or people – who would cause harm to her reputation. You must leave – now," said Joseph firmly.

"Aww, c'mon! Even just to say hi?" Lance asked.

"Even then. We are a close-knit community. Everyone

knows what everyone else is doing. Word gets around fast. If you had tried to come by here and I had been gone, you could have done some real harm to her reputation. I must ask you to leave. Now," Joseph said. His tone brooked no nonsense or resistance.

"Wow. You people are . . . Wow! OK. I'm leaving now. But, before I do . . . would you please give this to her?" Lance handed a small, gaily wrapped box to Joseph. Joseph barely looked at the box before giving it right back to Lance.

"No I cannot allow you to give her gifts. It would be highly inappropriate. Take that gift and please leave – right now!"

Sarah had come up to stand next to her husband.

"I don't know who you are, but I don't get a very good feeling from you. My daughter wants nothing to do with you. Please respect my husband's authority in this house. Go. Now," Sarah ordered.

"OK, whatever. Fine," Lance muttered, raising his hands in defeat. Jamming the box into his jacket pocket, he turned, bounding down the porch steps. A minute later, he was gone.

Sarah looked at Joseph with worry plain on her face.

"He is one persistent man," Joseph muttered. "What is that term the *Englischers* use?"

John, hearing his question, walked out of the kitchen. "'Stalker,' Mr. Beiler. He's stalking Miriam. I heard about this when I spent some time in the city."

***

Miriam was grateful that she was so busy with the quilting. The only times she wasn't in the quilting room at her sewing machine, she was helping Sarah or spending time with John or Anna.

Joseph hired a young Amish boy to help him with the chores that Miriam had previously helped him with – milking and caring for the livestock.

He noticed that, on several days as he returned to the house, he saw the by now very familiar black truck driving slowly up and down several roads around Ephrata. It was Lance, looking for an opportunity to encounter Miriam. Joseph was grateful that he had told Miriam that, when she needed to leave the farm, she was to be with him, Sarah, John or Anna.

Miriam continued her daily work on the Amish Wedding quilt. She had allotted several weeks for its completion and she was just a little bit ahead of the schedule she had planned for herself. On one day when Sarah needed several crafting supplies, she realized she would be forced to ask Miriam to buy them for her.

"Joseph, can you take her to town?"

"I can't. I have this order to finish – my customer told me he needs it earlier than he had realized, so I need to get it done fast," Joseph said. "You can't go with her?"

"*Nee*. I am rising the bread for supper right now."

Joseph sighed, feeling helpless. "Well, it's early. Maybe, if she leaves now and hurries, she can be back before that Lance character comes here. He's been arriving after dinnertime for the past several weeks."

"I don't like it, but I have no choice. Okay. I'll tell her to leave right now and get back as fast as she can," Sarah said with a worried sigh.

In the house, Miriam's jaw dropped as she heard Sarah's instructions.

"Alone? But *mamm*! He's still out there, from what *daed* says! I can't go out alone," Miriam said.

"We don't like it, but I can't leave home and your *daed* is trying to finish a rush order. Just go now. Here's my money and list. Get what I need and get home as fast as you can," Sarah said, worry in her voice.

Miriam swallowed, feeling fear swirling in her belly.

"OK, but I have to leave right now. I want to be back before dinnertime." Tucking the cash and list into her apron pocket, she hurried to the barn and quickly hitched the horse to the buggy.

"Daughter, be very watchful. Keep an eye on all the roads and look for his truck. If you see him and he tries to stop you, ignore him and get back on the road. Take back roads if you must, and get home as fast as you can," Joseph instructed Miriam.

"*Ya. Daed*, you are scaring me!"

"Good! Let it keep you alert. Go now and be careful."

Miriam left, driving the buggy as fast as she could. Arriving at the market, she picked up everything her mother needed and stopped at the counter to pay.

Hurrying to the buggy, she put everything in the back, untied the horse from the post and climbed into the buggy. Driving back as fast as she could, she kept a worried eye out for an all-too-familiar black truck. As she got closer to home, she began to breathe a little more freely.

Lance, driving to an outlying *Englischer* community to talk to a baseball prospect, kept moving his eyes over the countryside, looking for Miriam. As he got closer to the edge of the Amish community, he felt disappointment. Then, he spotted her buggy moving quickly down another road. By now, familiar with the roads in and through Ephrata, Lance whipped his steering wheel around, taking a side road so he could shortstop Miriam. Driving quickly, he slammed on the brakes and turning his steering wheel so he could angle his truck, blocking Miriam's ability to get away.

Miriam, seeing him and how he had angled his truck, was scared for her safety. "Let me go! I have work to do and my *mamm* needs her purchases!" she called out.

"I'm not going to hurt you. I just need to know something – why is everyone and their uncle reacting to me the way they have?" Lance asked.

"Because the Amish *Ordnung* – the rules we live by – forbid me from spending time with any man who is not my fiance. If anyone from the Amish community were to pass by and see me talking to you right now, it would destroy my reputation. I would be seen as damaged," Miriam said. As she spoke to Lance, she tried to measure the gap between the back of Lance's truck and the edge of the road. *I think I can pass by and get away.* Slapping the horse's back with her reins, she began moving slowly between the edge of the road and the back of Lance's truck.

Lance, seeing her moving through the gap, finally realized that his interest in her could ruin her reputation. Climbing into his truck with reluctance, he set the gear into "drive" and moved it forward slightly, allowing her to get through.

Miriam turned to him. "*Denki* for understanding. Please don't come after me any more. Respect my life and how I live it." Facing forward again, she flicked the reins, urging the horse on – she didn't want to be seen in his company at all.

Getting home, she told both of her parents that he had found her and that she had told him to leave her alone.

"Did he try anything to you?" Sarah asked, hand at her

throat.

"*Nee*. When I told him that his interest could destroy my reputation – about the *Ordnung*, he realized we were serious. He let me go then. That's when I came home," Miriam said.

After that, Miriam – and all of Ephrata – had several weeks of peace. Her message to Lance seemed to have worked. Joseph didn't see his truck rolling through the community at any time of the day or night.

Miriam, finding this out, began to feel as though she could breathe freely. Now that Lance had stopped snooping around Ephrata, Miriam felt a little more freedom to visit Anna and go to the market when she needed to do so. On days when she and her parents had to go into town, she felt happier and more excited, knowing she was not likely to bump into Lance.

\*\*\*

In Philadelphia, Lance struggled with his resolve to stay away from Ephrata and Miriam. On some days, it was difficult for him to resist the drive to the small Amish community.

As the weeks wore on, however, his resistance began to crumble. As April slid into May, he began to question his decision to stay away.

*What are ya, some kinda' wuss? You go for what you want and you take it, dude! Are you gonna let some stupid, old-fashioned religious rules get in the way of what you want? You want that woman, so go take her. Besides, you know she was just putting up a show of resistance. She wants you just as bad as you want her. She was kissing that Amish dude, but before long, she'll be kissing you. Don't let her parents and her boyfriend get in the way. Take her, you idiot!*

These thoughts and more ran through Lance's mind. As the academic year at his university finally ended, he decided he was going to take a day off and pay a little visit to Miriam.

Striding into his boss's office, he plopped into the chair across from his boss.

"Hey, Dan, I need to take a personal day. I'll wait until finals are over," said Lance.

"Sure, long as everything is up to date, you can take a day. Shoot me an email," Dan said.

"You got it. Thanks, man!" Lance stood up and went back to his office, feeling relief. *You're doing the right thing, dude – for you.*

At the end of the semester, Lance jumped into his truck, anticipating seeing Miriam's quiet beauty. *She's a looker, all right, but take that ridiculous bonnet thing off her head, curl that beautiful hair and put some makeup on her and WHOA! She'll look even more beautiful. I might be able to convince her to come away with me by the end of the summer. That's what I'm going to plan on, anyway. Besides, it's been a couple months since I've been in Ephrata. It won't matter. They won't mind. I obeyed their idiotic rules.*

Setting his cruise control once he hit highway speed, Lance drove quickly to the Amish community.

\*\*\*

In Ephrata, Miriam was taking a rare day off of her own. Humming a hymn under her breath, she made sure her hair was neatly combed, then set her black prayer *kapp* on her head.

"*Mamm*, I'm going to Anna King's. We're going to spend the day together and I'm going to look through some cross stitch patterns to see if she has any patterns I might be able to use for future quilt orders," she told Sarah.

"Okay, but be watchful, daughter. That Lance character hasn't been around for some weeks, but that doesn't mean he won't try to come back," Sarah warned.

"*Ya, mamm*. I will. I'm going straight to her house and coming straight home. It will be before supper when I get home," Miriam promised.

"Okay. Eat some hot breakfast first," Sarah instructed.

After spending an enjoyable day with Anna, Miriam was riding back, using side roads to get home.

In the distance, Lance smacked his steering wheel, laughing.

"Bingo! There she is!" He stopped his truck, looking at her direction, then took the road she turned onto. Angling his truck as he had before, he jumped out of the truck and, bending down, began plucking wildflowers from the side of the road.

Miriam spotted the black truck and got scared.

"What are you doing here? My fiance and father told you to stay away from me!" she said. "Go – no! I don't want those," Miriam said, edging away from the small bouquet that Lance was holding out toward her. Seeing the display of affection, she grew even more scared for her safety and reputation. She didn't try to look for any side roads – there were none that connected with the road to her parents' farm.

"Please, just give me a few minutes of your time. I know you're engaged, and I respect that. I just want to get to know you a little better – as friends," Lance pleaded.

"No. That is not possible. Our rules make no allowances for a woman to be friends with a man not her fiance or husband. I can't be friends with you. Now, please let me pass. I have to get home and help my mother with supper," Miriam said. She refused to plead or beg. She had to be strong.

"Please. Just enjoy the sunlight with me? For a few minutes? Please? That's all," Lance said.

Miriam sighed. *If the only way I can get him off my back is to sit with him for a few minutes, I will do so, then I will hurry home. Why didn't I take that other side road?*

Climbing down from the buggy unassisted, she walked slowly to the side of the road and, crossing her arms stiffly, she faced the sun quietly. After a few minutes, she uncrossed her arms and said, "I have to go home now."

Lance nodded and moved his truck out of the way.

Climbing back into the buggy, she was startled when she saw Samuel Fisher rushing up to her.

"Miriam! What are you doing, talking to a strange man? Are you all right?"

Miriam looked at Samuel with wide eyes. She knew just what could happen. Looking at Lance Newman, she said, "This is what I was telling you about! I don't want to spend time with you because . . . because I don't like you. And because, doing so will ruin my reputation!" As she spoke, she flung the nosegay at Lance.

"Mr. Fisher, you can ask John to confirm this. In fact, I beg you to do so. This is the man who nearly ran me over at the beginning of spring. I have spent most of the spring trying to avoid him, but he won't listen to me." Flicking the horse's reins, she sped away, trying not to cry and scream.

That evening, John knocked hard on the front door even before Miriam could sit down to supper. Dreading the coming scene, she opened the door.

"Miriam, I just talked to my *daed*, and he told me that he saw you talking to that Lance! What were you thinking?"

Miriam looked frantically from John to her shocked parents.

"Miriam? What were you doing? I told you to watch out for him and to get home right away!" Sarah said.

"Wait. Everyone, please wait. John, I told him exactly what could happen to me if anyone saw me talking to him. You know that I have been trying to avoid him ever since he first came here! The last time he tried to stop me, I told him his interest could ruin me and he seemed to understand what I was talking about. That's when he stopped coming here. *Mamm, daed* and I agreed that I could spend the day with Anna King today as long as I went straight there and came straight home. That's what I was doing. I had no idea that that Lance had decided to try and come back here," Miriam said forcefully. She was angrier than she had ever felt before.

"Okay. I am sorry, Miriam. You're innocent – that's clear. But, please. Don't talk with him at all. Don't spend even one minute in his presence. Ignore him! If he tries blocking you again, get around him on the side of the road," John pleaded.

Miriam, upset, nodded sharply, agreeing with John.

Meantime, Lance, not knowing that John was at the farm, knocked at the door.

Joseph, already upset by what Miriam had done, was even angrier when he saw the tall, blonde *Englischer* standing on the porch.

"Do you know what you've done to my daughter? You've put her good reputation at risk! Her fiancé's father – his *father*!

Saw her talking to you. Stop acting *mupsich* – stupid – and leave my daughter alone! Don't come her and don't talk to her. Don't even look at her. Go on! Get out of her!"

Miriam had taken too much. About to break down crying, she threw the pot holder onto the kitchen table and ran upstairs into her room. Sitting forcefully on her bed, she began to cry.

Downstairs, Sarah and Joseph Beiler, along with John, stood shoulder-to-shoulder. Joseph mutely pointed to the door, not trusting his ability to speak. John took a menacing step toward the interloper. Sarah crossed her arms and took several steps toward him.

Lance, belatedly realizing his blunder, raised his hands, palms out.

"Hey, man, I'm sorry. I didn't realize I'd put her at risk by just passing a few minutes with her. I'm outta' here," he said. Backing up fast, he bumped into the edge of the door. Correcting his path, he backed out and, turning around, ran down the porch as fast as he could. Looking up to the second story windows, he spotted Miriam's downcast head and her shoulders framed in a window. He paused for just a second, hoping she would look down. Then, thinking of his self-preservation, he ran to his truck and gunned the engine. Leaving a huge dust plume rising in the air, he took off as fast as he could.

The atmosphere in the Beiler house was quiet and sad for the next few days. Miriam, feeling pulled between two forces, tried to find her usual happy mood, but couldn't. Joseph and Sarah were worried for her safety and good reputation.

That Sunday was a meeting Sunday. After the three-hour service had ended, Bishop Stoltzfus asked Sarah to join him.

Sitting on a bench that was at a distance from the lunch crowd, he began to speak.

"I have heard that you were seen in the company of an *Englischer* man, Miss Beiler. Is this the same man the drives the black truck?"

"Yes, Bishop, he is. I . . ." Miriam sighed, trying to stay calm. "I have been trying to make him leave me alone. I've tried to avoid him. When he was coming here every day, I stopped running errands for my *mamm* and *daed*. I didn't go into town to visit friends or to buy supplies for my quilting. Bishop, that man has tried to express his interest in me. John and my *daed* told him that John and I are courting and to leave me alone. I told him about the *Ordnung* and how we are expected to live. Before I stopped going about Ephrata by myself, he blocked my buggy once. This last time – the first time he had returned after several weeks – he blocked me once again. We – John and my parents – told him to leave me alone and never to contact me again. I don't know what else I can do!" Miriam said, swallowing her tears.

"Okay. It is clear that he doesn't want to understand the *Ordnung* and how we are all expected to obey the rules. I see, too, that you have done everything you could to avoid him.

Miss Beiler, for the sake of your good name, I am telling you to do everything your parents tell you to do, from today forward. Do you understand?" asked the bishop.

"Yes. *Denki.*" Miriam quickly returned to sitting with Anna, and began playing with her food.

That night, after Miriam had come home from the singing with John, her parents called her into the kitchen.

"Daughter, until this Lance character moves on, you can't go out around by yourself. It's clear he doesn't respect you, your reputation or our rules. If you need to go out, you will go out with us or John," said Joseph.

Miriam was scared. Lance had nearly destroyed her life and her reputation. Nodding quickly, she agreed with her father.

"What about going to see Anna?" she asked.

"One of us will take you to go spend the day with her, then go to pick you up. Until that man understands our rules, that's how it has to be," Joseph said.

Miriam didn't like this arrangement, but knowing the alternative, agreed to it.

"*Denki, daed.* I know you're trying to protect me," Miriam said.

# CHAPTER FIVE

Two weeks later, Miriam told her parents that she needed to go to the Amish market for items she needed. Her father told her he would take her. As they were on the way to the market, Joseph spotted the black truck.

"He's back. I'm taking that side road there," he told Miriam.

Miriam sighed, grateful now that her *daed* was now with her.

Lance, driving down the quiet roads, spotted Miriam's buggy in the far distance. Figuring out which road the buggy was on, he veered onto that road. As he approached Miriam, he realized, too late, that Miriam was with her father.

*Oh, no, no way! I don't want to tangle with him again!*

Pulling abreast of the buggy, Lance floored the accelerator, speeding down the dirt road. He left a huge, brown cloud of dust behind him, causing Miriam and Joseph to choke on it.

Once they had gotten the dust out of their mouths, Joseph drove straight to the market, where Miriam bought everything she needed.

"I'm ready, *daed*," Miriam said.

"Home, then?"

"*Ya*. I have a Wedding quilt to finish," Miriam said.

Spring slowly melted into summer and the outside temperatures increased. Miriam's new pattern of traveling about Ephrata continued. Her last encounter with the determined *Englischer* had truly scared her. On some trips to town, she spotted the black truck at a distance. On other days, she sighed in relief as she got home without spotting the truck.

\*\*\*

*She's being escorted everywhere like a prisoner. I know she goes to that Amish market place, looking for new clients. Maybe I can get her attention then and get her to spend some time with me.*

The next market day was bright and cool. Miriam and Anna were together, each buying the supplies they needed to continue their work. As Miriam was standing in line to pay for her purchases, she spotted the all-too-familiar black truck.

"Look!" Miriam tapped Anna's shoulder. "See that truck? That's the man – the *Englischer* who's been bothering me," she whispered.

Anna, a very traditional Amish woman, heartily disapproved of Lance's action. She grabbed Miriam's arm and pulled her in the opposite direction.

"Let's pay for out things over there, then get out of here," she said. Looking around, she spotted Sarah and caught her eye.

Sarah swiveled her head around and spotted the truck. Hurrying behind Miriam and Anna, she paid for her items and trotted out behind the two young friends. Clambering into the buggy, she waited as Miriam jumped in. Flicking the horse's reins, she sighed as the buggy began moving ahead.

"*Nee!*" she whispered under her breath.

Lance had come around the opposite side of the market in his truck. Sarah pulled in a deep, shaky breath and pulled to the front of his truck. Stopping the horse, she looked down at him.

"Your efforts to get Miriam's attention are not appreciated. Please leave – and do not come back!" Sarah said angrily.

Lance looked at Miriam, who was refusing to acknowledge him. Finally, Miriam laid her hand on Sarah's shoulder and whispered into her ear.

Miriam looked straight ahead and spoke. "Mr. Newman, I love John Fisher and that's why I am engaged to him." Now, looking at Lance, she glared at him. "Leave me alone! Once and for all, just leave me alone! *Mamm*, let's go home."

Lance hearing what Sarah and Miriam had to say, decided she was being forced to rebuff him. Heaving out a gusty sigh, he thought.

*I need to find a way to get Miriam to understand that I'm attracted to her and I want to get to know her better. It's probably best to stay away from here for the time being until I have a good plan to . . . get to her.*

# CHAPTER SIX

Miriam, pacing in her bedroom, wanted to believe that Lance would let her be, but it was becoming more and more clear that this would not happen.

*What can I do? I want to be free to go about Ephrata and see my friends and be with John, but, as long as that Lance character is coming here, I can't. All I can do is to continue going around with my parents, Anna and John.*

\*\*\*

On the Fisher farm, Samuel and Emily spoke quietly together, worried about John's engagement to Miriam Beiler.

"I saw her standing with that *Englischer*. She threw flowers back at him and yelled at him, but, Emily, that doesn't mean anything," Samuel said.

"I saw her talking to Bishop Stoltzfus at the last meeting. She was trying not to cry. I don't know what they were saying," said Emily.

John, passing by, overheard the quiet conversation. Veering into the kitchen, he asked his parents if he could join them.

"John!" Emily gasped.

"*Mamm*, I don't think you need to worry as much as you seem to think you do. Miriam has done nothing to encourage that Lance character. He's done all the pursuing and she's tried to push him away. I'll admit – I'm feeling impatient and I want him to just stay away from here – but she cannot do more than she is already doing. Her parents, Anna King or I take her to where she needs to go. She doesn't drive around Ephrata by herself anymore, because we all know he could be here and he could see her. She doesn't want to run into him, so she's agreed that it's best for us to take her everywhere," said John.

"*Denki*, John. I'm glad you told us all of this," said Emily gently.

After John had gone out to go and visit with Miriam, Emily sighed.

"I think we should go and visit with Joseph and Sarah. I want to find out what they have been doing – what they know," Emily decided.

"I don't like it, Emily, but I think you're right. Just . . . don't poke around too hard. From what John says, they have the situation well in hand," Samuel advised.

Two days later, they drove out to the Beiler farm.

"Emily – look. That black truck. He's back," Samuel said. "He's looking for her."

At the Beiler farm, Joseph let the Fishers in. "We are doing everything we can to discourage that Lance character," Joseph said. "Miriam, too. She does not like his attentions any more than we like them. She yelled at him the last time he tried to come here to visit her. You must understand, this situation has put her under a great deal of stress and pressure. She is working on her largest quilting order ever. When she runs out of thread, we have to take her to the Amish market so she doesn't have to face him alone," Joseph said.

"We saw him while we were driving here, Joseph," said Samuel. "He was just driving up one road and down another, looking for the buggy."

"*Ach,* yes. We know. He is one very persistent man. But we can wait him out. We are patient, where he is impatient. For as long as it takes, we will be protecting her. Emily, Samuel, I can assure you – Miriam does not want that *Englischer's* attention. She just wants to be left alone so she can make her quilts, prepare for her baptism and get ready to marry John," Sarah said with a smile.

Miriam, who had been thinking and praying on the back porch, walked into the kitchen as Sarah finished speaking.

"Ah, Miriam! I'm glad you're here," said Emily with a

strained smile. "I have a question for you regarding this *Englischer* man – I know you spent some time with him recently, and I am worried for my son. Have you decided whether you're going to stay here in our community – be baptized and become a full member?"

Miriam's eyes widened at the pointed question. She opened her mouth to answer and relieve Emily of her worry, but Joseph beat her, speaking up first.

"Emily, both my daughter and your son are still completing their 'running-about' times. Besides, Miriam has already spoken to the bishop about her desire to take her Kneeling Vow – and about her efforts to rebuff this Lance character. Everything she has done, with the exception of those few minutes she spent with him a few weeks ago, has been above reproach and in compliance with the *Ordnung*.

"Remember – she is Sarah's and my daughter, and it is up to *us* to correct and discipline her when she does wrong. We have spoken to her about her error in consenting to spend even a few minutes with that man, and we have put measures in place that protect her, her reputation and her relationship with John."

Emily, taken aback by Joseph's words and tone of voice widened her own eyes behind her eyeglasses.

"Well. It seems that we have all been worried and concerned, Joseph. I hope you'll understand where my own concern and question came from – a worry for my own youngest child. If Miriam is . . . confused about her decision and commitment to John, we need to know that now. If, on the other hand, she is attempting to deal with this 'Lance character,' as you call him, then that eases my own mind."

"Emily, I hope you'll understand that we've all been worried about what that man has been trying to do to Miriam," Sarah said. "Do you remember in our nurse's training, when we went through the mental health instruction?"

"*Ya.* Are you saying that you believe . . ."

"That this man could have a mental condition and put Miriam in danger? I've had that thought more than once, Emily. We have all been very direct, none more so than Miriam. John and Joseph have also told him, using that *Englischer* phrase, to 'take a hike.' He's not understanding what we've all been telling him. He keeps coming back and coming back and . . ." Sarah broke off, unable to continue for the tears that suddenly began falling down her cheeks.

"Emily, what we're all worried about is that this character believes that, if he just keeps coming back and making contact with Miriam, that one day, she'll suddenly decide he's the man for her. I have no doubts about her commitment to John. My concern isn't the chance that she'll suddenly change her mind and cause hurt to John – it's that this man is dangerous to her. She yelled at him the last time he came here. *Yelled* at him, Emily. That is not our meek Miriam, but she is feeling the stress from this man's harassment. She is doing everything exactly as she should be doing. I don't want to have to rely on the *Englischer's* law enforcement, but if it comes down to that, I will. If Miriam needs more protection than we can offer her, I will contact them and ask them for their advice and help," Joseph promised as he rubbed his hand on Sarah's back.

"Okay, then, thank you. Samuel and I were worried when he saw her in plain sight with that man. John knows that you and Miriam are doing all that you can, but he's also worried . . ."

"More for her physical safety than about anything she might do to destroy their relationship, I would think," Joseph said.

"*Ya*, Joseph, that is what he said. But when I saw Miriam standing next to that man, I began to worry. You must admit that, if you had seen John standing by an *Englischer* woman, you would have the same thoughts," Samuel said.

"Possibly, but, since we're going through this situation, I might – *might* decide that there is more to the situation than meets the eyes," said Joseph.

Sarah, recovered from her crying, sighed deeply.

"Emily, Samuel, rather than quarreling, what we should be doing is thinking of ways to support and protect Miriam and John. Don't you agree?" she asked.

Emily looked at Samuel, who had the grace to look shamefaced.

"You are right. We are sorry. We should not have accused Miriam without . . ." Samuel began.

"Excuse me," Miriam interjected. "I'm right here. I don't want to be disrespectful, but *mamm, daed* and John have all been very supportive as I tried to figure this out. I . . . I do not want this man's attention. I don't like him! I just want him to leave me alone and stay away from Ephrata forever. When John told me that this man lied about how he learned about my quilting – that he learned of my business through a . . . *business card*, that's when I got scared.

"He is *not* listening to me and my wishes. In fact, he's ignoring them and continuing to come here. He's finding ways to get to me – and what's so scary is that he's, I don't know, disguising his attempts as some horrible romantic interest in me. Mr. Fisher, I'm sure you saw me throw those wildflowers back at him. When he saw me coming down the road, he picked them from the side of the road. When he gave them to me, I got scared – really scared.

"I haven't invited his interest because I love John and I want to spend the rest of my life with *him*! Again, I apologize, but, as you and my parents talk about this whole mess, I would appreciate being addressed as well – because this all affects me and John the most," Miriam said, gazing directly at the Fishers.

"Bishop Stoltzfus has already asked me about what happened and I told him everything, honestly. Yes, I made a *mupsich* mistake agreeing to spend even two minutes with that man. But I don't know what else to do!" Miriam now began to sob, feeling her frustration and fear bubbling over.

"Okay, I think we've all upset you enough, Miriam. Your parents tell us that you have begun taking measures that protect you from this man. We – Emily and I – both apologize for doubting your commitment to John. We would like to demonstrate that by adding our efforts to yours, your parents' and John's as you try to keep that 'Lance character' away from you. If we spot him, we will make him leave. Joseph, I hope you won't have to call law enforcement – have you spoken to the bishop or any of the deacons about this matter?" Samuel asked.

"*Nee*, not yet. I plan to speak to the bishop this weekend, after service ends. I just want to protect Miriam and respect the *Ordnung*. That is all," said Joseph, balling his hands into two large fists.

"We are all frustrated. Miriam, we are sorry. I hope you will be able to forgive us," Emily murmured.

"*Ya*, Mrs. Fisher. I do . . . I know that you are affected by this whole situation as well. And, please understand, I have kept, not only myself and my family, but you, John and the entire Amish community in mind as I've tried to push this man away from me. He doesn't respect us, our beliefs or our culture. That's clear to me. He wants what he wants and he's going to try and get it by whatever means he has available. Even if it means forcing his will on me. I am relying on my parents and my faith even more than I ever have before. Please . . . I would appreciate having your understanding and support as I keep that man away from me!" Miriam stopped as her sobs overtook her once again.

"Emily, I think we have our answer, now," Samuel said, looking very uncomfortable. "We . . . we were wrong in our too-hasty assumption. Miriam, Sarah, Joseph, you have our support. Miriam, we apologize," he said, resting his hand on Miriam's shaking shoulder.

"*Den . . . denki*, Mr. Fisher," Miriam said, her words broken by her sobs.

"I will see you out. This has been a very long day and Miriam needs to try and relax," Joseph said, standing. He walked the Fishers to the front door, giving them a small smile as they left.

"Sarah, I am going to go and speak to the bishop. I will be back by suppertime. Please leave the doors closed and stay here at home with Miriam. I don't want her being alone – not now," Joseph said, placing his straw hat squarely on his head.

"*Ya*, husband. We will be all right here. It is not often we lock our doors, but I think it is high time we began doing so. What do you plan to discuss with the bishop?" asked Sarah.

"Everything that you, Miriam, John and I have been through with this man. Our efforts to make him leave her alone. And to let him know that we might need to rely on the *Englischer* law enforcement for help if he doesn't stop," Joseph said.

"Please tell him that Miriam is doing everything she knows, within the *Ordnung* to make him leave her alone – that she has been horribly affected by all of this," Sarah suggested.

"*Denki*, wife. I will." Placing a soft kiss on her face, Joseph turned and left, going straight to the barn. As he walked, he scanned the area, looking for any vehicles, particularly a black truck. Seeing none, he let out a huge sigh of relief and walked faster to the barn.

Knocking on the bishop's front door, he smiled at Mrs. Stoltzfus.

"Good afternoon, Mrs. Stoltzfus. Is your husband here? I have a . . . need, a situation . . . to discuss with him."

"*Ya*, he is in the barn," said the bishop's wife, gesturing behind the house

"*Denki*. I won't be long," said Joseph with a small smile.

In the barn, he stopped to allow his eyes to adjust to the dimness inside.

"Ah, Joseph Beiler, how are you? Come in! I take it you are here on the matter involving your daughter?" the bishop asked with a sharp look.

"*Ya*. Her . . . situation continues. She is doing everything . . . *we* are doing everything we can think of to make this man stop bothering her. Samuel and Emily Fisher came by just a little while ago, to ask her if she still planned to be baptized and marry John. Miriam came in and heard us talking and it became . . . quite a discussion," Joseph said with a huge sigh.

"No! I know she intends to be baptized. She has assured me of that! I will go talk to . . ." at an abrupt shake of Joseph's head, the bishop paused. "You don't want me to talk to the Fishers?"

"*Nee*. Miriam made it quite clear to them that she is doing everything she knows to do . . . that she loves John. They left, understanding out situation much better. Bishop, we have been telling this man to leave her alone. We have not used force or violence. Still, he does not stop. He continues to stop by and harass her. I wanted to let you know, before I do it, that I am thinking of contacting *Englischer* law enforcement. Sarah and Mrs. Fisher both believe that he might have some mental condition that is causing him to act like this. I don't know about that, but I do know that my daughter is hurting badly over all of this. I know that we don't rely on law enforcement, but our *Ordnung*, to work out various issues. This man doesn't know or respect the Amish way of life and belief in humility, modesty and the Plain life. He tried to give Miriam a gift when he stopped at the house! Gave her a bunch of wildflowers – which she threw back at him. When he tried to give her the gift, I gave it right back to him and told him that it was very inappropriate for him to do so," Joseph finished, pacing back and forth.

"Let me understand this. You are saying that this man

doesn't understand our belief or culture." As the bishop spoke, he ticked individual points off, finger by finger. "That he keeps bothering your daughter. That our usual ways of handling someone are not working. And that you want to contact *Englischer* law enforcement. Am I right?"

"*Ya*. Normally, I wouldn't even think of this, but because he is an *Englischer*, he won't understand our orders to leave her alone – that a visit from the police may be the only thing to stop him," Joseph said.

"Hmmmm. I have one question for you – does Miss Beiler know this man's address in the city?"

"*Nee*." Joseph said with a frown.

"They would need to know where he lives to make contact with him, no?"

"*Ya*." As Joseph spoke, he clenched his fists convulsively, betraying his agitation and level of frustration.

"That may be a problem – or not. I don't know how they operate. Go ahead and call them. Maybe they have a way of finding him. If they do, maybe they can talk to him and let him know that his actions are bothering your daughter, you and the Fishers," Bishop Stoltzfus suggested.

"I will, *denki*. But I don't know if they will be able to find him. The city is huge," Joseph said.

Back home, he went straight to his carpentry shop and the

phone installed there. Picking up the thick phone directory for Philadelphia, he thumbed through the "N" listings, looking for Lance Newman. His heart fell as he saw listings for over 10 men with the same name.

*Is it worth calling all ten to see if I can find the right one?* Thinking of Miriam's pain, he decided the time and long-distance charges would be worth it. Before he did, he tried to find a reason for making the calls. Remembering that Miriam had said something about the man visiting high schools to talk to ball players, he decided to ask if Mr. Newman would be visiting high schools in Lancaster County.

Beginning, he went down the list, from name to name. On the fifth name, he got an affirmative answer.

"*De* – Thank you. I'll tell my son. Goodbye." Hanging up, Joseph wrote down the phone number and address, then looked up and called the non-emergency number for the Philadelphia police. After several frustrating minutes, he hung up after finding out that the city police wouldn't visit a man who had been bothering someone outside the city. *At least they told me I can call the sheriff in Lancaster county.* Finding the phone book for Lancaster county, he called the sheriff's department. Here, he had better luck.

"So, you're Amish and you're saying this "Englischer" man has been coming to your community. He's been bugging your daughter, and, no matter what you tell him, he refuses to stop. Well, that could be considered stalking," said the dispatcher.

"Yes? So, can you do anything?" Joseph asked.

"Well, technically, no. But . . . we can go visit him and tell him that someone from Lancaster has filed a complaint and that he really should cease his visits to your daughter and home. In order for us to arrest this guy, he has to do something that puts your daughter or someone else in your family at risk of harm. Then, we can arrest him. It's up to you, sir."

"I don't want to make you do anything that goes against your own rules," Joseph said. "But I also want him to leave my daughter alone. Yes, please, go and talk to Mr. Newman. And, thank you," Joseph said.

"Not a problem, sir. I know the Amish try to resolve things their own way, but it seems he's not getting your message. It might be a few days before we can visit him – but we will," said the dispatcher.

"Thank you."

# CHAPTER SEVEN

Several days later, a unit from the Lancaster County Sheriff's Department drove into Philadelphia and located Lance Newman's apartment complex. Using the information Joseph Beiler had given them, they climbed the stairs to Lance's apartment and knocked on the door.

"Yes – whoa! Hey, I had nothing to do with that robbery," Lance said, telling a bad joke. The fear in his eyes gave him away.

"Mr. Lance Newman?" one deputy asked.

"Yeah, that's me. What's up?" asked Lance.

"We received a complaint several days ago from a man in Ephrata. He tells us that you've been trying to spend time with his daughter and that she and her parents want you to leave her alone."

"Yeah, what of it? I thought she was pretty. Besides, I

haven't gone back in . . . phht . . . several days," Lance said as his eyes narrowed.

"Good. Keep it that way. Because they've complained, that's considered to be potential harassment. She's told you that she doesn't want your attention or gifts. Respect that. If you don't, and we find out you've gone back, we can arrest you for stalking and harassment," the sheriff's deputy said with a warning tone.

Lance had been about to make a sarcastic remark, but at the words, "arrest, stalking and harassment," he shut his mouth.

*No way can I withstand another mark on my record. If the university gets wind of this – if I get arrested, then I'll be fired. But I want her so much! And I know she wants me. She's just so restricted. I'm sure she's being forced to marry that Amish dude. Isn't that what they do, arranged marriages? Of course they do. They treat her like a prisoner, but when she's mine, I'll treat her like a princess. A queen. My queen.*

For a moment, he lost himself in the fantasy. Miriam, in his tiny apartment, smiling sweetly at him from beside the stove.

*She wants me and I want her. I'll just have to be more careful next time so that we can be together. Forever.*

"Officers, you won't have any problems from me. No way can I be arrested. All I wanted to do was express my interest in the young lady and see if she returned that interest. Now that I know she doesn't . . . well, sure, I'm disappointed. But, oh well! You win some, you lose some. I promise you – I won't go back," Lance said with his widest smile crinkling his face and his hands raised, palms out.

"Okay, then, just as long as you're aware that the family's not happy and neither is the 'young lady' in question. Stay away from Ephrata! Period. Got that?" asked the bulkier officer with a frown on his face.

"In spades and crystal-clear, sir." Lance shrugged. "I'll just nurse my broken heart heart here at home and move on. What else can I do?"

"Thank you. As long as you understand," the smaller officer said.

Lance stood in the doorway, watching the officers as they walked down the hall. All traces of humor had been wiped off his face. Moving slowly, he shut his door quietly, being careful not to slam it. His anger pushed him to do something physical – slam that door, punch a wall, kick the fridge – something.

*I'm gonna have to be much more careful when I—*

*Hold your horses and Amish buggy, Lance. They recognize your truck. When you go back, you're gonna have to use a different vehicle. Maybe borrow Eddie's old beater and promise to replace the brakes on it for him. They won't recognize a brown Saturn. Yeah, I think that's what I'll do . . . but Miriam, love of my heart, that's just gonna have to wait. I'm not about to let myself be arrested, so you're just gonna have to bide your time. We'll be together, in the end. I promise.*

In Ephrata, Joseph decided the time was right to tell Miriam and Sarah what he had done to stop Lance's visits.

"Daughter, wife, we need to talk," he announced one evening after supper. "Miriam, I went to talk to Bishop Stoltzfus about your situation and I told him that you, your *mamm*, John and I have been doing everything to make that Lance character stop bothering you. I had the idea of asking the law enforcement in Philadelphia to go talk to him, but they said they couldn't. Something about 'jurisdiction.' So, they suggested that I call the sheriff's office here in Lancaster County. They said they couldn't really do very much, but they did send two officers to visit that man and tell him to stay away from you. I don't know what they told him, but I think they did talk to him. I haven't seen him here now for a few days, so maybe he'll stop coming here."

"*Daed, denki!* I haven't seen him either, but I haven't gone anywhere either. I've only stayed here and worked. When I've gone out, it's been with John or you. Do you mean it's over? I can start driving myself again?"

"*Nee*, not yet. I want to make sure he really won't be coming back here. We'll take you where you need to go. My biggest worry was John's parents. Now, I'm glad we talked to them. They understand that you've done everything you could possibly do. But . . . until we know for sure, we will take you everywhere," Joseph decided.

"Okay. I understand. I feel better than I have in . . . in weeks! I feel like I can breathe again," Miriam said happily.

She didn't know that Lance had decided to leave his truck at home. Instead, he had borrowed a nondescript, older-model Saturn from his friend. The vehicle he chose to use was a golden brown sedan. In addition to using a different vehicle, Lance had decided it would be more prudent to restrict his activities to figuring out the comings and goings of her parents. Not knowing of his continued activities in Ephrata, she focused completely on her quilting. She had finished the Amish Wedding quilt and now, she was working on one of the three children's quilts she had agreed to make.

Spring slowly edged into a hot, sunny summer. Miriam's work on her quilts moved along smoothly. And Lance continued coming to Ephrata in secret, making note of the Beiler family's comings and goings.

"Miriam, your *mamm* and I are going to the Amish market. We want you to go with us . . ." Joseph said.

"*Nee, daed,* I can't. I still have too much to do on the quilt order. I've only just started on one of the children's quilts and it will take me a good two months, at least, to finish it. Then, I have the two remaining children's quilts to make. I'm sure I'll be okay at home alone. I'll shut the doors and lock them – I promise you," Miriam said with regret.

Sarah looked at Joseph, questioning.

179

Joseph let out a long sign and ran one hand down his long beard, a sign that he was thinking.

"Miriam, this worries me. It really does. But . . . OK. As soon as we walk out the door, you lock it. I want to see you lock the back door before we go. We will be back as soon as we finish our errands."

"*Denki, daed.* I will stay inside. I promise you."

Miriam hurried to the back door in the kitchen and locked the door to Joseph's grim satisfaction. Standing by the front door, she waited until both of her parents walked out. Shutting the door securely behind them, she locked it and jiggled it in the frame, showing Joseph that it wouldn't open without a house key.

"We will be back! Stay inside the house,"

"*Ya, daed*, I will." Miriam promised.

Hurrying back to the quilting room, she continued pinning and cutting out quilting shapes for the green-on-green blanket. As she worked, she was unaware that the front door remained slightly cracked open to provide natural cooling to the inside of the house.

Joseph and Sarah rode down the road from their house on the way to the Amish market. Joseph's eyes swept the countryside, looking for that familiar black truck. As his gaze roved over the roads and fields, he nearly missed a nondescript brown sedan idling on a side road – his gaze swept past it –

then returned to the vehicle. Peering through the smeary windshield, Joseph tried to see if he could recognize the driver. Forcing himself to look calm and relaxed, he and Sarah continued moving down the road. Looking through the side of his eye, Joseph spotted a tall man . . . but couldn't make out any features. The niggling fear he had felt when he and Sarah returned ten-fold.

"Sarah, don't make it obvious you're looking, but there's a brown car to our left," he said. "Can you recognize the driver?"

Sarah kept her eyes aimed forward, but looked out the side of her eyes as well.

"He's . . . it's a tall man, Joseph. It's hard to tell, but I think I saw blonde hair!"

"This is what I'm going to do. I don't know . . . is he driving toward the farm?" Joseph asked.

"*Ya*, I think he is! We have to go back home! We can go to market next week!"

"I can't make it look like I just recognized him. I'm going to keep driving down the road, then take the road next to the Zook farm and go home that way. Once we get home, you run into the barn and call the sheriff's office," Joseph directed.

"*Ya*," Sarah said.

As they reached the road, Joseph yelled to the horse, who began to gallop down the road. The horse, knowing the roads, headed straight for home. Once Joseph and Sarah arrived back home, he jumped out of the buggy. Sarah was close behind him.

Lance, not knowing he was seen, drove to the Beiler farm. Looking around carefully, he didn't see anyone nearby. Easing the old door closed, he continued looking around as he moved to the front porch. Walking up the steps, he paused as he heard one step creak. Sweeping the windows with his eyes, he saw no motion inside the house. *Good. She's inside, all alone.* Taking slow, careful steps toward the front door, he tried the doorknob. Locked. He looked along the long, deep porch – *Bingo! They left a window open on the first floor! Don't you know you're inviting me inside?* Removing the window screen, he put it on the porch and began to push the window open in the casement. He stopped when he heard a soft *clunking* sound coming from the window frame. His heart pounded and he felt sweat running down the sides of his face. Nobody came to the door, so he continued sliding the window open.

Back in the quilting room, Miriam looked up from her fabric-cutting. *Did I just hear something?* She looked from window to window. Nothing. No noise. *Probably just an old house settling.* Turning her attention back to her fabric-cutting, she kept working, unaware that Lance was slowly easing his lanky body through the now-completely open window.

By now, Lance was completely in the house. Pausing for a few seconds to get his bearings, he looked around at the placement of the large, open rooms. *I'll check downstairs first.*

*If she's not down here, I'll go upstairs. Her parents won't be back for hours yet.* However, Lance was unaware that Miriam's parents had turned around and were, by now, nearing the house. He tiptoed down the wide hall, checking each room for Miriam.

Hearing a soft sound from a room at the end of the hall, he continued to tiptoe down the hall. He smiled greedily as he saw the object of his affections, bent over a long table, cutting fabric out in various, angular shapes. He stood there for precious seconds, just drinking in the sight. After several seconds, he continued sliding into the room like a tall, blonde, upright snake, keeping his eyes focused on Miriam's back.

Miriam was so focused on cutting out the fabric pieces for the green-on-green quilt that she was completely unaware that someone had joined her – and was, by now, directly behind her. Feeling a kink in her shoulder, she finished cutting a shape out of bright-green fabric. Setting the long, sharp scissors down, she stretched her neck and massaged her shoulder with her fingers – and, as Lance slipped one hand over her mouth, her eyes widened and she gasped. Lance slipped his other arm around Miriam's torso and hauled her against his chest, lifting her slight form off the floor. He began backing up quickly now, knowing he just needed to get her into the car.

Miriam tried hard to fight. She had the benefit of the hard physical work required of all Amish, but Lance had a much bigger advantage – surprise. Because of her strength, unusual in a girl so slight, Lance had a fight on his hands.

Lance swore to himself, realizing that this tiny slip of a girl was making it harder for him to get out of the house. *I should be getting outside the door by now, but she's making it too hard!* He felt sweat beading on his forehead and temples, then sliding down the sides of his face. He gasped, working to keep Miriam in his arms. *Finally! I have to open the door so I can get her out* . . . Lance took his hand from Miriam's mouth and reached for the doorknob . . .

# CHAPTER EIGHT

The door flew open as if under its own power. The corner of the door caught Lance on the back of his head. He grunted as stars exploded behind his eyes, and he staggered.

Joseph, seeing Lance holding his youngest daughter, let out an inarticulate growl and grabbed her from Lance's arms. Holding her protectively, he kept his eyes on Lance, who was still dazed from the knock to his head. Joseph backed up, bumping into Sarah. "Take her," he said to Sarah, who nodded and pulled Miriam in tightly.

Miriam grabbed the fabric of Sarah's dress convulsively in between her fingers with a sob.

"*Mamm*, I didn't know he was out there! He . . . grabbed me while I was cutting quilting pieces out!"

"Shhh, shhh, daughter. Come, sit down," Sarah murmured, glaring at Lance.

Joseph grabbed Lance's upper arms clapping his hands hard on the younger man's arms.

"Sarah, *nee,* go to the barn and call the Lancaster County sheriff's office and tell them what just happened," he ordered.

"Miriam, let's go. I am not letting you out of my sight," Sarah said.

Miriam nodded, not wanting to be alone.

Joseph began forcing Lance out of the house. On the front porch, his mouth dropped open as he saw Samuel and John Fisher pulling into their front yard.

Samuel and John both leaped out of their buggy and ran to the porch, grabbing Lance by his neck and forearms. As they forced Lance to the towering oak tree in the front yard, they were all surprised to see Bishop Stoltzfus driving quickly into the yard.

Joseph, Samuel and John struggled to keep control of Lance, who was struggling to get loose.

Bishop Stoltzfus strode quickly to the four men.

"Mr. Newman, if you ever return to our community, you will find yourself thrown out again and again. We don't hold with depending upon law enforcement, but if we have to, we will . . ." as he spoke, he sent a questioning glance to Joseph.

"Ya, Sarah is calling the sheriff now. She has Miriam with her," he confirmed.

"Good. Mr. Newman, it will be up to the sheriff what he wants to do. As far as we are concerned here in Ephrata, I very strongly suggest that you leave . . . and never come back. Miss Beiler does not want your attentions at all. She has told me that she has tried to get you to stop bothering her – and you *are* bothering her. Ah, good, the sheriff is here," the bishop said, almost conversationally.

"Agh! I can't go to jail! I'll lose my job!" Lance growled.

"You should have thought of that when you decided to ignore my daughter's wishes," Joseph said, his voice a low growl. He tightened his grip on Lance's neck and upper arm as Lance redoubled his struggles to break free.

"Mr. Beiler? We understand you had an intruder. Mr. Newman, we meet again. It seems you decided to ignore our warning when we visited you in Philadelphia. You do know what this means, don't you?" the tall, bulky deputy asked.

"I'm not saying anything!" Lance shouted as he continued to struggle.

"Mr. Beiler, where is your daughter?" asked one deputy.

"She's probably either in the barn with her mamm or coming out," Joseph said.

"Thank you. I'll go take her statement."

Ten minutes later, he returned, tucking his notebook into the breast pocket of his uniform shirt.

"It looks like Miss Beiler was alone in the house, working, when you broke in and grabbed her. She says you covered her mouth with one hand and lifted her from her chair, attempting to force her out of the house. Under Pennsylvania law, that is breaking and entering, assault and attempted kidnapping. If we present this to the district attorney, you could be facing quite a few years behind bars, Mr. Newman, but I'm going to defer to the wishes of these good men here. Sir?" asked the deputy, looking at Joseph and swinging his glance to the bishop.

Bishop Stoltzfus glanced at Joseph, who was struggling to hold onto Lance and thinking of what would be best for Miriam and the community.

"Mr. Beiler, I'll hold onto this joker," the huge deputy offered, grabbing onto Lance.

Joseph let go and heaved out a deep sigh.

"Officer, normally, we don't rely on law enforcement, but this Englischer has refused to get our message that my daughter does not want his attentions. He tried to kidnap her. I don't know what's wrong in his head or not. My worry is for the other young women of Ephrata, should he turn his sick attentions to them. Our warnings to him fell onto deaf ears. With our bishop's permission, I am going to allow you to take him – my understanding is that we would have to file a criminal complaint, correct?"

"That's correct. We'll be happy to write everything up for you. We will also need to dust your home for his fingerprints and we'll be taking his car into . . ."

"ARGHH, NO!!! That isn't my car!" Lance screamed. "Don't arrest me! I get the stupid message and I'll stay away from that stupid woman and this insane community! Just don't . . . arrest me!"

"Ahhh, yes, I remember something about you owning a black truck. Is that Saturn what you came here in?" asked one deputy.

Lance clamped his lips shut, refusing to say any more.

Joseph spoke.

"We've seen you here often enough in Ephrata so that we recognize you. You don't have to be in your truck for us to know you're here. Bishop Stoltzfus offered help and I accepted it. Miriam's fiance and his father also offered their help. I accepted it. Now, go. Get out of here and don't you ever try to come back again. You will not be welcomed."

Four men, three bearded and all wearing straw hats, glared at Lance, who allowed his angry gaze to drove from one hard, rawboned face to another. A sneer gathered on his face and he spat into the dirt at their feet.

"Okay, we're cuffing him and taking him off your hands. We have another unit coming by to take evidence in a minute or two, then we'll be out of your hair," one deputy said.

Lance, now securely handcuffed, was marched to the back

of the squad car and forced to sit in the back. The deputies got in and drove away.

Miriam, knowing that Lance was gone, finally came out of the barn, shaking. She allowed John to hold her as he wrapped both arms around her and pulled her head against his chest.

"OK, it's OK, Miriam. He's gone and he probably won't be back. Those are some serious charges he's facing. It's clear that he had no good intentions in coming into our community, other than to force himself on you," John murmured.

At his words, Miriam, dissolved into shaky tears.

"I'm just glad he's gone," she said through hiccups and sobs. "What if he had tried this to someone else?"

Sarah spoke up with a frown on her face.

"I don't know all the specifics, but Miriam still isn't eighteen. He's over twenty-one. I think, if we call them again, the sheriff's office and that attorney man could talk to us about whether that Lance character could be charged with harming a minor."

"I think you're talking about someone called a sex offender, Mrs. Beiler. Talk to them, but unless he actually did something – sexual – to her, I don't think that will happen," said the bishop.

"Denki, Bishop. I will," Sarah said. "I know we don't know Englischer law, but what he tried to do to our Miriam – he's sick!"

The Lancaster evidence van pulled into the front yard and Joseph broke from the group of men to introduce them to Miriam. The two of them went with the law enforcement officers to show them where Lance had entered the house. As they showed them around, Miriam shivered from her fear. While the officers dusted for fingerprints and walked slowly through the house, Joseph calmed Miriam down.

"You did the right thing. You made sure the doors were locked. I should have remembered the window was open for air – that's how he got in. It's my job to protect you, daughter. That's what I'm doing now and why I had your *mamm* call the sheriff. I didn't want to involve them, but sometimes, we have to. That man wasn't going to listen to anything we said, so he needed to get the message from someone whose language he understands. Now, I'm praying that they will charge him with crimes so he won't be back here for a good, long time, if ever. You are safe, now, Miriam. Give thanks to the Lord that I had a bad feeling and had asked both the Fishers and Bishop Stoltzfus to come by here today," Joseph said.

As they walked outside, Joseph saw that the law enforcement vehicle parked outside had drawn an audience. Miriam spotted Anna King's worried look.

"*Daed*, there's Anna, and she looks very worried. I ned to go and calm her down," Miriam said, feeling somewhat calmer.

"*Ya*, you go ahead and tell her what you need to say. You probably shouldn't say anything about what that man tried to do. Just tell her that he tried to get to you and we had him arrested," said Joseph.

"Okay, denki, *daed*." Miriam scurried over to Anna, who gave her a big hug.

"Are you all right? I was driving by, on my way home from the market, when I saw this car. What happened?" Anna asked, her eyes huge.

"I can't say very much yet. Lance Newman tried to get to me again – and that's all I can say," Miriam said with a shaky sigh.

"Well, it had to be bad if the police are here," Anna said. "Do you see what I meant when I told you that he was no good for you??

"*Ya*, Anna, I do. I've been trying to get him to leave me alone for a long time, now. My parents, John, his parents, Bishop Stoltzfus, and now, the sheriff are helping me. They arrested Lance just a little while ago and took him off to jail – thank the Lord."

As Miriam finished speaking, a law enforcement investigator came trotting up to her.

"Miss Beiler, we need to talk to you, if you could come into your house."

"Yes." She led the investigator in to show her where she had been when Lance grabbed her.

The investigator walked slowly from the quilting room and down the hallway. As she did, she looked over every inch for any physical evidence she could take in building a case against Miriam's attacker. When she spotted anything out of the ordinary, she took the evidence, explaining her actions to Miriam as she did so.

"If you could get one of your parents in here, I need to look over you – your clothing to see if there's any proof of his grabbing you," the investigator said.

"Okay. Mamm! We need you here," Miriam said, motioning Sarah over to her.

"Ma'am, we need to have you watch while we look over your daughter for any evidence that Mr. Newman might have left on her clothing or body. Can we go into a room for this?" the investigator asked.

"Ya, come with me," Sarah said, bustling to the quilting room and shutting the door.

The investigator began by having Miriam standing up with her arms spread out at her sides. As with the house, any time she found anything, she plucked it off with tweezers and slipped the item into a sealing plastic bag. When she had finished looking at Miriam's clothing, she moved to her body, looking for cuts and bruises.

Miriam flinched slightly as the investigator prodded around her mouth, chin and under her nose.

"I'm sorry. Does that hurt?"

"Ya," Miriam said.

The investigator sighed. "I know how the Amish feel about photographs, but I assure you, this is only for evidentiary purposes, not to glorify you. I need to take a picture of the bruise that's starting to show up around your mouth. He gripped you pretty hard, Miss Beiler."

"Bruise? *Mamm*?" Miriam's eyes widened in shock at the thought that Lance had actually hurt her.

"Yes, miss, take the photos. We understand. Miriam, yes, I can see a bruise beginning to form. I think the bishop will give permission since this is to prove that Mr. Newman tried to hurt you. Miss, before you take the photograph, I need to get the bishop in here," Sarah said, holding her hand up.

"Go right ahead, ma'am. We just want to make sure we get all the evidence on the first go-round," the investigator said, unzipping the pouch of a digital camera.

Sarah came hurrying back in with the bishop close behind her.

"Miss, go ahead and take the photo. We understand the purpose. One question, however. Would you please photograph only the lower part of Miss Beiler's face, the part with the bruise? This way, her full face will not be shown and she will not be in violation of any of our rules," asked the bishop.

"Normally, we'd need to have a picture that shows her full face, but I'll include an explanation that she's Amish," the investigator said after some thought.

Miriam, feeling odd about the picture, stood stiffly with her eyes shut. She flinched as she saw the bright flash from behind her closed eyelids.

"*Mamm*? This feels . . . strange," she said.

"It is all right, Miss Beiler. I understand why the investigator needs this photo. That bruise must show up as evidence against that man, if he is to face justice in an Englischer court. You have done no wrong. Instead, the wrongs were committed against you. Just remember to follow the Ordnung in all other matters," said Bishop Stoltzfus.

Finally, the sheriff's investigators had collected all the evidence they needed. Before leaving, they reminded Miriam and her parents not to say anything about Miriam's attempted kidnapping.

"*Mamm*, I really have to get started on that quilt. I'll be in the quilting room, if you need me," Miriam said.

"OK. If you need me, I'll be making supper."

"Let me know when you need my help and I'll come in,"

Miriam said, walking into the quilting room.

"Nee. Your work is more important. Besides, most of the supper preparations are done already, so all I have to do is assemble the stew and cook it. The bread is risen and only needs baking."

"Denki, *mamm*!" Settling into her chair, Miriam resumed cutting the pieces of fabric for the green-on-green quilt she had just begun. When she had finished, she looked up. "Hmmm. I think I have time to start stitching pieces together," she whispered to herself. After another hour and a half, she had pieced together about one-quarter of the top of the quilt.

Shutting the machine off, she placed the unstitched pieces to the side on a table. Before leaving the room, a wave of apprehension hit her and she doubled back into the room. Going straight to the window, she shut and locked it. Letting out a shaky sigh, she thought to herself.

*Until I know he's not getting out, I won't feel completely safe.*

# CHAPTER NINE

In the kitchen, Miriam shakily told Sarah how she might never feel safe enough to leave the doors or windows open again.

"Miriam, he's behind bars. He's not getting out. We need to keep air moving through the rooms so we don't get too hot in here," Sarah said.

"I know, *mamm*, but . . . I keep thinking that he's going to get out and come back here," Miriam said.

Sarah was about to speak when Joseph came in.

"What? What's happening?" he asked.

"Miriam shut the window in the quilting room because she thinks that Lance character will be getting out of jail and coming back here," said Sarah.

"Miriam, he's in jail. I don't think he's getting out, but I can call the sheriff to ask if he knows where Mr. Newman is,"

Joseph offered.

"*Daed*, could you? I don't like this feeling. I feel as if I have to be watchful – I didn't feel like this while I was working, but when I finished, it hit me," Miriam said.

"Come with me and we'll call together," Joseph suggested. In the barn, he found the phone number and called the sheriff's department.

"I'm calling about Mr. Lance Newman. My daughter, Miriam, is afraid that he is going to be able to get out and come back here . . . please, if you would. We would be very grateful," Joseph said.

After a few minutes, the dispatcher came back on the line,

"Mr. Beiler? I just checked with the county's detention center. Mr. Newman is definitely still a guest of our facility. He can't get out until he's gone before a judge, who may or may not set bail for him. Even then, he might not get out because the amount the judge orders him to pay might be too high for him."

"So, he's still in jail? When could this change?" Joseph asked as he looked at Miriam's apprehensive expression.

"Within two days. If he makes bail, the district attorney's office would call you at the number you gave us when you filed the criminal complaint. That would allow you to do what you need to do to protect her and your family," explained the dispatcher."

"OK, denki – thank you, miss. That's what I thought, but I wanted to be sure. Oh, one more question. Do you know what his bail amount might be?"

"No, I don't. That's up to the judge who hears his case. If he gets out, you will get a call. OK?"

"Thank you, I understand. Yes, goodbye."

"He's still in jail?" asked Miriam.

"Ya, he is. He has to appear in front of an Englischer judge, who decides if he gets out of jail or not. If he gets out, he has to put up some money that is his promise that he won't try to flee the county before his criminal trial. The dispatcher just told me that, if he gets out of jail, the district attorney's office will call me. That way, we can set up some kind of protection for you – just in case that Lance character tries to come back here. You, your *mamm* and I have to talk after supper. In the meantime, you go open that window back up."

After supper, Miriam and Sarah had just finished cleaning the kitchen when John knocked on the front door. Joseph answered, saying, "Before you and Miriam begin visiting, we need to talk."

"Certainly, Mr. Beiler," John said, seeing the serious expression on the older man's face.

Joseph explained what he had learned from the dispatcher.

"So, we don't know if he'll get out of jail or not. If he does, we don't know if he'll try coming back here – although, if he does try, he's *mupsich*. I am thinking that, if he does, we should have Miriam stay somewhere else."

"*Daed*, me stay somewhere else? But . . . my quilts! I . . . I want to obey you, but I have to finish those quilts!" Miriam said.

"*Ya*, I know, daughter. I want to ask Mr. and Mrs. King if you could stay with them for a few weeks – if that man gets out of jail. If he doesn't, then, you stay here at home. John, we won't know for a few days if he's going to get out or not. I plan to visit the district attorney's office tomorrow – or the sheriff's office – and find out when the hearing is supposed to take place. I also want to find out if I can be there. No, Miriam, you can't be there. I've decided that I don't want you anywhere that man is. You will stay here and I'll be at that hearing," Joseph said decisively.

Miriam saw the resolute look on Joseph's face. She knew better than to protest. "Yes, *daed*. I understand. I don't want to see him anyway."

"Mr. Beiler, if this comes to a criminal trial, what will you do if Miriam has to testify?"

"If she has to testify, that is one thing. But being in the court room for this first hearing? No, she won't be there. Once I know what's going to happen, then we will know whether you will go to the King's or stay here, Miriam."

"Yes, *daed*."

After the discussion about Lance and upcoming legal matters, John and Miriam went for a buggy ride.

"That bruise is getting darker, Miriam. What are you going to do if you have to go out to the market?"

"I'll stay here and ask mamm to get my purchases for me. There's not much more that I can do until it fades. I'm just grateful that this coming Sunday is not a meeting Sunday," Miriam said.

"That's true," John said as he guided the horse down the dirt road. "Does it hurt?"

"It's a little tender, but that's all."

"How are you feeling . . . emotionally?" asked John.

Miriam sighed. "Open windows scare me. Do you know that he came in through the living room window? *Daed* had me lock the doors before they left for the market today."

John stopped the horse and slipped his arm around Miriam's shoulders.

"Miriam, he's in jail. I don't know how the Englischer legal system works, but I know he has to be given the chance to pay bail to get out of jail. I don't know how much they'll want him to pay. If he doesn't have the money, he can't get out of jail. That means you'll be safe. But if he does get out of jail, I agree with your *daed*. I want you to go stay with Anna until we know it's safe."

John pulled Miriam against his side, nestling her close to him. As he thought about what had so very nearly happened that morning, he trembled, partly from fear and partly from anger.

"John? Why are you shaking?" asked Miriam.

"I . . . I'm thinking about what happened to you this morning. He could have kidnapped you today . . . how did you keep him from pulling you from the house?"

"I fought, John. I fought hard. I'll probably feel the soreness tomorrow because I tried so hard to keep him from getting me out of the house. Still, he picked me up, covered my mouth with his hand and carried me from the quilting room to the living room. *Daed* pushed the front door open and hit Lance on the head, and I think that's how he was able to get me out of Lance's arms. That's about when you, your *daed* and Bishop Stoltzfus showed up. John, I'm sorry, but thinking about it just brings it back. Can we talk about something else? Please?" Miriam asked.

"Okay. I don't want to cause you any more pain and fright, Miriam."

"There is one thing I want to say about this morning, though," Miriam said. "I want to thank you for trusting me through this whole mess. You could have believed that I was breaking my promise to marry you, but you didn't. You believed me, even when Lance tried to trick me into spending some time with him and your *daed* saw us."

John gently slipped his arms around Miriam's body, holding her to him. He rocked her back and forth, giving her the comfort she seemed to need.

"Ya, I could have, but I saw your fear of him, Miriam. Yes, there were a few moments where I wondered what was happening. But, when we – you and I – talked, I could see that you didn't want to get to know Mr. Newman. You only wanted him to leave you and your family alone, and when he wouldn't stop bothering you, that's when all of us started trying to help you. Ya, you made that one mistake, and when you realized it, you took steps to correct it. I have always trusted and loved, you, Miriam.

"We're both about to start almost five months of instruction before we are baptized. Once we're baptized, we can marry each other. Because our instruction will end when this year's wedding season ends, we won't be getting married until the next wedding season. My *daed* has a *grussmudderhaus* next to his house, and that's where we would live until we move into their house," said John, thinking into the future.

Miriam, caught up in the happy planning, forgot the terrible events of the day. "You know we won't be able to move into their house until after we have our first child, right?"

"*Ya.*" John looked at Miriam, seeming to see someone else. "I keep imagining a little girl with light brown hair and golden eyes, just like yours."

Miriam blushed, thinking of children and the future.

"I have a confession to make," she whispered. "When I imagine us married, I know it won't always be very easy. I know we'll have challenges and problems. But . . . I also see myself as the *mamm* of little boys with dark brown eyes and hair. Little boys who will grow up to look like their *daed*. And . . . it's fine that we'll live in the *grossmudderhaus* at first. It's small, but that's all we'll need at first, until the *bopplis* start to come. We're young, John, and we're strong. We love each other and we will have a strong marriage," Miriam said.

John leaned down, pressing his lips to Miriam's, mindful of the bruise on her lower face.

"Tell me if that hurts, because I don't want to make you hurt," he whispered.

"It's . . . tender," Miriam confessed.

"Then, no kissing until that bruise and the soreness go away. I don't want anything to ruin our time together," John decided.

"John, are you going to continue working with your *daed* on his farm after we marry?"

"*Ya*. There's a shortage of farm land, so that's how I'll earn money after we marry. I'll till several acres and plant seed. What grows will be ours for harvesting. *Daed* and I have talked about this already. He has about five hundred acres and he'll give me about one hundred. I'll use the money from that to buy land when some goes on sale, then we will build our own house. What will you do? Continue making and selling quilts?"

"Yes. I'm working on that huge order and I expect that I'll continue to get a lot of orders, especially if I have good customers like the ones I'm working with now. That's what I'll be doing to bring money into our family. I can work from home to help you while we raise our *kinner*."

"I like that. Ya, keep making quilts and ask your customers to let their families and friends know about your work. You know, as artistic and expert as you are at your age, imagine just how in demand you'll be in even 10 or 20 years!"

"Oh!" Miriam said with a breathless laugh. "Thank you, John, but I have a lot yet to learn about quilting. *Ya*, I'm making some beautiful quilts now, but I have to thank my *grossmuder* for everything she taught me. I just enjoy making the quilts and giving pleasure and happiness to my customers. Every time I sit down to work on a quilt, I imagine the *kinner* and the adults, happy to go to sleep at night under their warmth. If they choose to hang my quilts on a frame or on the wall, I am happy with that."

"I have always wondered one thing, Miriam. Have you ever had unhappy customers?"

Miriam thought back on her short quilt-making career.

"Hmmm. Only one, but that was because she wasn't sure of

the colors. I showed her patterns, then she asked me to make the decision about the colors. I told her that, because I didn't know what colors she had in her home, it would be very difficult for me. So, she finally told me what colors she had in the bedroom and we decided on colors. Well, when I delivered her quilt to her, she brought it back to the market, unhappy because it wasn't an exact match to the drapes and carpeting in her bedroom! I told her that's why I needed to know precise colors so I could make something she would enjoy displaying. I ended up giving her back her money – and going into debt to *daed* and *mamm* on that quilt. That taught me to be very clear with customers on what colors and patterns they want in their quilts."

"That's why I'm happy to plant crops and harvest them. The harvest is what we get. That's what we use to feed our livestock, save up more seed and sell at market. No disputes about color or size. All we need to know is how many bushels a customer wants. We sell that to him and it's done," said John.

Before the sun began setting, John and Miriam rode around to other picturesque areas of Ephrata so they could enjoy each other's' company without the fear of an unwanted visitor intruding on their courting time. As they spent that evening together, they discussed their plans for their future in more detail. As the sun began to descend in the evening sky, he started the slow drive back to Miriam's parents' house.

Miriam rested her head on John's solid shoulder, feeling tired from the events and stresses of the day. Her eyes began to droop as the buggy moved slowly down the road, and she slipped into a light daze. As John stopped the buggy and set the brake, she came to full wakefulness, raising her head from John's shoulder and stretching.

"I think you'd better go straight to bed when you get inside," said John.

"*Ya*, I plan to. I'm more tired than I thought," Miriam said, yawning. John walked Miriam to the front door, kissing her softly.

## THANK YOU FOR READING!

And thank you for supporting me as an independent author. I hope you enjoyed reading this as much as I enjoyed writing it! If so, I hope you also enjoy the sample of the next book in the series, THE WEDDING SEASON, in the next chapter. Click on the link to be notified when the next book in the series is available for purchase.

Also, if you get a chance to leave me a review, I'd really appreciate it (and if you find something in the book that – YIKES – makes you think it deserves less than 5-stars, drop me a line at Rachel.stoltzfus@globagrafxpress.com,   and I'll fix it if I can)

*All the best,*

*Rachel*

RACHEL STOLTZFUS

# THE WEDDING SEASON

## CHAPTER ONE

Miriam woke up the morning after Lance Newman's arrest, feeling oddly . . . free, like his passing into the hands of the law had opened the door to her prison. And in a way it had. No longer did she have to look over her shoulder or live with that persistent, itchy certainty that he might at any moment come back and attempt to do horrid things to her in the name of his own twisted sense of love.

*Out of my distress I called on the Lord; the Lord answered me and set me free.*

The psalm came to Miriam's mind and she glanced upwards, the sense of peace and happiness that she'd felt upon awakening seeming to fill her even more. Yes, today was a new, wondrous gift, and Miriam was going to seize it.

With that thought firmly in mind, Miriam dressed and

combed her hair, twisting the gentle waves of light brown hair into a bun and pinning it beneath her prayer kapp. When she was ready for her day, she walked with light feet and a light heart down the stairs to the kitchen where her mamm had started making breakfast.

"*Guder mariye, mamm!*" Miriam said, grinning at the smell of fresh bread. On the skillet, thick strips of bacon sizzled.

Her mamm, Sarah Bieler, returned Miriam's smile before waving the spatula towards a metal bowl on the counter beside the sink. "Whisk these eggs for breakfast, if you would, please?"

"Ya," Miriam said, crossing the room in easy strides and taking up the whisk to start at beating the eggs with quick, practiced motions. "I just—it's a beautiful morning, isn't it?"

Outside the window, the skies were a charcoal grey, clouds hanging heavy the wheat field. By the barn, the horse stood idly, nibbling at the grass once before taking a couple of slow, heavy steps and bowing his head again.

"Some days, it's like we carry the weather inside us," Sarah said, her eyes sparkling.

Miriam laughed. "That is true. I feel like I've been slogging through a storm for so long. As long as he stays in jail, I can live again."

"You live no matter what, in God's hands," her mamm said cryptically, "Now add some onions and peppers to those eggs.

"It's just good that daed called the Englisch police. I didn't want him to at first, but I also worried that Mr. Newman wasn't getting the message – that he didn't want to get the message."

"Nee, he didn't. Did you add the milk already?"

"Ya, it's in there. Miriam sniffed the fragrant smell of bacon sizzling in the pan as she scraped the diced vegetables into the egg mixture. "Mmmm. I love making omelets."

"*Gutt*, now put some hustle to it. All of this worrying has the whole family hungry."

Ten minutes later, Joseph Beiler walked in, sniffing appreciatively. Miriam and Sarah were dishing up the hot breakfast and placing it at the long kitchen table.

"Denki, Sarah!" Mirian's daed said, giving her mamm a warm smile. "You must have known I was extra-hungry after yesterday," he said.

Sarah smiled back. "We are all hungry now that we don't have to worry for Miriam's safety. Dig in! We all have busy days ahead of us."

"Miriam, I don't know the particulars, but you will have to testify in court hearings. Everything you can tell the judge that will keep that Lance character away from you, you'll have to remember," Joseph said.

Was—did that mean she had to face him again? Miriam looked out the window into the fields. The clouds hung as charcoal heavy as before, but now she felt the weight of them. "Why? I mean, didn't I already— "

"He has the right to face his accuser. That's Englischer law."

"So Lance Newman has rights and I have—"

"If you want him to stay in prison, it's what you have to do."

"That's not fair!"

"Stop whining, Miriam. You're becoming a woman, not a child. And we will be with you. Your mamm and me."

Miriam wanted to cry. She knew she wasn't a child, but she'd done nothing to provoke this man, and just when she thought she was finally free of him, the law that was supposed to protect her was dragging her back into his clutches. Miriam pressed her lips together and took a deep breath through her nose. When she could speak without her voice cracking, she said, "If this is what I have to do to keep him in jail, then I will do it."

"*Gutt*," her father said, putting a comforting hand on her shoulder. "I know you are strong. Stronger than this and stronger than him. You're our daughter and God's child. We'll be with you and so will God. What does this criminal Lance have to match that?"

Miriam nodded, and her dead squeezed her shoulder, the strength of his grip comforting. "You will do yourself and us credit, Miriam," her daed said.

Miriam desperately wanted to believe her daed, but she feared that when the time came for her to step into that courtroom and tell her story again under Mr. Newman's cold gaze, she might freeze up, the truth turning to ashes in her throat.

*\*\*\**

Indeed, a day later, Joseph came in from the carpentry shop, saying that he needed to go to a hearing.

Miriam's stomach twisted. "Do I have to—"

"Nee, not at this time. A driver is coming by to pick me up," he said as he raced past Miriam.

"OK, I'll let you know when he is here," she said, watching him run upstairs.

Ten minutes later, Joseph came down, wearing his Sunday clothes and a straw hat. He put on his black meeting jacket before stepping out the door.

Late that afternoon, he returned.

"Miriam, Sarah, here's what happened," he announced. "Mr. Newman will not get out on bail. It's not a matter of not having the money. The judge was going to make him pay bail, but when the district attorney told him that you were nearly kidnapped, Miriam, he changed his mind and said 'no bail.' Mr. Newman was not happy.

"You didn't need to be at this hearing, but you will have to be at what they call a 'preliminary hearing.' At other hearings, you will also have to be present. Your memories and truths will be important to keep him away from you so you can be safe here at home," pointed out Joseph.

At hearing that Lance was still behind bars, Miriam let out a huge sigh she hadn't been aware she was holding.

"Good! That means I can go where I need to go without having to take you away from your work."

"Ya, but this incident has taught us to be more careful. Miriam, if you see any strange Englischer cars, please avoid them," pleaded Joseph.

"He asked me for directions. How was I supposed to know—"

"Just, be careful, Miriam."

It hurt Miriam to know that her parents were blaming her, but she understood their worry. The thought of Lance getting free or of some other man like him following her, making her a prisoner in her own life, was terrifying. "I will be careful, daed, I promise." She took a breath and squared her shoulders. "But, I also have to buy some new supplies. I'm just about finished with the green-on-green quilt and I need the thread to finish it. Then, I can start the second child's quilt." And she wasn't going to let Lance's ghost hold her back from her dreams.

"When will you go to town?" asked Sarah.

"Tomorrow. I would like to go with Anna – I still feel safer having someone with me," Miriam said as she moved the large salad bowl to the table. Moving back to the refrigerator and stove, she loaded her arms with food and set it on the table.

"Ya, that is fine, but don't be too long," Sarah said with entreaty in her voice. "I still worry for your safety. I know, Joseph, I need to leave that up to the Lord, but it's not too easy!"

"Ya, I know, wife, but He will protect her." Joseph reminded her. "And so will we."

# CHAPTER TWO

The next day, Anna stopped by the Beiler house for Miriam.

"You two have fun, but don't be too late," reminded Sarah. "It looks like it might rain, and, you just never know who's out there and what they might do."

Miriam nodded. "Mamm, we'll be careful. Please don't worry."

As Anna drove, she and Miriam discussed the events in Lance Newman's court case.

"Nee, Anna, I don't know much. All I know is that the Englischer judge wouldn't let him get out of jail, even though he said he had the money to pay that bail. Daed told me that I have to be at hearings – and being in the same room as Lance Newman scares me!"

"Ya, and it should," Anna said wisely. "He is very smart, very mupsich or very sick. Now that you know he meant to do you harm, will you be less trusting of some Englischers?"

"Some. When I see some of them at the market, they're just curious. Some try to take our photos because they don't understand why we avoid having our pictures taken. Some are just curious and they want to respect us. Them, I like the best," asserted Miriam.

"Ya, me, too. I will tell you which ones to av-"

"Avoid? Anna, there's no need. I've figured that out already! Mr. Newman just made himself seem harmless, but I still picked up on . . . something," mused Miriam.

As the friends drove slowly down the road, they took in the bucolic scene – the deep-green leaves adorning the trees, the long road as it wound toward town, the sunlight splashing over everything and, dotted here and there, farmland and large, two-story houses. Miriam, remembering her mother's warning about the weather, gazed around until she spotted the towering, fluffy white and gray clouds. While they were still a long distance away, Miriam saw that they were definitely rain clouds that could bring thunder and lightning with them.

"Let's hurry, Anna! There's that storm mamm told us about," Miriam urged.

In response, Anna lightly flicked the horse's back and she began to trot more quickly. Within half an hour, the friends were at the Englischer craft store.

Miriam quickly found what she needed and made a mental

note to return for some brightly patterned fabric for children's quilts. Anna found several cross stitching patterns and stocked up, tossing them into her basket, along with several skeins of embroidery floss and more even-weave fabrics.

After they paid, Miriam felt the coolness of the breeze on her cheek as it picked up. Looking in the direction of the clouds, she gasped.

"Anna, let's go fast! Look!"

"No need to warn me! Blackie will move fast as well – she doesn't want to be in the rain, either," responded Anna. She didn't have to flick Blackie's reins. Instead, the horse took off at a fast clip, wanting to beat the storm home.

"Okay, I'll drop you off, then I'd better get right home," Anna said tensely. "I don't want to be out in this because I think it's going to get bad."

As she promised, she stopped momentarily at the Beiler farm, allowing Miriam to jump down with her purchases. As soon as Miriam was clear of the buggy, Blackie took off, at nearly a run. Miriam ran inside, feeling the wind speed picking up.

"I hope Anna makes it home in time!" she muttered to herself.

Sarah, hearing her, nodded. "I do, too. Do what you can on your quilting because you'll need to light the lanterns once this storm hits."

As windy as it was, it still took another forty-five minutes for the clouds to release their heavy burden of rain on the land. Instead of coming in after finishing his carpentry work, Joseph stayed in the barn, tending to the livestock and handling the milking, along with the Amish boy he had hired several months earlier.

Once the outside chores were done, he brought the boy in with him.

"Abram will stay here until the worst of the storm is over, then I will take him home," he told Sarah.

"Abram, welcome to our home. Enjoy some supper until the storm eases," Sarah directed the young teen boy.

"Denki. This storm threatened, but I didn't want to leave Mr. Beiler without help," he said.

"Ya, and I appreciate that. Dig in! There's plenty of food," he ordered.

Abram was happy to comply – his appetite was no different from any other teen boy his age.

After supper, the storm finally abated, allowing Joseph to take him home. Sarah and Miriam did the dishes and cleaned up the kitchen and Miriam finished the quilt for her wealthy Englischer clients.

Coming to the kitchen, she smiled and announced, "Mamm, my green-on-green quilt is done!" She poured herself some lemonade and sat down with her mother.

Sarah grinned, rejoicing with Miriam. "Good! Do you plan to start another one tomorrow?"

"Nee. I want to help you with the housework and give myself a day's break. I'll be fresher for a day's break," Miriam said decisively.

Sarah smiled in approval. "Good. I will welcome your help. We need to make a dessert and bread for Sunday's meeting. You will have a two-day break because Sunday is a day of contemplation and rest," she reminded Miriam.

"Ya, I know. Because I normally quilt on Saturdays, I counted only tomorrow as a break day. It will do me good!" Miriam exulted as she stretched. She and Sarah read the Bible before going to bed.

The following day, Miriam and Sarah baked, then cleaned the kitchen so they would not need to do very much work on Sunday. In the evening, John Fisher drove by to visit with Miriam. They chose to stay inside the house, where it was cooler and less humid. Drinking lemonade and eating oatmeal raisin cookies, they chatted and laughed in the kitchen as Sarah and Joseph chaperoned in the living room.

"What has your daed told you about having to testify against Mr. Lance Newman?" John asked, cocking his head in curiosity.

"I will go to the next hearing sadly, and for every other

hearing, ya, I do have to go," Miriam said with a deep sigh. "I really don't want to, but if it means he can't get out, I will. God will give me the strength I need."

"He will. If I can, I'll go with you. Just ask me and I'll let you know if I can," John offered.

"Don't you need to be at the hearings?" Miriam asked, confused.

"Only the criminal trial," said John.

After John had left, Miriam was about to go upstairs. Instead, Joseph called her to the door.

"Miriam, you have company!"

Miriam stopped, confused. Had John come back for some reason? Running lightly back downstairs, she saw Esther Zook at the front door.

She waved. "Esther! How are you?" What was she doing here?

"I'm fine – I just have a question for you. I have been quilting for several years now, but I am not as good as you. I want to start selling my quilts, but I've been told that I need to work on my technique. Will you teach me?"

Miriam felt a sense of warmth, a gentle pride that her skills were enough for someone else to ask for her guidance and instruction. "I'll be happy to! I plan to start on a new quilt for a customer on Monday morning, if you want to come by then,"

Miriam said.

"Ya, that's good. What time?" Esther asked, wringing her slender fingers.

"After breakfast. If you could be here by eight in the morning, we'll get started from scratch. I've already cut out the quilt pieces and hemmed them I'll start sewing them . . ."

"You *hem* your quilt pieces? You mean each individual small shape?" Esther asked with surprise in her voice.

"Ya. You don't?"

"Nee. Maybe that's my problem . . . Okay, I'll be here. Should I bring some of my own work?"

"It would be helpful so I could see it, ya, if you would," Miriam decided.

# CHAPTER THREE

The next morning dawned sunny, hot and still. After taking care of the livestock and eating breakfast, the Beilers left for the meeting, which was being held at the Fisher home.

In the barn, Miriam settled with Anna and her friends on the women's side of the barn. Looking over, she saw John gazing at her with a smile on his face. She smiled back, then grew confused when the smile faded. She put one hand out on the bench to support herself when she was unexpectedly jostled.

"I'm sorry, Miriam! I . . . tripped," Esther said, nervousness in her voice.

"It's okay. I'm just glad you didn't fall," Miriam said, wondering why Esther was so nervous.

Esther quickly settled herself right next to Miriam, smoothing her dress and smoothing her hair under her kapp. As she did, her gaze settled on John.

Miriam, seeing this, looked at Esther, then at John. She saw that John was focusing his attention on the front of the barn as he waited for the deacons and bishop to start the service. Feeling a nudge on her ribs from Anna, Miriam turned her attention to her.

Anna leaned over to Miriam, gesturing for her to scoot over slightly.

Miriam did so, leaning over toward her friend.

"She's sitting by you so that, in case John turns to look at you, she can try to distract him," Anna whispered.

"What? No! Everyone knows John and I are courting!" Miriam whispered back.

"You do know that Esther doesn't like the Ordnung, right?"

Miriam nodded. "Ya. Everyone knows that . . . she's probably going to leave us. That's what everyone says. Oh, they're getting started," Miriam straightened and faced forward.

Three hours later, Anna and Miriam, followed by the other women and girls, went into the Fisher kitchen to start serving the lunch. When their eating shift finally started, Anna indicated a bench at the far end for her and Miriam. The two friends scooted in next to their friends, filling the bench up and making it impossible for Esther to join them.

"Okay. Esther Zook likes John. She wants him to court her

instead of you," Anna said bluntly.

Miriam was stunned. She stammered as she tried to organize her thoughts.

"But . . . but he's . . ." she managed to say.

" . . . Courting you. If you've made true promises– and please don't say anything – nobody knows this, including Esther. She has never liked following the Ordnung."

"I know!" Miriam exclaimed, and then lowering her voice to a whisper added, "That's why it doesn't make any sense she'd wish to court with John. I don't really know why she's not working to save money and move to the city, so she can live an English life."

"She doesn't want an English life. She just wants things to be easy. Esther's always been lazy. Remember in school, when she would write her sums on her wrist and peek at them when the teacher gave us quizzes?"

Reluctantly, Miriam nodded. Esther had given it up when a couple of the older students had spoken with Mrs. Stoltzfus, but she'd never truly been shamed.

"Esther would rather pick and choose the parts that get her what she thinks she wants. She likes John. She's not married yet and neither is he. In her mind, that means she can make him aware of her."

"But—" What if John liked Esther too? What if he decided

Miriam was too much trouble with the trial and the fact that she was determined to make a success of her own business. Not that she didn't want to be a good wife to him – she desperately wanted that, but she also didn't lie to herself and pretend that her quilting wasn't important. She got lost in her work, and the sheer act of creation delighted her.

"Don't look at me so sad sack," Anna said. "You have nothing to worry about. John cares about you."

Miriam sat on the bench, trying to take in everything Anna had just said. As she did, she ate slowly, not feeling very hungry.

"Esther came by yesterday, asking me to help her with her quilting. I said I would," Miriam said.

"We; she needs the instruction. Go ahead and do it because you're the best, other than old Mrs. Lapp," Anna said. "Just...be careful okay?"

Seemed like everyone wanted to tell her that these days. Miriam wondered what she'd done to make her life so dangerous.

And what she could do to make things as they were, when she'd been happy.

\*\*\*

At her own table, Esther chatted quietly with her friends about John and her efforts to get his attention.

"Esther, he's courting Miriam Beiler," Rebecca Miller, her best friend, said. "They're both receiving instruction from the Bishop for their kneeling vows, so it's only a matter of time until they publish their intent to marry each other. You'd better stop."

"They haven't published any intentions yet. And if he's really in love with Miriam, nothing I do will change his mind." But if he wasn't, if he was only courting with Miriam out of convenience or pity for her situation, that made him available. She'd only be helping the pair of them to break them up.

"I don't like this, Es," Rebecca said. "Seems like a sin."

"I'm doing them both a favor," Esther said. "I'll be the fire through which they test their bond. First Corinthians 3:13: *Every man's work shall be made manifest: for the day shall declare it, because it shall be revealed by fire; and the fire shall try every man's work of what sort it is.*"

"I don't think that's what it means."

"Stop worrying. It will all work out. Now, tell me, is there anyone you're interested in courting with..."

\*\*\*

After the adults and younger children had all left the Fisher farm, the youth returned to the barns for the singing. Miriam and John sat at the same table on different benches. Miriam giggled as one of the boys shouted out the name of a well-

229

known hymn, which everyone began singing. She was jostled once again as Esther slid in next to her. Now that she was aware of Esther's interest in John, she paid closer attention to the other young woman.

Esther, sitting across the table from John, gazed at him and smiled. "I love this song. And you sing it very well," she said, fiddling with a curl of hair that that she'd allowed to artfully slip from beneath her prayer kapp.

"Denki," John said, averting his gaze. He didn't like how Esther was sitting, though there was nothing overtly suggestive about any one thing she was doing. She leaned her forearm on the table, the position subtly calling attention to her chest, and when she spoke, she stared at him a second too long, fluttering her lashes in a way that was almost flirtatious.

No, it was ridiculous. Everyone knew he and Miriam were courting.

Miriam scooted over as Esther came ever closer and closer to her side.

"Did you get caught out in that storm on Thursday?"

John shook his head. "Nee, I was working in the shop."

"You're so lucky. I was hanging clothes, and I guess I got lost in it because the heavens just opened up on me. I was soaking wet. My mamm said it was..." Esther lowered her voice, gazing up at John, "*sinful* the way my dress was clinging, and had me come inside immediately."

John's eyes widened fractionally, and Esther smiled. She had his attention. But before she could follow up, Miriam elbowed her, a bit sharply, in the side and said, "Your friend is calling you."

Esther looked at where Miriam had gestured, and Rebecca was waving her over. A wave of fury washed through her, brief and a bit shameful. Esther took a breath. It wouldn't do to let her temper get out of hand. When she had collected herself, she smiled and said, "Denki, Miriam."

Actually, it was better that she was leaving now. Better to give John a hint of what he might have with her, rather than offering too much. Rebecca had done Esther a favor, in a way.

Now, she only had to see what the other girl wanted.

*\*\**

Once Esther had left, Anna quickly scooted over to Miriam's other side. Several other friends rearranged themselves so that the girls' side of the bench was completely full. After a couple of songs, Esther returned.

She looked at Anna, "That was my spot."

"You left."

"Hmmmph."

It didn't look like any of Miriam's other friends were planning to get up either. Esther nodded, and gathering as much dignity as she could manage, returned to Rebecca's side. At least Rebecca was a true friend. And John liked her. Esther could tell.

The rest of them could go hang.

# CHAPTER FOUR

The next day, Samuel and John were finishing their work in the fields. They paused to take long gulps of cool water and pour it over their heads and necks. Shortly after they had resumed working, Samuel looked up in puzzlement. He saw Esther Zook as she approached the farm.

Esther sat straight in the buggy, maintaining a cool, sober expression. Stopping the horse, she gave John a sweet, shy smile as he continued pulling weeds out of the earth.

John stopped his weed-pulling, confused and more than a little upset – he and Samuel were on a tight schedule for finishing the weeding. As he looked at Esther, he saw her wearing her meeting dress and newest prayer kapp. As she approached him with several questions, he closed his eyes and groaned inwardly, remembering that his parents would expect him to treat her politely.

Esther smiled a lot as she talked to John. It was annoying the fact that she seemed to either not know or not care that he and Miriam were courting with each other.

"John, what's your favorite childhood memory? What were you doing? Who were you with?" she asked him, one right after the other.

Putting one gloved hand up to stop Esther, John shook his head.

"Wait a minute. I think you're confused here – I'm courting Miriam Beiler, and I have been for several months. I am not available to spend time with any other young women. Nor do I want to," John said firmly.

Esther stopped cold. Her face grew hot, and she lowered her eyes. "Do you . . . do you like me?" she asked.

John, blindsided by the unexpected question, answered, but not in a way she expected or liked.

"I cannot answer that question because *I am courting Miriam Beiler*," he said through clenched teeth.

Twenty minutes later, Miriam responded to several sharp raps on the front door. She had just finished piecing the quilt pieces together for the primary colors quilt for the little Englischer boy. Along with that day's work and the instruction she had given to Esther Zook, she felt she had done a good day's work.

"Esther! Do you want some more . . ."

"You aren't being fair! I like John Fisher and I want to get

234

to know him better! Let him spend time with me!" Esther shrieked.

Miriam, not expecting this, took several seconds to respond.

"Esther, yes, we *are* courting. We have been for several months. Beyond that, I cannot say anything. You know what the Ordung allows to courting couples. We are able to meet and visit under supervision; at singings, we spend time with each other in accordance with what the Ordnung allows us to . . ."

"You're not being fair! All I want is to be friends with John Fisher!" Miriam screamed.

"Esther, when we were kids . . . before we became teenagers, we could spend time with boys in the district." Miriam spoke quickly so she could get her words out before Esther's next outburst. "When we became courting age, that had to stop, as it should. Beyond courting, male-female friendships are no longer allowed, and you know this!"

"Even the Englischers allow teens and young people to have opposite-sex friendships with each other!" Esther shouted.

Sarah, passing by, stopped at the front door.

"Esther, unless you want to find yourself in trouble with the deacons and bishop, you'll follow the Ordnung," she said sternly. "John cannot interact with you now that he is of courting age –and courting Miriam."

"You refuse to listen to me, Miriam. I am not coming back

for any more quilting lessons," she said quietly. As she finished speaking, she turned around and stalked away and down the porch back to her buggy.

"Mamm?" she asked in confusion. "What just happened?"

"She does not like the restrictions the Ordnung imposes upon her. Come daughter, let us get supper ready," Sarah said, turning and walking into the kitchen.

After supper, John came to the house. Again, because of the heat outdoors, they chose to visit inside the living room.

"John, Esther Zook came by today, very upset – because of you. She seems to think that, despite our courting, she can have a friendship with you – or expect you to court her."

"Ya," John said with a troubled sigh. "My daed and I were weeding in the fields when she drove up. She was wearing her meeting dress and prayer kapp. She started asking me 'getting to know you' questions and I told her that I can't spend time with her. I am very confused about this. I reminded her that we are courting."

"I didn't say anything about our being engaged because we haven't published it yet," Miriam said as she looked at John with worry.

"Nee, I didn't either. I wonder if we should tell her privately so she understands just what she is doing . . ." John broke off and ran his hand through his dark hair, frustrated.

"Nee, I don't think that's necessary, John. I don't want to violate any of the Ordnung . . ." Miriam broke off as Sarah walked past.

"Is this about Esther Zook? She came by here, screaming at Miriam about you, John," Sarah said as she shook her head. "She refused to accept the fact that someone she likes is committed to somebody else."

John and Miriam gazed at each other. Miriam's confusion was reflected in John's eyes. Miriam felt a shiver of apprehension slide over her body – she wondered if Esther Zook would be the Amish equivalent of Lance Newman.

# CHAPTER FIVE

"Let's go for a drive. I need the fresh air," John suggested restlessly.

"Yes, let's! Mamm, we'll be home before dark," she said absently to Sarah.

"John, I'm worried for you. I've been through this stalking thing with Lance Newman and I don't want the same to happen to you." Miriam wrung her hands together.

"Nee, I don't think it'll get *that* bad," John said, shaking his head. "If I start to remind her often that you and I are courting, she'll eventually understand the message and start leaving us – me – alone."

Miriam sighed. She'd believed the same thing herself, but Lance Newman hadn't gotten the message. But what could she say that wouldn't make her seem paranoid or wrong? "Okay, ya, I'll leave it up to God," she said.

As they drove around Ephrata, they encountered Esther, who was, by now on foot. John looked at Miriam with a question in his eyes. Miriam indicated they should continue driving past Esther.

Esther started as she saw John and Miriam sitting together in John's courting buggy. Then, as though molding her face into an expression like a clay mug, she smiled and gave John a wave.

John slapped the reins of his horse and urged him on, taking Miriam back to her parents' farm.

Miriam was quiet.

"Don't worry about it, Miriam," John said. "I was only a wave."

It was only Esther 'happening' to be where they were and only giving all of her attention to John. Right. When they had reached her farm, Miriam asked, "John, before you go, would you please come in with me? I'd like to describe to my parents what just happened," she asked him quietly.

John shook his head. "What for?"

"Please, for me?"

"Of course."

Inside the Beiler home, John and Miriam sat down in the kitchen with her mamm and daed to explain what had just happened between them and Esther.

Sarah, hearing Miriam's description of Esther's behavior, began to wonder what was really happening.

*Is Esther really having problems understanding that our Ordnung doesn't allow a courting couple to spend time with others of the opposite gender? Does she know that John cannot even be alone with Miriam until they marry? I know that Mr. and Mrs. Zook have described Esther's reluctance to obey the Ordnung, and I know they are all on rumspringa, but the girl should have some respect.*

"I have heard that Esther is wild," Sarah said slowly, trying to remember just what the girl had done to earn this reputation. "I don't know if this is why she is acting as she is – or if there is something . . . deeper . . . behind her behavior."

Miriam felt relief and frustration warring inside her. Relief because at least she knew she wasn't just imagining things. Frustration because Esther's attitude made it difficult for them to help her to understand why she couldn't spend time with a courting Amish man. Her Amish man. With that, she and John had to admit that they couldn't do anything more. John, accompanied by Miriam, went to the front door, ready to go home.

While Miriam and John were saying their goodbyes, her daed Joseph brought in the day's mail. John left, and Miriam walked back into the house.

"Miriam, here is a letter from the Lancaster County District Attorney's office. Let's see," he said, ripping the envelope open and pulling the single sheet of paper out. "Okay, we have to attend a hearing – and you will have to testify – so they can decide if they have enough evidence to bring Mr. Lance Newman to trial. I will call for a driver. I hope this will be taken care of in one day so we can return to our own lives," he said.

The next day the D.A.'s representative came to visit so she could explain just what would happen in court.

"Miss Beiler, you'll be called to the stand to testify about what Mr. Newman did to you and how you tried to get him to stop. Your parents will have to wait outside the courtroom so that what you say doesn't affect any testimony we might need from them."

"Will . . . will Mr. Newman be in there? In the courtroom?" Miriam asked, feeling very nervous.

"Yes, he will. He has the right to face his accusers and hear what they are saying about his actions. This helps him to develop his own defense," the representative said.

"Oh . . ." Miriam said. The news hit her like a kick to the stomach.

"Don't worry. He can't get to you. He'll be wearing handcuffs and shackles on his ankles so he can't get to you. We also have guards from the sheriff's department in there to protect witnesses. Now, when you are called to the stand, you have to raise your right hand and put your left hand on the Bible so you can take an oath . . ."

"Excuse me," Joseph said, with one finger raised. "We Amish are not allowed to swear an oath on the Bible. We are only allowed to make promises to God. Instead, we can make an affirmation of faith. That should be enough."

"An affirmation of faith. I'll let the D.A. know that you are Amish so he knows not to require you to take an oath, then. Thank you for pointing this out."

After finishing with the Beilers, the representative drove to the Fisher's farm to give them the same information.

"You do know we can't take an oath, correct?" Samuel asked the representative.

"Yes, I do. I just learned this from Mr. Beiler a little while ago," the representative confirmed.

"Good. We will be there," Samuel promised.

***

The two weeks before the preliminary hearing passed quickly, with Miriam, her mamm and daed, John and his mamm and daed taking care of their daily responsibilities. Miriam found that, as the days passed, they seemed to speed up, racing past much too quickly for her liking.

In her room the night before the hearing, she had already changed into her nightgown and taken her hair out of its customary thick braid. As she ran the comb through her long hair, she thought about the hearing, feeling her stomach squirming at the fear of the unknown.

*I really don't want to be there. I don't want to see Lance Newman, ever again, but if I don't go to town and testify, then there's the chance he'll get out and come back to Ephrata. And, I don't know what he'll do if he does get out. God, please help me to face this hearing and get through it! Give me the wisdom and courage to speak the truth when I have to testify.\*

John was going through a similar experience in his own parents' home. He had gone upstairs after reading the Bible and praying with his mamm and daed. Now, he was shirtless and pacing back and forth in his room.

*Lord, there is only so much I can do to protect Miriam and my family. I am afraid that, when I see Lance Newman in that courtroom, that I will want to express exactly how I feel about him. I know we disavow violence, but I confess to having thoughts of taking violent actions against him. He could have hurt Miriam when he tried to kidnap her. Please, Lord, give me the strength to be the Christian you want me to be!*

Once they had prayed, both Miriam and John went to sleep, blowing out the lamps in their rooms. The next morning, they woke early as the sun came up in the east.

That morning, Miriam toyed with her hot cereal as she struggled to keep the nervousness from overtaking her.

"Miriam, you must eat! It will be a very long time until lunch in that courtroom," Sarah said as she forced herself to eat.

"Ya, mamm, I know. But I am scared! And that's upsetting my stomach," Miriam moaned.

"Ach, okay. Let me make some tea for you. That will settle your stomach," Sarah promised, beginning to bustle around the stove.

Joseph came in, stomping the dirt from his shoes.

Raising one finger, he told Sarah, "I'll be back downstairs as soon as I change my clothing."

Miriam, smelling the ginger tea, sipped it apprehensively, hoping it would stay in her stomach. As she took small sips, she breathed deeply, willing her stomach to behave. After several minutes, she felt able to brave the bowl of oatmeal. Taking small bites, she waited to make sure she wouldn't become sick. After several minutes, the bowl was empty.

"How do you feel?" Sarah asked as she washed dishes and watched Miriam.

"Better, denki," Miriam said. "I'll dry so we can leave sooner. The sooner we get there, the sooner we can get start. And the sooner this mess will finish and we can come home."

Sarah chuckled. "Ya, that is one way of looking at it."

"The driver will be here soon," Joseph broke in. "I'll make sure the house is closed and locked."

Ten minutes later, the Beilers had just walked outside the front door as their driver pulled into their yard. After stopping for the Fishers, the driver made quick time driving to the county seat, where the hearing would take place.

The D.A. walked to both families as he saw them come in.

"Welcome! How was your ride down?"

"Good, thank you," Joseph said, looking around the cavernous entryway of the court house.

"If all of you will follow me, I'll explain what's about to happen," the D.A. instructed. In a small room off the hall, he explained that, until each of them had testified, they would have to wait in the hallway until their names were called.

"We'll begin with Miss Beiler, since we want to build our case from her testimony and recollections. I'm sorry. I know you're scared. I want to let you know that you have nothing to fear. Mr. Newman will be restrained in handcuffs and shackles. We have two guards standing in the courtroom to protect witnesses, the judge, attorneys and the general public. My assistant will call you when we're ready for you and she'll bring you to the front of the courtroom. There's a microphone in front of you that amplifies your voice. Speak directly into it, but don't put your mouth against it. All right?"

"Ya . . . yes. Thank you. I understand. Where will Mr. Newman be?"

"At a defense table located in front of the witness stand. You will be looking right at him, but if you're more comfortable angling yourself so you won't be looking at him, turn so you face the jury box. That's the area with the twelve chairs to the side of the room."

"Okay. I do feel better knowing I can do that," Miriam said as she let out a deep breath.

Five minutes later, they all sat on the long bench, waiting. As they waited, they talked quietly. Other visitors to the court house looked curiously at their unusual dress. Both families were used to the stares, so they simply waited for Miriam to be called.

"Miss Fisher? They're ready for you," the assistant said, holding the heavy door open.

Miriam started, feeling the squirmy-snake feeling return to her stomach. Holding her hand against her abdomen, she walked in next to the D.A.'s assistant, looking around the courtroom. She saw the visitors' gallery, the jury box, a low wall with a gate and two long tables. At the front of the room stood a high bench with a man in a black robe. A small box sat to the judge's left. Miriam saw a metal stalk aimed at the seat in the small box. As she walked slowly to the front of the room, she met Lance Newman's eyes. The stark hatred she saw in those ice-blue orbs filled her with a chilling fright.

*Dear God, give me the strength to do this.*

Miriam closed her eyes and took a breath. Fear made her

skin cold and her hands sweat.

*Face him, child. If you don't face him, you'll always be ruled by him.*

That voice in her head was gentle and strong. She felt herself warm. Her second breath came easier. She was strong enough, and she was not alone.

Miriam walked to the stand, rested her palm on the Bible, and swore to tell the truth. After giving her affirmation of faith, she sat down at the witness stand. The microphone seemed to loom in front of her mouth and nose, but she reminded herself that she could do this, that she was strong enough.

After several fairly innocuous questions, the D.A. started questioning Miriam in earnest.

"Miss Fisher, would you explain just when you realized that Mr. Newman was not going to leave you alone?"

"When he kept coming to Ephrata after I told him to leave me alone – that his attentions to me could destroy my reputation in the district. He kept coming to Ephrata, insisting that he wanted to get to know me. Even when my daed – my father – told him to stay away, he would ignore that and come to our district."

"What did your father tell him?"

"He came to our house after John – my beau – told him to stay away from me. He tried to bring me a gift. My father gave it back to him, telling him it wasn't appropriate for him to be doing that. I . . . I got angry and I screamed at Mr. Newman and told him to leave me alone."

"Did he leave you alone?"

"Ya, for a few weeks. Then my father and John told me that they saw his truck in Ephrata again. He would just drive from road to road, looking for me. My parents told me that, if he was going to be doing that, it was too dangerous for me to be out on my own. I had to wait for them, John or my best friend, Anna, to go with me when I needed to run my errands."

"Did you ever begin to feel as if you were in danger from Mr. Newman?"

"Yes."

"When?"

"I was with my mamm – mother – and Anna at the Amish market. We were buying items we needed to complete our work for our customers. Mr. Newman found our buggy at the market and tried to cut us off. My mother yelled at him and I yelled at him. Another time, he cut me off when I was trying to go home and tried to hand some wildflowers to me. John's father saw me standing in front of Mr. Newman and questioned what I was doing. That's when I really got mad at Mr. Newman and told him that, if anyone else had seen me in his company, my reputation would be destroyed."

"Explain what happened on the day that Mr. Newman broke

into your parents' house, please."

"My parents had to go to town to buy some groceries. They wanted me to go with them, but I had – have – a large quilt order to finish. I explained this and my father said that, if we locked both doors, I could stay at home. He didn't like it, but they left after I demonstrated that both doors were locked. I was working on a quilt in our quilting room." Miriam, remembering that horrifying day, shifted in her chair, forcing herself to breathe evenly. The strain showed on her delicate face.

"They had been gone for only a few minutes. I was cutting out pieces of fabric for the quilt I had to begin. I thought I heard something, so I stopped cutting and I laid my scissors down and listened. I didn't hear anything, so I started to cut the pieces out again. I kept cutting and cutting, then . . . then someone put his hand over my mouth and grabbed me around my middle. I dropped my scissors and he lifted me from my chair and started trying to take me out of the house.

"I fought, sir. I fought hard, trying to get out of his arms so I could get away. But he got me into the living room. He took his hand away from my mouth to open the door. I wanted to scream, but his arm was pushing too hard on my stomach and I couldn't get the breath in.

"The front door pushed open and it hit Mr. Newman on the head. My father grabbed me and put me into my mother's arms. Then, he grabbed Mr. Newman and started pulling him to the porch. He told my mother to call the sheriff, then John and his father, Mr. Fisher came to the house. My mother and I ran to the carpentry shop, where the phone is and she called the sheriff's office. As we ran to the shop, I saw Bishop Stoltzfus riding into our yard. I watched from the shop and saw my father, John and Mr. Fisher holding Mr. Newman while the bishop talked to him." Miriam finished with her heart pounding.

"In other words, he attempted to force you to go with him."

"Yes."

"Did he have his truck with him?"

"Nee – I'm sorry. No. He had borrowed a different vehicle."

"Can you describe it?"

"Brown. It's a car, not a truck," Miriam said.

After the D.A. finished asking questions, the defense attorney attempted to get Miriam to admit that she had tried to attract Lance Newman's attention.

Miriam told the defense attorney that Mr. Newman had been the pursuer, trying to get her name, seeking to get her to spend time with him and attempting to give her forbidden gifts. By the time the defense attorney finished with her, she was struggling to hold tears back.

"You can step down, Miss Beiler. You're done," the judge said.

"Denki." The single word wavered out of Miriam's trembling lips as she stood quickly to leave the courtroom. With her eyes downcast, she left the courtroom.

Two hours later, the preliminary hearing was finally over. The families still waited outside, wanting to hear the judge's decision.

After the final Amish witness had testified, the D.A. brought them all back into the courtroom, where they sat in the visitor's gallery.

"After hearing everything that everyone in this case has had to say, I find that sufficient evidence exists to bring this case to trial. Mr. Newman, I will be scheduling your criminal trial and you will remain housed in the county jail," said the judge.

Miriam, glancing at Lance, saw him scowl heavily. She looked down quickly at her clasped hands as she saw him turning his head in her direction.

What does this mean? It sounds like the judge thinks there's enough to have this trial. That news is too good to believe!

Miriam looked up and focused her eyes on the judge, then she swung her gaze to the D.A., who was sitting back with a look of relief on his narrow face. As the hearing came to an end, the D.A. strode to the families and told them that he needed to meet with them in his office.

"Do you have a driver hired?"

"Yes, we do," Joseph said with a single nod. As he focused on the D.A., he was aware that the sheriff's deputies were leading a fuming defendant out of the courtroom.

"Ask him to bring you to my office. I'm leaving now and I should be there within the next twenty minutes, depending on the traffic," the D.A. instructed.

"Ya, we'll be there. Denki," Samuel said with a nod. As he had watched Lance leaving, he finally relaxed. *I'm glad we realized Miriam was telling us the truth, or she would have been seriously hurt!*

Twenty-five minutes later, the D.A. was sitting at his massive desk, facing the two Amish families.

"Okay, we just won the first round here. What I mean by that is that the judge decided we presented enough evidence to bring Mr. Newman to trial. All of you did well, testifying. The next step is for us to develop the evidence we have to the point that we can put on a full trial and prove that he intended ill will toward Miss Beiler, that he tried to kidnap her and that he was stalking her. The judge will set the trial on his own calendar and let everyone know. As soon as I know, I'll be sending letters out to each of you. Now, does my office have phone numbers for one or both families?"

"We have a phone in my carpentry shop," Joseph said. He gave the number to the D.A.

Miriam, hearing that there would be one more hearing, was

stunned.

"Excuse me, sir, but I thought this was the hearing that would send Mr. Newman to prison," she said with a look of confusion on her face.

"I'm sorry, but this was only the hearing that determined if we had sufficient evidence for a trial," the D.A. said. "This next hearing is the one that will determine Mr. Newman's guilt or innocence. Hopefully, a jury will find him guilty and the judge will sentence him to prison. Then, it's over."

"Oh. So, you mean a jury could decide that he's not guilty? But . . . how?"

"We have to make sure our evidence is so strong that a jury will have no choice but to decide he's guilty. My assistant will be working with you on this over the next few months. We will be getting even more evidence from you and your family. We have the physical evidence that we will present at trial. We have to prove that Mr. Newman had the motive, the means and the opportunity to stalk and attempt to kidnap you. When the jury sees this, it's more likely that they will come back with a guilty verdict."

"So we have to meet with your office more? And come back here for a trial?" Joseph asked.

"Exactly. We'll make this as easy for you as possible. Miss Beiler, are you OK?" the D.A. asked with concern.

Miriam's mouth opened and closed.

"I . . . facing him was frightening. When he turned and looked at me when I came in to testify, I saw hatred in his face . . . Mr. Williams, he frightens me!" Miriam said, trying to keep tears from falling.

"He should . . . but every time he comes into the courtroom, he's very securely handcuffed. He can't get to you. I don't think you saw it from where you were sitting, but his handcuffs are connected to his ankle cuffs with a heavy chain. That, along with the deputies stationed in the courtroom, makes you and everyone else safer."

"Mr. Williams, what measures have you taken to protect everyone in the courtroom? Just in case Mr. Newman tries to do something, I man," Joseph clarified. "I, too, saw the hatred in Mr. Newman's eyes today. He could still try to harm my daughter."

"As I said, Mr. Beiler, we have security in the courtroom should Lance Newman try to do anything," the D.A. said, pushing a pen back and forth on top of his desk.

"Well, that's good. But I think you need to have a talk with Mr. Newman and remind him that, if he hadn't tried to force his will on Miriam, he wouldn't be facing Englischer criminal charges. Now, would he?" Joseph asked with a keen look in his eyes.

"I'll have the defense attorney have that talk with Mr. Newman. In addition to that, I'll have him remind Mr. Newman that, if he tries anything, he'll be facing even more time behind bars," the D.A. promised.

"Mr. Williams? If Mr. Newman is found guilty, for how long could he go to prison?" Miriam asked.

"That depends on the severity of the charges that he could be convicted of. See, there's degrees of severity. Say he murdered someone. If he was found guilty of premeditated murder, that's murder in the first degree. He gets more time behind bars for that than he would for, say, involuntary manslaughter. For what he's accused of doing to you, he could be facing about 10 years behind bars," the D.A. said, giving Miriam a solemn look.

Miriam was stunned. "Ten years! That's . . . that's all? But he could come back and try to hurt me when he gets out!"

"Hopefully, by then, he will have forgotten all about you, Miss Beiler. I'm sorry, but that's the best I can offer right now," the D.A. said with a look of regret on his lean face.

# CHAPTER SIX

After returning to Ephrata, Miriam, her parents and the Fishers all struggled to understand and come to terms with the short sentence Lance Newman was facing. After thinking about it for several days, Miriam realized that she needed to let go of her very human reaction and allow God to take care of the situation.

"You look like you're feeling much better, Miriam," Sarah said, mixing cookie dough one afternoon.

Miriam had come into the kitchen for a glass of cool water.

"Ya. I cannot do anything about what might happen to Lance Newman, mamm. All I can do is give it to God and allow him to handle the situation," she said. And she knew that God's strength would be enough. She stood as living witness.

"I think we all realized that, daughter. We want to see him spend the rest of his life in prison, but it's not up to us, is it?"

"Nee. I'm tired of thinking about that horrible man. Instead, I want to think about my baptismal instruction. Bishop Stoltzfus will begin working with me next week!"

"Ya, I know! You're beginning about four months of instruction, my girl, so make sure you attend to what he teaches you. That will give you the basis for a life as a good Amish woman," Sarah said as she added walnuts and raisins to the cookie dough.

\*\*\*

The following week, Miriam met with the bishop in her home.

"Let's begin with Christ's forgiveness of those who wronged him," the bishop said, opening his Bible. "What do you remember from your Bible lessons?"

"He forgave Judas and made the Pharisees forgive the fallen woman," Miriam said, thinking of what she remembered.

"Ya. And, how can we apply that willingness to forgive to our lives today?" the bishop asked, seeming to look deep into Miriam's soul.

Miriam shifted uncomfortably, thinking of her recent struggle to let go of her anger at Lance Newman.

"Bishop, we went to the preliminary hearing for Mr. Newman a few weeks ago. When we talked to the district attorney, he told us that Mr. Newman could get – maybe – 10 years in prison if he's convicted by a jury. I . . . I have to admit to you that I am having a very hard time, or at least I was, when I heard that."

"And, what have you remembered from your Bible reading?" he asked.

"That God is the only one who decides whether to hold people bound to their sins or not . . . it's so difficult for me! He tried to kidnap me!"

"Ya, ya, I know. I was there, remember? I don't really like to talk about this very much, Miss Beiler. But do you remember the shooting of the ten female scholars in Nickel Mines back in 2007? What did the residents of that district do after the shooter injured and killed those children? Hmmm?"

Miriam's stomach squeezed uncomfortably and she shifted, feeling the weight of her anger.

"I remember that day. It was . . . horrible. I also remember that, even though everyone in Nickel Mines was hurt so badly by the shooter's actions, they forgave him. They took a meal to his family. They held his father when he started crying. They didn't want to make things any worse by hating an innocent family, bishop. But . . ."

"No, Miss Beiler. No 'buts.' You remembered everything perfectly. Even though they were hurting so badly at the loss of ten such precious lives, they forgave the shooter and his family. Now. I know you struggle with anger and forgiveness in regards to Mr. Newman. Despite the Englischer trial that's coming up, will you be able to forgive him? Remember, if you cannot unbind him from what he tried to do to you, you will be bound to your own sins forever."

Miriam sat, looking down at the smooth wood floor of the kitchen. As she did, she rubbed one finger against the binding of her Bible and thought.

"Ya. I know. I'm working on forgiving him, but it is so hard!"

"You are human. It is natural for it to be hard. Just think — when you finally do manage to forgive him, the feeling of lightness will be so precious to you! I have another question for you. When you have to testify at Mr. Newman's trial, will you be able to do so truthfully?"

Miriam realized that, if she was going to truly have God in her heart, she needed to release her anger at Lance Newman — that her anger bound her, not only to his sins and hers, but to Lance Newman himself.

"Do you mean that I'll be able to testify without hatred or wanting bad to come to him?" Miriam asked. As she asked this question, her forehead crinkled.

"Exactly."

"If . . . if I am to be a true Amish woman with love in my heart for everyone . . . I . . . I will have no choice but to forgive him completely," Miriam said slowly, thinking as she spoke.

260

Nodding firmly, she said, "Yes. Yes, I can. It won't be easy, but I can . . . and I do . . . forgive him." Miriam felt a strong sense of relief as she made this realization.

"Do not forget, Miss Beiler . . . forgiveness is not just a one-time event. Your memories and fears will come back. You will experience more anger and frustration at him. And . . . you have to work at forgiving him, day after day. Make it one of the first things you do when you rise in the mornings."

"But, bishop, that means I have to think of a man every day that I just want to forget!" Miriam said, dismayed.

"Ya. Christ struggled with the same issues. I imagine that, when Judas Iscariot betrayed him, the Lord knew he had only a few short hours to forgive him. And, as he went through that horrible pain before he died, he had to forgive Judas, again and again and again."

"Oh," Miriam said on an outward breath. She realized that her own experiences paled next to what had happened to Jesus.

# CHAPTER SEVEN

Within a few days of this baptism instruction, Miriam received a letter from the D.A.'s office, announcing the date of Lance Newman's criminal trial. When Sarah came in, Miriam showed her the letter.

"Good. I am glad we have this now because it allows us to plan and finish everything we have to do," Sarah said as she scanned through the words.

"They say the trial will take several days. Mamm, I can't be away for a long time. I have to finish the last two quilts," said Miriam as she looked at her progress on the third quilt.

"Your daed will not want to stay in any hotels. He'll want to come home every day, so we're probably going to hire a driver," Sarah said, looking at Miriam.

Miriam sighed in relief, knowing that, in the evenings and on Saturdays, she could finish the quilts.

When Joseph came in from tending the livestock, they talked about the trial.

"Nee. We won't stay in hotels," Joseph decreed.

Sarah glanced at Miriam, who nodded.

"We will ride back and forth from home to the court house, every day until the trial is over. We'll have to compensate the driver well for taking us back and forth. We'll come home every evening to take care of our chores and remember what God has taught us."

***

The next few weeks were very busy for both the Beiler and Fisher families. Miriam worked from early morning until after it was dark, finishing the third quilt for her wealthy Englischer customers. Once she finished that child's quilt, she began on the lavender and purple child's quilt, cutting the pieces and beginning to stitch them together.

Sarah took care of the household chores and cooking on her own, relying on her older daughters to help her out. Joseph, who was working on a large set of bookshelves for an Englischer professor, finished putting the pieces together and staining the furniture just days before the trial was set to begin. The professor hired a van to pick up and transport the bookshelves to his university office, paying Joseph handsomely for his work and finishing a few weeks earlier than originally planned.

John and Samuel were facing an even harder deadline imposed by nature. Knowing they needed to keep caring for the corn crop while they were at the trial, they hired a neighbor who promised to take care of the crop and ensure that it would be ready for harvest by the time the trial came to an end. At the Amish market, Miriam was hired to make a quilt. Knowing the trial would take up at least one week, she told her customer that she wouldn't be able to start it until October. The customer, eager for an Amish quilt, agreed to Miriam's terms, making her down payment.

***

While John and Samuel Fisher were hard at work, making their corn crop ready for their neighbor to tend, Esther Zook, who had been unable to get John out of her mind, decided it was time to try and get his attention one more time. She was unaware that John was so hard at work in preparation for the Newman trial. Putting on her best dress and newest prayer kapp, she boarded the buggy after telling her father that she had to run errands.

Nearing the farm, she wished she had a mirror so she could check her appearance. Instead, she satisfied herself with a quick smooth of her fingers over her hair. Widening her mouth into what she thought was a shy and winsome smile, she slowed the buggy as she saw John pause momentarily, wiping sweat from his face.

"Hello, John. How are you?" she asked softly.

John turned, breathing heavily. His slumped posture showed how tired he truly was. As he saw Esther, he frowned.

"Esther, I am very sorry, but daed and I are extremely busy, doing three weeks' worth of work in one week here. We have to be at a criminal trial and it might last longer than a week," he said, struggling to keep from yelling.

Esther's mouth dropped open. *How . . . how rude!* Well, all I did was stop by to say hello and see how you're doing! You don't need to be that rude! I know harvest is coming!" she said defensively.

Samuel heard the young people beginning to argue. Sighing because he was just as hot and tired as John, he threw down his weeding tools and marched over to John's side.

"Miss Zook, we are working and don't have time for idle visiting. I must ask you – what are you, a young Amish woman, doing visiting an Amish man who has been courting another young woman for over a year? You know this is wrong!" Samuel snapped. As he stood next to John, he crossed his arms and took a wide-legged stance.

Esther placed her hand over the high neck of her dress, glaring at the two men.

"Anything could happen between him and Miriam! Anything!"

"They will take their Kneeling Vows and get married. And you are going to go home. Now! That's what will happen. I will be talking to your mamm and daed about this!" Samuel said, glaring at the young woman.

Esther, hearing this, quickly snapped the reins on her horse's back. She didn't want yet another argument with them so she pressed her lips tightly together, forcing hot words back, and drove off fast.

Samuel, watching the buggy move down the road, asked John, "How long has Esther been trying to pursue you?"

John, grateful for his daed's assistance, shook his head.

"It's been several weeks. I told her that I'm courting Miriam, unavailable and not interested, but she refuses to listen," he said, wiping his face again.

"John, don't be mupsich! You saw what Miriam went through with that Newman character! I don't want Miss Zook to become another one like that Englischer! Let's finish this work," Samuel snapped at John.

The two men finished in a glowering, uncomfortable silence.

After supper, Samuel cleaned up, telling Emily he needed to go talk to the Zooks. Hitching the horse to his buggy, he took off, still feeling unsettled and worried.

At the Zook farm, he knocked at the front door and waited.

Micah Zook answered the door.

"Samuel! Come in!" he said, opening the door wide.

At the kitchen table, Samuel gulped thirstily at the cool water given to him by Rebekah, Micah's wife.

"How are you? I understand the trial begins tomorrow," Micah said, sitting across from Samuel.

"Ya. John and I have been putting in many long hours, getting the corn ready for our neighbors to tend while we are at the trial. There is . . . something I need to discuss with you," he said, hesitating to bring trouble on them. *Nee, it is not you bringing the trouble. It lives here in Esther's refusal to accept the facts.*

"You know that our youngest son, John, has been courting Miriam Beiler, right?" At two affirmative nods, he sighed heavily. "I do not want to cause or bring trouble to you. I respect and like both of you greatly. But Esther has been attempting to pursue John – even though he has been courting Miss Beiler for over a year, now. John tells me that this has been going on for several weeks, and that she refuses to accept reality. I told her that she is in violation of the Ordnung and that I would be making you aware of this – behavior your daughter has been displaying."

"Samuel, she has always questioned why the Ordnung is so restrictive, but we have told her more than once that it is a set of guidelines that we use to follow and distinguish ourselves from the Englischers. We have had many . . . discussions on this," Micah admitted sadly. As he spoke, he twirled his own water glass back and forth on the table.

"Denki. Then, you are aware that this could be a factor for why she refuses to leave my son alone?" Samuel asked, peering closely at the other man.

"Ya. It's not only with her desire to be courted by John, Samuel. In big matters and small, she questions the Ordnung," Micah admitted. "We will talk to her tonight. Denki."

***

After Samuel had left, Micah called Esther downstairs. After calling her several times and waiting, he glanced at Rebekah, shook his head and ran upstairs to knock on Esther's bedroom door.

"Esther! Open the door! Now!" Micah ordered.

In her room, Esther shook her head, bringing herself out of a daydream that felt . . . so real. Hearing her father's loud voice and knuckles hitting the door, she looked around, orienting herself again. Scurrying to the door, she opened it.

"Ya, daed? What is it?" she asked.

"Come downstairs. Your mamm and I have to talk to you," Micah ordered.

"But . . ."

"Esther, no arguments. Come downstairs now," Micah said. He sighed tiredly, wiping his hands over his eyes.

Esther followed him slowly, wondering what was wrong.

"Sit," said Micah, pacing back and forth in front of the kitchen sink.

After taking her seat, Esther looked up at her father with questioning in her eyes.

"Esther, it has come to our attention that you have been . . . pushing . . . your attentions onto John Fisher, and he does not welcome them. *He is courting Miriam Beiler and you can get into significant trouble with what you are trying to do!*

I forbid you from ever trying to get that young man's attention ever again.

His father was here a few moments ago, telling us what you have been doing. He told us that his son raised his voice at you, and that *he* raised his own voice at you. Are you aware that they have been putting in many long, hard hours, getting their crops ready for a neighbor to care for while they attend and testify at a criminal trial? They do not need or want your silliness, Esther. It will stop. Today," Micah said, glaring at his wayward daughter.

"But, daed! He hasn't promised to marry her officially! He's still free to meet and interact with other young Amish women like me!" Esther said, with an obstinate set to her chin and mouth.

"No, you will not! If I must restrict you to the house except for meeting days, I will. Do you understand me?"

"Daed! You will not do that! I have my friends to visit. You and mamm send me to the store on errands . . ."

"That is stopping. You are no longer allowed to take the horse and buggy. How could you ignore the Ordnung's rules on courting, Esther? How?"

"I should be able to associate with anyone I want to! That includes my female friends from school – and Amish men my age. I don't believe the Ordnung can restrict my life so severely," Esther said with confidence.

"Esther, if you keep up with this behavior, you will ruin yourself in this district and other Amish districts. No decent Amish man will want to associate with you, much less marry you," Micah said, glaring at Esther. "He is courting another young woman! You cannot try to attract the interest of a man who is courting another. Go upstairs, think and pray about what I have been telling you," ordered Micah, striding back and forth in the kitchen.

Esther, released, popped up out of her chair, running upstairs. Tempted to slam the door, she forced herself to shut it quietly, beginning to fume about the injustice of it all.

*I should just leave Ephrata and have the rest of my rumpsringe in New York City or Philadelphia, where I can be free. Who knows? I might not even come back for my Kneeling Vow! I know I won't be able to take part in very many family activities, but I want to have a free life.* As Esther thought and fumed, she quite overlooked the fact that, if she didn't become a full member of the Amish community, John would not be able to marry her.

The evening shadows in Esther's room lengthened as she began fantasizing about being John Fisher's wife. Standing up slowly, she began to act out the fantasies as they filled her mind.

*John, come in! Supper will be ready in a few minutes. Go ahead and wash up. There is hot coffee on the table. Ya, I made your favorite chicken and dumplings with vegetables . . . washing and putting his clean laundry away, smoothing her hands over the freshly washed shirts, dark pants and underwear . . . caring for their bopplis and kinner, breast feeding them, making pureed baby food and feeding the bobblis as they grew . . . reading to the children as they grew up, running outside in the huge yard . . .*

If John, his parents and Miriam and her parents had been aware of that last fantasy, they would have been much more than just irritated and concerned – they would have been frightened at what was happening in Esther's mind.

# CHAPTER EIGHT

Very early the next morning, Miriam woke up. Remembering what this day was, she sighed, not wanting the day to begin. Looking at the dark window, she saw it beginning to lighten. Finally, she knew she could no longer hold the day off. Sighing once more, she threw the covers back and got dressed. Combing and braiding her hair, she coiled it into a large bun, which she covered with her prayer kapp.

Downstairs, she tried to smile.

"Guder mariye, mamm. How are you?" she asked.

"Nervous. But God has it in his hands. How about you?" Sarah asked as she made breakfast.

Miriam, helping Sarah, thought.

"I want this over, but I wish I didn't have to be in the same room as Lance Newman," she said, turning the slices of bacon.

"How is your stomach?"

"Fine. It's my spirit." Miriam lifted the cooked bacon out of the sputtering fat and set it on a folded paper towel. Next, she scooped fluffy, steaming scrambled eggs into a large bowl. Hearing Joseph walking in, she surveyed the table and turned to pour the fruit juice while Sarah poured the coffee.

Forty-five minutes later, with the kitchen clean, the three waited in the front yard for their driver. He pulled up smiling at them.

The Beiler family climbed into the mini-van, greeting the Fisher family.

"Mr. Andrews, we will alternate paying you every day so you can put gas into your vehicle," said Joseph as he struggled with the seatbelt. Miriam, turning slightly, took it from him and pushed it into the catch until it snapped.

"Denki, daughter," murmured Joseph with a gentle smile.

Twenty-five minutes later, they were at the court house, arranging a time to meet the driver for the return trip home.

As they had for the preliminary hearing, both families waited in a small room just off the courtroom.

"Miriam Beiler!"

On the stand, Miriam breathed deeply and said a quick prayer for calm and help. With a shaking hand, she sipped water from the glass on the witness stand.

"Miss Beiler, thank you for coming her today. Would you

please describe your first encounter with the defendant?" asked the D.A., pacing back and forth.

"I was coming home from the Amish market . . ." Miriam began. Hearing Lance's soft, derisive laughter, she stopped distracted.

"Excuse me. Mr. Newman, please stop laughing and distracting the witness," ordered the judge. "You can proceed, Miss Beiler."

"I was thinking of the huge order I had just gotten from a tourist couple. It was my largest order and I was quite excited and worried . . ."

"Mr. Newman! Please stop your laughter!" the judge ordered.

"I was thinking of all the work I would have to do to make all the quilts the family needed. My horse whinnied and reared because Mr. Newman nearly hit him with his vehicle. I told Mr. Newman to be careful. He told me he was lost, looking for the Englischer high school north of our district, so I gave him the directions. I just wanted to get home so I could begin working on my plans. Mr. Newman wouldn't let me go unless I told him my name. I told him . . ."

"*Liar! She's lying!*" Lance shouted, standing at the defense table.

"Mr. Adams, *make your client sit down and make it clear he's to stop disrupting these proceedings!*" the judge ordered.

"I told him I couldn't tell him my name. He wouldn't back his truck up and I couldn't move my buggy because I would have gone off the road. The only way he would allow me to get past and go home was if I told him my name," Miriam finally finished.

At the defense table, Lance glowered at Miriam from under light-brown eyebrows. Two beefy sheriff's deputies stood on either end of the defense table, just waiting for Lance to burst out again.

"Now, would you tell me how Mr. Newman tried to get you to spend time with him?"

"He came back to Ephrata. My beau – boyfriend – and his father were working in their field when Mr. Newman stopped at their farm, telling them that he was lost. He told them he needed to find me so he could hire me to make a quilt for his mother. He told my beau that I had given him a business card. But we Amish don't use business cards. That goes against our beliefs.

"Instead, we rely on word-of-mouth for advertising. John told him that and he also told him to stop trying to find me. When John came to my parents' house, we talked and I told him what Mr. Newman had told him. My parents also talked about him and we all decided to go for a ride. My parents took their buggy and I rode with John in his buggy.

"Mr. Newman was parked at the side of the road, just waiting. My father pulled up to him and asked him what he wanted. When Mr. Newman admitted he had come to Ephrata to find me. My father called John and I up and I saw Mr. Newman with an angry expression on his face."

"Objection! She can't know what his expression meant!"

"Overruled. Go ahead."

"We told Mr. Newman to leave me alone and not come back to Ephrata. I told him that I didn't want his attentions, that John and I are courting. Finally, he left and we went back home."

As Lance listened to Miriam's testimony, he grew more and more angry.

"Miss Beiler, would you please educate the jury about how your Ordnung affects Amish youth?"

"Certainly. When Amish youth, who are in their "running-around time" begin to pair off, they court only with each other. They cannot see anyone else. We're allowed to test the limits, but not break rules. But our parents make it clear what we are and aren't allowed to do. When I told this to Mr. Newman, he scoffed . . ."

Lance couldn't stand it anymore. He stood up from his seat and tried to rush to the witness stand and Miriam. The deputies, alert to anything he might try, grabbed him by his shoulders and arms, forcing him out of the courtroom.

Miriam sat back in the witness box, frightened. She had never before witnessed this level of violence or force.

"Miss, I'm sorry for that. Do you need a few minutes to compose yourself?"

"Ya – yes, please," Miriam said in a shaky voice. The D.A. escorted her back to the small room, explaining to her parents what had just happened. After several minutes, she had pulled herself back together.

"Are you feeling better?"

"Yes. I can continue," she told the D.A.

Lance was brought back to the courtroom.

"Mr. Newman, if you have even one more outburst, you will be watching these proceedings from a video camera feed in a holding cell. Do you understand?"

"Yes, your honor. I'll behave," Lance promised sullenly.

Despite Lance's promise, he grew visibly angrier and angrier with every recollection Miriam testified to regarding his refusal to accept her wishes.

Miriam, seeing the progression of Lance's anger, continued to testify, but she scooted back once again in her seat, becoming ever more fearful that Lance would burst out and attempt to attack her once again.

Miriam was relieved and worn out when she was finally allowed to leave the stand. John came in and gave her a small smile, then took the witness stand.

"Mr. Fisher, would you please explain your relationship to Miss Beiler?"

"I have been courting Miriam Beiler for over a year and we are engaged to be married," John said.

Hearing this, Lance let out a long, rolling and rude snort. He restricted his reaction to this noise, so the judge gave him a stern warning about any outbursts. Lance, wanting to hear everything, promised he would behave.

"Mr. Fisher, please explain to the jury what you told Mr. Newman about his attentions to Miss Beiler."

"Mr. Newman stopped at our farm, telling us he was lost and trying to find the Beiler farm. He told me that he had a . . . business card . . . from Miriam, that he needed to order a quilt from her. I told him that we don't rely on any of the traditional Englischer ways of advertising, only on word-of-mouth. Then, I told him that Miss Beiler and I have been courting and that any attentions from other men could ruin her reputation in our district and beyond."

Finally, Lance could restrain himself no more.

*"He's lying! He never told me that! I wanted to get to know her, but when she told me she wasn't . . . AGGHGHGHG! Let go!"*

The deputies had grabbed him and began to pull him out of the courtroom. This time, he stayed in the holding cell, forced to watch the proceedings via the video feed.

Miriam, hearing the commotion, heard his voice becoming more and more faint. Despite his outburst, she felt better. She knew that, from the holding cell, Lance could not hurt her.

\*\*\*

The rest of the week took on a boring sameness for Miriam. She, her parents and the Fishers rose early every morning, had breakfast, met their driver and spent the day in the county court house. Upon returning home every evening, Joseph and his young helper cared for the livestock, Sarah made supper and Miriam did an hour or two of work on the final quilt of the large order.

The D.A. called his witnesses to the stand as he built his case against Lance Newman. Joseph, Sarah, Emily, Samuel and even Bishop Stoltzfus all testified. Miriam was surprised to see Lance's Englischer friend testifying against Lance. He testified that he had loaned his old Saturn to Lance, believing that Lance's truck was in the shop and that he needed to meet with a college baseball prospect.

Finally, the district attorney rested his case, and the defense attorney began.

Again, Miriam was the first witness called. In stark contrast to her treatment by the district attorney, the defense attorney was derisive, attempting to show the jury that Miriam had been playing Lance and John against each other.

"You were bored with your farm life down in Ephrata. You

decided you wanted a little excitement, didn't you?"

"No! No! I love my life in our dist--"

"You tried to attract my client so you could find an easy way out of that little community. Then, you got scared that you'd get in trouble. You got cold feet, didn't you, and you falsely accused my client of a crime!"

Miriam was stunned. Remembering the D.A.'s instructions, she looked at him, her eyes huge and questioning.

"Objection! Badgering my witness!"

"Sustained. Go easy on her. Ask your questions and allow her to get a word in edgewise!"

"Didn't you try to get Mr. Newman . . ."

"*Objection!*"

"Sustained . . ."

"Were you bored . . ."

"*Objection!*"

"Sustained! If you try to lead this witness once again, you'll be facing a contempt of court charge!"

"No more questions for this witness," the defense attorney muttered.

"Miss Beiler, you can go now."

Miriam escaped from the witness box, sobbing and wiping hot tears from her face. She felt dirty, as though she had tried to entice Lance Newman.

After Miriam's testimony, the defense attorney called the rest of his witnesses – former girlfriends, former coworkers and fellow students Lance had gone to school with.

After he rested his case, the judge gave his instructions to the jury and sent them to the jury room to begin deliberating.

Miriam waited in the small room for the jury to return.

"If they aren't back by about four, I'm going to call the driver so we can go home," Joseph decided.

"Ya, that's good. At least we'll get home a little earlier," Samuel said.

However, the jury worked fast. Going through the exhibits and testimony, they arrived at a decision in about two hours.

"Jury's back. You can sit in the visitor's gallery and listen to what the jury decided," the bailiff announced.

Sitting in the front row, both families watched, wondering what would happen next.

Lance was finally permitted to come back. Miriam felt a cold shiver run down her body as she saw his cold glare. She inhaled as she saw him mouth, "I'll get off and I'll come and get to you." She began praying for her safety and that of her family and the Fishers. Looking at Lance's ankles, she saw the heavy shackles, relieved that he was restrained.

# CHAPTER NINE

Lance sat on the hard bench, shackled at the ankles and wrists. He shifted, trying to find a comfortable position as he waited for the jury to march in with his fate.

After the judge gave his instructions to the witnesses, visitors and defendant, the foreman stood, holding a folded piece of paper.

"Mr. Foreman, what say you?" the judge asked in the archaic language of the courtroom.

"Your honor, we find the defendant, Lance Newman guilty of stalking; guilty of assault and guilty of kidnapping."

"Is this the verdict of . . . SIT DOWN, Mr. Newman!" the judge shouted.

Lance had erupted once again. Shouting, he turned toward Miriam, anger and madness in his eyes. Forgetting about the shackles and cuffs holding his ankles and wrists restrained, he stumbled toward the low wall separating the visitor's gallery from the rest of the courtroom. Raising one knee, he tried to climb over the wall and, teetering precariously, he overbalanced. He was unable to regain his balance and fell forward, hitting his nose and forehead on the hard wooden bench.

Miriam screamed as she saw Lance lying on his belly, not moving. She screamed again as she saw blood seeping from his nose, mouth and one ear.

Lance had hit his face against the bench, knocking him out immediately. As his body continued to fall, he struck his nose hard on the floor, breaking it. The impact forced bits of bone backward into his brain.

Lance, transported to a nearby hospital, was diagnosed with a huge blood clot which pressed on his brain. The clot began to grow even larger, causing a dangerous buildup of pressure on his frontal lobe and the top of his brain. Despite having a piece of his skull removed, he slipped into a coma. The pressure continued rising in his brain and he was soon declared brain-dead.

After conferring with his family, his doctor removed him from life support.

\*\*\*

Because of Lance's sudden death, there was no need for the legal proceedings to continue. Even though the jury had found him guilty, there was no Lance to serve any prison sentence.

In Ephrata, Miriam struggled to return to her usual life. As she worked on the quilt, she kept seeing Lance falling awkwardly over the low wall and striking his head on the seat and ground. At night, she woke from the same kinds of dreams.

Sarah and Joseph both noticed Miriam's inability to focus on anything at home.

"I'll talk to her, wife. I think she's experiencing the stress of what happened to Mr. Newman when he learned he was found guilty," Joseph said as he paced back and forth in the kitchen.

"Husband, she is probably dreaming of this at night. She looks tired, like she isn't sleeping well at all," Sarah observed, watching Joseph pacing back and forth.

That evening after supper, Miriam sat in the quilting room, her hands motionless. She simply stared into the distance.

Joseph walked in, looking at his youngest child's troubled expression.

"Miriam. We've watched you for several days. You are not your usual self. You pace. You stare into the distance. You look exhausted, as though you aren't sleeping well. What is bothering you?" Joseph asked as he sat down in one of the chairs.

Miriam gazed at him with her chin trembling. She covered her mouth with one hand as she struggled to force tears back.

"Daed, I keep seeing Lance Newman falling onto his face. I see the blood coming out of his ears, mouth and nose. I knew that he would die! Daed . . . I was praying . . . before they said the verdict." Miriam sobbed once. "I'm worried that my prayer might have led to his fall and injury." Tears poured down Miriam's drawn and pale face.

"What did you ask God for, daughter?"

"Protection," Miriam said.

"And that is all? Protection?" Joseph asked, leaning forward in his chair.

"Ya."

"Miriam, you need to realize that Lance acted all on his own, without any regard for the laws of the state or of our own Ordnung. By your asking for God's protection, you did not cause him to fall and hit his head. It was his own inability to understand that his choices and actions led to the charges against him. Miriam, this is very important, so you must listen," Joseph said sternly.

Miriam, caught by the strict urgency in her father's voice, fastened her eyes onto his face.

"Yes, daed?"

"When he heard the verdict against him, that inability to take responsibility was what led to his injuries and death. You simply asked God to protect you. You didn't ask him to kill that man."

Miriam began to get a glimmer of understanding of the events of that day. Beginning to weep, she said, "Now that it's over, you mean I can get back to my own life?"

"Ya. You can. Now, you need to start focusing on your baptismal instruction, taking your Kneeling Vow, then getting to marry John Fisher," Joseph said with a gentle smile. He reached one hand out toward his daughter's face and wiped tears off one cheek.

*** 

In another part of Ephrata, Esther Zook was obsessively thinking about John and devising ways that she could see and be with him, despite what her parents had decreed.

*I don't care that he's courting Miriam Beiler. I like him and he's not even engaged to her. As far as I'm concerned, I can still let him know that I'm interested in him. If he likes me back, he'll start courting me.*

# CHAPTER TEN

Esther was in her room one cool evening after helping her mother clean up from supper. She had begun routinely coming up to her room after supper, closing her door and entering her fantasy world as she dreamed of a future as Mrs. John Fisher. Every evening, she closed the door and acted out one fantasy or another.

Esther's fantasies had begun to become more real than her everyday life. During the day as she helped her mamm clean, wash and iron, cook, bake and can fruits and vegetables, she impatiently looked forward to her time alone in her bedroom at night. She had begun to withdraw from her parents – and they had noticed that distance.

On this evening, when Esther came out of her fantasy world, she looked toward the window and saw that it was black-dark outside. She realized how dim it had become in her room – her lamp was nearly out of kerosene. Undressing and putting on a warm nightgown, she quickly brushed her teeth and returned to her room to go to bed.

*** 

The following Sunday was a meeting day. All families in the Ephrata district prepared for the meeting, putting on their meeting clothing, hitching their horses to their buggies and putting their lunch contributions into their buggies.

In the Zook home, Esther Zook got ready for meeting with extraordinary care. She ran her hands over her already smooth hair and carefully arranged her snowy-white apron over her dark-maroon dress. Her heart hammered in her chest and her cheeks carried a hint of flush in them.

*Today's the day! John loves me and he's going to admit to that today! He'll begin courting me instead of Miriam Beiler. I have to look my best. I wish we could use mirrors!*

She was silent on the ride to the Beiler farm, caught up in her sick fantasy.

"Esther, take the vegetables into the kitchen and we'll meet you in the barn," instructed her mother.

"Ya, mamm. Denki," Esther said quietly. Walking calmly with the large bowl of mixed vegetables, she entered the kitchen, full of women and teenaged girls. She spotted Miriam Beiler, busy arranging foil-covered containers in the large oven. She glared at the other girl, convinced that she had stolen John Fisher from her.

Miriam, busy helping Sarah, missed the glare. Once she was released to go to the barn, she sought out Anna and the two friends walked to the barn, giggling as they did so. Esther was behind them and she continued to glower at Miriam.

John, looking around the barn, saw Miriam and Anna enter, going to the women's benches. He frowned as he saw Esther sidle in after Miriam, wearing a heavy scowl and staring fixedly at the other girl.

*We will leave the singing early and spend time in her parents' house. She doesn't need to be exposed to Esther's ugliness.*

After the lunch ended and families had gone home, the Beilers opened their barn to the district's Amish youth for the customary singing. John sat across from Miriam, making sure that Esther could not sit near him or Miriam. All of their friends had gathered to sit on the bench with them. Still, John felt very uncomfortable, knowing that Esther was in the background, nursing an irrational anger, if not hatred, towards Miriam.

"Miriam, let's go into your house," he said in between songs.

"Okay," she said, puzzled.

In plain sight of Esther, John walked right next to Miriam and escorted her into her parents' house.

Esther was stunned. She had expected that John would approach her with love shining out of his eyes, and ask to court her instead of Miriam. Flushing, she looked down with a scowl at her fingers as they tangled together. At ten that night, she was still unpaired with any of the young Amish men. Finally, one of the unattached youth approached her unenthusiastically and said, "I'll take you home." Nodding jerkily, she agreed to the ride home.

Inside the Beiler home, John asked Joseph for his guidance.

"Mr. Beiler, I have been telling Esther Zook for several months that I am not interested in a courting relationship with her. I've told her that Miriam and I are courting – that we have been for well over a year. Because we haven't published our engagement, I haven't said anything. I doubt Miriam has either.

"Today, I saw her glaring at Miriam and acting rudely toward her. Miriam has tried to ignore Esther's attitude so as to keep the peace. She's turned the other cheek, more than once. Before the singing began, I talked to several of our friends and asked them to sit at our bench so Esther could not sit with me. I don't know what else I can do!" John finished in frustration as he clenched his long hands into fists.

"John, we saw the same thing you did. During meeting, it was obvious to several district families what she was up to," Sarah said.

"So? What do we do? This has to come to an end . . . somehow," John said, giving an anxious look to the Beilers. His head swiveled around as he heard several courting buggies rolling out of the graveled yard. He tried to pick out who had offered to give Esther a ride home, but couldn't see through the glass in the kitchen window.

"It's long past time to go talk to the Zooks – didn't your daed already go and have a discussion with them?" Joseph questioned John.

"Ya, he did. It seemed to help . . . for a little while," John said, sighing.

"I think we should also talk to the deacons and, quite possibly, the bishop as well. Maybe we should start with him before visiting the Zooks," Joseph said, sending a questioning look around the table.

"Ya, husband, that is good. Let's go visit him tomorrow, all of us, and tell him what we've been seeing. John, your mamm and daed should be there, too," Sarah said, nodding emphatically now that a decision had been made.

The following day, both families drove to Bishop Stoltzfus' house. Mrs. Stoltzfus answered the door.

"Hello! Do you need to speak with my husband?" she asked.

"Ya, denki. It is an important matter and we need his advice," John said.

"Come in. He's about to come in from the barn. Sit down. Would you like something warm to drink?"

"Coffee or hot cocoa would be welcome," Sarah said with a

grateful smile.

Ten minutes later, both families, along with Bishop Stoltzfus and his wife sat around the long, wooden table in the kitchen. John spoke first, explaining what he had experienced and witnessed. He also informed the bishop of what he had tried to do to correct the situation.

"I saw her interactions as well and knew it would be only a matter of time before you came to visit me. We need to inform Esther's parents of what is going on with her. Has anyone already tried talking, either to Miss Zook or her parents?"

Both John and Samuel raised their hands.

"John, what have you tried to tell her?" asked the bishop.

"That I'm courting and not interested in her. I do admit that I got mad and shouted at her one time," John said as his cheeks reddened.

"I spoke to her mamm and daed and they said they would have s strict talk with her," Samuel said. "I cannot blame my son for becoming angry. We were in the midst of readying the crops for our neighbor before the trial."

"Good. Tomorrow is a working day for all of us. I propose that we all meet at the Beiler home and drive to their farm and talk to them. John, if Miss Zook tries to come to you and talk to you, do not let her know what we are planning. Simply tell her to leave you alone. Reference the Ordnung. If she argues, walk away. Just walk away," said Bishop Stoltzfus, stabbing a stiff forefinger against the smooth wood of the kitchen table.

"Ya, I will, bishop. I promise," John said in a low voice. "Now that you're helping, I feel much better."

***

Waking the next morning, Miriam saw that clouds covered the sky. It was cooler than normal, showing that fall was imminent. After finishing breakfast, she lit her kerosene lamp and started working on her quilt.

At the Fisher farm, John and Samuel discussed the weather and their day's work plans.

"It may rain or simply stay cloudy. We need to get as much of the field ready for harvesting as we can. I want to get this crop ready for sale as soon as we can," Samuel said as he finished the last of his coffee.

"Ya. I have instruction later this week, so I will need to finish early," John said, putting a warm coat on over his long-sleeved shirt.

"Well, let's get busy," Samuel said, rinsing his coffee cup.

Starting at one end of the long rows of corn, the duo moved, weeding and looking for any ears of corn that would not be fit for harvesting. Samuel started in one row and John took his position in the next so they could cover more ground. By dinnertime, they had gotten through almost half of the field.

As they rode the wagon back to the house, John scanned the cloudy sky.

"It's not going to get sunny for today, at least. It's also cooler than it's been," he said, stretching his tired legs.

"Ya. Autumn is right around the corner. What do you plan to tell Mr. and Mrs. Zook?"

"The truth. That Esther hasn't listened to our message – or she hasn't *heard* what we've been telling her. And, daed, it's not for lack of honesty. We've been blunt, haven't we?" John asked, looking at Samuel.

"Ya, that we have, John. I think she's going to need to hear it directly from your mouth, son. If she refuses to stop bothering you, I'm going to suggest that her parents send her to stay with relatives – until you and Miriam are married," Samuel said, frowning as he spoke.

"Ya. I like that," John said with a smile.

After supper, Emily washed the dishes quickly so she, John and Samuel could ride to the Beiler farm.

At the Beiler farm, Miriam helped Sarah clean the kitchen, wash and dry the dishes. As they were hitching the horse to the buggy, the Fishers and Bishop Stoltzfus drove into their yard.

"Hello! How was your day?" the bishop asked.

"Busy, but productive," Samuel said.

"Nearly finished with a set of bookshelves," Joseph said.

"OK, let's go. Before we leave, though, John, you must be blunt with the Zooks. They won't fully understand everything unless you tell them everything. I will ask them if they saw her behavior at the Beilers this weekend."

"Denki. Ya, I will," John said, nodding slowly.

The bishop started out of the yard, leading the small procession. The Fishers were next and the Beilers brought up the rear.

In the Zook home, Esther was upstairs, deep in one of her nightly fantasies. Walking back and forth and acting them out as they occurred to her, she started as she gazed out her bedroom window and started as she saw three buggies and three families pulling into their yard.

*What are they doing here? That's Bishop Stoltzfus and the Beilers – with Miriam. What are the Fishers . . . John's here! What's going on?*

Stepping quickly and lightly to her bedroom door, Esther opened her door, straining to hear what was being said downstairs. Unable to hear very much, she eased out into the hallway and tiptoed toward the top of the stairs.

She was better able to hear the low rumble of conversation now . . .

" . . . *not* interested in Esther. I have been courting Miriam now for over a year and that's going to continue. We have a strong relationship and that will not end. Your daughter has been trying to make me interested in her. She drives by the farm when my daed and I are hard at work on the crops. Mr. and Mrs. Zook, *it has to stop*!"

# CHAPTER ELEVEN

Esther, hearing this, was crushed. In an instant, the dreams and fantasies she had built up crashed down around her ears, shattering like so much glass. Almost without awareness, she shot to her feet and raced down the wooden stairs, into the kitchen. Breathing heavily, she became hysterical and loud. Seeking and finding Miriam, she began to scream at her:

"You stole him from me! I liked him and wanted him to start courting *me*! I noticed him a year ago and thought what a fine Amish husband and father he would be! I will not be working outside my home – therefore, I need a strong, industrious husband," Esther babbled as she drew in a long, shaky breath. Swiping angrily at the tears pouring down her face, she glared at Miriam.

Miriam sat back in her chair, stunned at the loudness and irrationality of the attack. Focusing on Esther's face and eyes, she froze – there was madness there.

John, sitting next to Miriam, saw the same thing. He placed

one hand on Miriam's forearm, warning her.

Joseph and Sarah Beiler sat, frozen in their chairs. Sarah fell back on her nurse's training. Focusing on Esther's face, eyes and posture, she saw rage building. Behind that rage, she caught glimpses of insanity. She stood slowly, moving to the end of the room, then began to move closer to Miriam.

Joseph simply saw an out-of-control young woman. Seeing her breathing heavily, he realized, almost too late that she was about to blow and attack Miriam.

Emily saw the same things that Sarah did. Feeling strong waves of apprehension rolling through her body, she stood and quickly moved next to Sarah. Looking at her old friend, she communicated silently with her.

*She's about to attack. Be ready to move.*

*Ya, I don't know who she'll attack. Be ready.*

Esther stood as if frozen, staring. Her gaze moved wildly from person to person. Finally, it settled on John. She saw his hand resting on Miriam's forearm. Seeing that sight, seeing the hand of her beloved on the arm of another woman, enraged her. Esther felt her anger ratcheting even higher.

"How could you? I love you! I planned an entire life with you! Having our own home, finding out what your favorite meals are, how you like your shirts and pants ironed! Having little bopplis with you! Raising our kinner! And you do *that*? You reject me and you start courting . . . courting *that*? That *girl?* She cannot love you like I can, John! She was spending time with that Englischer! We all know that! How do you know she didn't betray you with that Englischer? How? Tell me, John!"

"Esther, I began courting Miriam before you even noticed me. Before last winter's blizzards, I spoke to her mamm and daed and got their permission to begin courting her! You didn't start approaching me until last spring! By then, we had been courting for . . . for months! I am going to be very direct with you, Esther. I love Miriam. I. Love. Her. And she loves me back. There is no future for you with me. None. Please. I encourage you to look past me and find another young man who can be interested in you, who wants to build a future with you. I . . ."

John paused, knowing what he was about to say could be considered cruel. "I am not interested in building a life and sharing it with you. You do not interest me in that way. Not at all. Please leave me alone. I am going to continue courting Miriam. God willing, when the time is right, we will decide to marry. If that time comes, we will set up our own home and have our own kinner," John finished, feeling breathless and wondering if he had gone too far.

Because Esther had become even more angry. John's breath caught in his chest as he saw her face grow splotchy-red. Looking at her posture, he saw her tense up. Looking at her hands, he saw them clenched into fists. His eyes swung from Esther to his daed and Mr. Beiler. His heart thumped crazily in his chest as he began squeezing Miriam's forearm in warning.

Both fathers saw the same things that John noticed – Esther's tension, clenched fists and the madness in her eyes. They both sensed danger at the same time and, pushing their chairs back at the same moment, they stood, readying themselves for action.

Esther's mamm and daed sat in their chairs, stunned by the anger and violence they now saw in their daughter. Micah placed his hand on Rebekah's shoulder as Joseph and Samuel stood up.

Bishop Stoltzfus moved next to John's and Miriam's fathers, ready for anything.

Esther finally tore her eyes away from John and Miriam. Looking wildly around the large kitchen for something, anything she could use, her gaze landed on the wide, deep silverware drawer. Running to it in two long jumps, she wrenched the drawer open and shoved forks, spoons and knives around, looking for . . .

*Ah! There it is! This will convince him of my love!* Wrapping her trembling hand around the wooden handle of a large knife, she pulled it out and whirled around. She held the knife above her head with the point aimed right at Miriam.

Letting out a loud, high-pitched scream, she rushed at Miriam, intending to bury the knife deep in her perceived rival's chest.

Miriam pushed herself back in the chair. *I'm going to die! Lord, I'm not ready!*

John's eyes widened as he saw the extent of Esther's insanity. Wrapping his arms around Miriam, he curled around her, protecting her.

Joseph Beiler and Samuel Fisher simultaneously bounded forward and grabbed Esther's arms before she could reach her target. Joseph grimaced as the knife plunged home, deep into his upper arm.

"Joseph! His arm!" Sarah shrieked running to him.

Bishop Stoltzfus jumped up and slid in between Esther and Joseph.

"Go, sit down. I have her," he told Joseph.

Sarah grabbed Joseph and made him sit down as she tore the sleeve of his shirt so she could assess the stab wound. Emily helped her.

"Mrs. Zook, go call the ambulance now! Your daughter and Mr. Beiler need medical assistance!" ordered the bishop.

Mrs. Zook was frozen in her chair, unable to believe the violence that had just taken place in her own kitchen.

"Go, wife! Make the call!" shouted Micah as he helped the three men restrain Esther, made strong in her insanity.

As the kitchen erupted in mayhem, John continued

crouching over Miriam, refusing to expose her to any danger. Instead, he turned his head so he could keep an eye on what was happening with Esther.

"Stay here. My daed, the bishop and her daed have her restrained, but she could get loose," he murmured to Miriam.

Miriam was unable to move. Instead, she whispered, "OK."

Emily, after looking at Joseph's arm wound, moved by the men who were holding Esther immobile.

"Sit her down. Keep your hands on her arms and don't let her stand up," she told the men.

All three of them struggled to pull Esther to an empty chair. Determined to get to Miriam and harm her, she was difficult to budge. Finally, they were able to force her to sit down. All three men kept their hands on her shoulders and arms. Mr. Zook positioned his hands on top of Esther's knees so she could not jump back up.

"Let me stand up! I have . . . I have to show Miriam Beiler that she doesn't steal what belongs to me! Let me go!" Esther shrieked.

Because of Ephrata's distance from the nearest hospital, it took about twenty-five minutes for an ambulance to arrive at the Zook farm. Pounding on the door, the paramedics waited.

Emily ran to the front door and let the paramedics into the house. As they walked to the kitchen, she briefly explained what had happened and the behaviors Esther was exhibiting.

"She stabbed the other girl's father. She's been screaming that the young man she wants was 'stolen' by the other girl? So, are you saying she's mentally ill?"

"Yes. She's being irrational and demanding that the young man stop courting the other girl and begin courting her."

"OK, we'll take over here . . . uh, we were only told about one patient. If she's dangerous, there's no way we can transport him in the same vehicle," the paramedic said as he noticed Joseph's injury.

"We have his bleeding under control. We'll take him to the doctor ourselves. Miss Zook needs your help more," Emily said.

"OK. Miss Zook, how are you today?"

*"Let me go! She stole him from me! I have to show her that she will pay for her actions! Let me go!"*

The paramedics observed Esther's struggles to break loose. The lead paramedic looked at her face and eyes. Seeing her wide, staring gaze, he dropped to his haunches.

"OK, Miss Zook, I'm going to ask you some questions. Can you tell me the day and date?"

"Ya, it is Saturday, April 21st."

"Where are you?"

"Being held as a prisoner in *her* home. She wants to lock me up so she can continue to distract my husband."

"What is your name?"

"Esther Fisher."

"Are you married or single?"

"Married. John Fisher is my husband. We . . . we are to have a boppli," Esther said, with a shy, yet mad smile.

"'Boppli?' What is that?" the paramedic asked.

"Pennsylvania Dutch for 'baby,'" Emily said, standing close by.

"Ah, thank you. Where are Miss . . . uh, Zook's parents?"

"Right here. I'm holding her legs down," said Micah, trying not to cry.

"Uh, I have to ask you a question that might be hard for you to answer. I apologize in advance, but it's necessary. Do you know if she has ever . . . been with a man . . . in that way?" asked the paramedic.

"You mean, in the Biblical sense? Nee! No! Never! She has never courted!" responded Micah angrily.

"OK, then. I'm sorry, but she needs to be taken to the hospital and given a mental health evaluation. Given that she's rather . . . confused about person, place and time, she'll be involuntarily committed to the mental health unit for that evaluation. It's likely she'll be put on a mental health hold for about five days. Depending upon the diagnosis, if any, she might be prescribed medications and discharged. Or she might be admitted longer-term, to a mental health hospital so she can get the help she needs," the paramedic finished.

"Oh! No! She can't be . . . she can't be!" Rebekah Zook began to cry helplessly.

Emily and Sarah wrapped their arms around her, shushing her and rocking her back and forth.

"It is OK. If she is mentally ill, she cannot help it. She'll get the help she needs," Sarah said softly.

Rebekah heard the hope in Sarah's words. She continued sobbing, but nodded her understanding.

"OK, take her to the hospital. I just don't . . . don't want her to be a danger to anyone," she said, wiping tears out of her eyes.

The paramedics descended upon Esther picking her up and forcing her to walk to the stretcher that had been set up on the by-now-dark porch. Lifting her up, they buckled the straps around her torso, ankles and wrists, securing her.

"Mamm! John! What's happening? Husband, make them unstrap me so I can make your supper!" she screamed irrationally.

Both of her parents turned away from the painful scene, their faces crumpling in grief.

Now that Esther no longer posed a threat to the others in the house, John slowly unwrapped himself from around Miriam. Looking around, he paled as he saw the blood on Joseph's shirt.

Miriam gasped, seeing her father's injury.

"Daed, are you all right?"

"Ya, I'm fine, daughter. Your mamm and Mrs. Fisher will have me set to rights in no time," Joseph said, nodding his head. "What's important is that you are not hurt. John, are you OK?"

"Ya, denki. Shaken, but I am all right," John said, forcing the quaver out of his voice.

"Well, now we have our answer. Sadly, mental illness was the cause of her belief that you, Mr. Fisher, were courting her and that you intended to marry her. Mr. and Mrs. Zook, we will pray that Miss Zook gets the help she so badly needs, that she makes a swift recovery and returns to your home," the bishop said softly. "Mr. Beiler, make sure you get that wound cleaned and dressed. You do not need an infection."

The Fishers, Beilers and bishop all returned to their homes, allowing the Zooks to take in the events that had pulled their daughter out of their home.

Sarah and Miriam treated Joseph's arm wound at home, wrapping it in a gauze bandage. He took acetaminophen for the pain and went to bed so he could return to his carpentry work the next day. Miriam, still quivering inside, sat in the kitchen, holding her mamm's hand.

In the Fisher home, John ran to the bathroom, where he was sick, before he came back to the kitchen to sit with his parents.

"Mamm, I never suspected that she was . . . "

"Mentally ill? None of us did, John. Certainly, I never did. I just thought she was being particularly stubborn about the Ordnung and its provisions on courting. Do not feel guilty. She has been suffering for a long time. We can thank God that she is going to get help from the Englischer hospital that she so badly needs," Emily said.

"Ya," John said, feeling better. "I did everything I knew to do – telling her I wasn't . . ."

"Interested. Ya, John. I was there. You handled things correctly. We didn't know until almost too late, that Miss Zook suffers from a mental illness of some kind. Blame that illness and not yourself, son. Continue your baptismal instruction, take your kneeling vow and prepare to marry Miss Beiler," Samuel said as he rubbed his face. "I am very tired and we have a long day tomorrow, preparing for the harvest. I suggest that we all go to bed. It has been a very long and stressful day."

"Husband, I want to give John some tea to settle his stomach. I will be up later," Emily said, pouring water into the tea kettle.

"Ya. OK. Good night."

# CHAPTER TWELVE

Life slowly returned to normal in the Beiler and Fisher households. Miriam made steady progress on the final quilt for her wealthy Englischer customers. Her instruction for baptism continued with Bishop Stoltzfus. Joseph finished making the bookcase for his customer and began constructing a dining room set for his newest customers.

In the Fisher household, John finally came to terms with the facts of Esther Zook's mental health issues, which helped him to realize that he wasn't responsible for her actions. As he slowly came back to his usual good mood, he was able to throw himself fully into helping his daed with the large corn harvest they were planning.

"Mr. Fisher, I think you – and Miss Beiler – are ready to be baptized. You have reviewed your Bible study and developed a very good understanding of Christ and his love for the world. When you request to take your Kneeling Vow, your request will be approved with no disagreement between me and the district's deacons," predicted the bishop.

"Denki, bishop! This is good news! I will tell Miriam the next time we court," John said with a broad grin across his handsome face.

And, in the Zook household, Micah and Rebekah learned that their daughter would be kept in the mental hospital for the foreseeable future. After getting a ride to the mental hospital to visit with Esther, they met with her doctor and social worker.

"Mr. and Mrs. Zook, we have a diagnosis for Esther. She is suffering from schizophrenia – with symptoms of paranoia. This means that she lacks a chemical in her brain that would allow her to think rationally. She believes that others plot against her. Fortunately, there are medications and therapies available that can help her return to a normal thought pattern. She'll be able to resume a normal life – as long as she takes her medication faithfully every day," the psychiatrist said.

The Zooks reeled as they heard the news. Hearing that she could have a normal life, they breathed sighs of relief.

"How long does she have to take this medication?" asked Micah.

"For the rest of her life. Because she lacks a certain chemical in her brain, that medication substitutes for it. If she doesn't take it, she runs the risk of the same disordered thinking and paranoia that brought her in here," the doctor said.

"Oh," said Micah.

"You . . . don't carry health insurance, do you?"

"No. It is forbidden . . . is this medication expensive?"

"The form of medication I am prescribing is an older, reliable medication. It gives good results and has few side effects. Because it's been on the market for several years, it will cost you less. If you visit one of these stores . . . "here, the doctor gave Micah a piece of paper with the names of two stores . . . "You should be able to get her monthly prescriptions for a very low amount."

"Denki. Can we . . . can we see her?"

"Of course!"

How is she?" asked Rebekah.

"Much better," answered the social worker. "She's aware of who and where she is. She isn't experiencing the sane disordered thoughts that brought her in here. But she's not completely back as you know her. That will take another couple weeks until the medication reaches a therapeutic level in her body. Once you see her, she'll be able to follow your conversation, but she may need to be brought back to the present time."

"Does she . . . know that she isn't married to John Fisher?"

"We are working on that. She clearly likes this young man. Deeply, in fact. For that reason, I am going to ask that she stay here in the hospital until she understands that there was no relationship between her and this young man. Until then, she could still pose a danger to him and his . . . girlfriend?"

"Thank you," Micah murmured.

After visiting with Esther, they were driven back home.

*\*\*\**

One month later, the harvest completed, first John, then Miriam took their Kneeling Vows, becoming full members of their Amish district. After both had taken their vows, they began seriously planning their wedding, set to take place during the next year's wedding season.

The holidays began with prayerful observations of Thanksgiving. Families gathered, celebrating the day and enjoying their time with each other. Miriam worked to finish the last quilt in her large order. As she sewed the back to the quilted front, she smiled, satisfied with how it was turning out. Two weeks later, just before Christmas, she sewed the last binding onto that child's quilt and, releasing a long sigh of relief, she cut the thread holding the quilt to her sewing machine.

Unfolding all four quilts, she spread them onto the work tables in the quilting room. Walking slowly from one quilt to the next, she looked closely for any imperfections. When she saw a stray thread, she cut it loose, brushing it off the fabric.

Sarah came in and, seeing all the quilts spread out, she

gasped.

"Miriam, they are beautiful! Your customer will love them!"

"Denki, mamm. I hope so! I've been looking over them to make sure they are perfect – after all, they paid a lot of money for them," Miriam said.

"You are still due the last half of the payment, right?"

"Ya. I am. I will call them after supper and make arrangements for their delivery," Miriam decided.

"Ya, that is good. How many other orders do you have waiting?"

"Two! I want to give some of the money to you and daed for the bills. The rest, I'll save for our wedding and for after."

"That is good, Miriam. Have you and John talked about where you will live?"

"Our grossmudderhaus here. It will allow us to save money to buy our own farm, either here in our district or another district, depending on where we find land," Miriam said.

"Another district . . ." Sarah said, her words trailing out.

"I hope it will be close by, if we have to leave the district. I want to stay here because you, my sisters, brothers and daed are here."

"God will provide, daughter." Sarah said, feeling a little sad. Seeing Miriam's eyes, she opened her arms and Miriam slipped into them.

*\*\**

Miriam delivered all four quilts to her customer. Upon seeing them, both husband and wife were very excited.

"Miss Beiler, they are perfect! I love the detail! Oh, and I have some good news for you! My wife and I talked and we're going to pay you a bonus for all your hard work. Also, my sister-in-law and her mother found out about your work. They will be meeting with you after Christmas so they can place their orders with you. I'll be bringing them up here," said the husband, who took his wallet out and counted out $2,500, handing it to Miriam.

"Oh! You don't have to pay me that large a bonus!" she said, stunned.

"Miss Beiler, please. You do exceptional work. They are perfect. Also, we heard about your troubles with Mr. Newman. That you were able to continue working through all that stress is truly amazing. Please accept it as a token of our gratitude and acknowledgement of your talent. Save it or buy supplies you need."

"Well . . . I am getting married. I can save it for a rainy day. Denki!"

The couple left, bearing all four quilts. Before they did, they set a date to bring their relatives to Miriam after Christmas.

"Merry Christmas!"

"Merry Christmas to you, too! And thank you for the bonus! I do appreciate it!"

Joseph and Sarah came up after the Englischers had left.

"Miriam, daughter, save that money! Those bonuses are far and few between, and you need to save," Joseph said.

"Ya," Miriam said, tucking the bills away.

*\*\**

Christmas came and went. Unlike the previous winter, this one was more mild. While it snowed, Ephrata didn't experience the same violent blizzards and deep snows that had fallen the year before.

John worked on the next season's crops with his father. In addition to helping him, he began to work on land his father had given to him – 200 acres. John, his father and brothers tilled the land and readied it for the crops that John wanted to plant.

Miriam began making a large quilt for her newest customer. On the date she had arranged to meet with the customers who had bought four quilts, she drove to the Amish market through several inches of snow. Greeting the relatives of her clients, she discussed the details of what they wanted to order.

"Our bedroom is painted light yellow and we have blue and

green furnishings in the room. So I would like this pattern . . . right here, in blue and green with a yellow back," the customer decided.

"OK," Miriam said, jotting down all the details. "A full-size quilt will cost you $800. And, you, ma'am? What are you thinking of?"

"I love bright colors. I want to display a quilt in my family room on a quilt stand. I understand you made a quilt using red, blue and yellow?"

"Yes, I did. Do you want those colors or . . .?"

"I have winter-white walls. My carpet is blue, so I'd like my quilt to be, oh, a sapphire blue, like this, then an emerald-green, like this and a royal purple like this. They're all cool colors and they'll pull the decor together beautifully," said the younger Englischer woman.

Miriam quickly jotted her notes down.

"Your quilt will be a full-sized quilt as well, so it will also cost you $800. I need payment of one-half of that as a deposit, as well as your phone numbers. I have just begun working on another order, which should be done in about four months. Once that's finished, ma'am, I'll start on yours. When I've finished each of your quilts, I will call you and we can arrange delivery."

"Girls, you are going to love her work!" gushed the woman's' relative. "We love the quilts Miss Beiler made for us. The kids love them!"

"Thank you!"

January slipped into February and Miriam worked steadily on her quilting orders. When she needed new supplies, she and Anna King got together and drove to either the Amish market or to an Englischer fabric and crafting store.

"How are your wedding plans coming along?" Anna asked.

"Not bad at all! Mamm and I are getting family to help with the food and John and I are making arrangements to visit all our family for our honeymoon," Miriam said. As she thought of the honeymoon, her cheeks heated up and she loosened her neck scarf slightly.

Anna giggled. She had begun courting a young man from the district.

Miriam looked at her with a saucy grin on her face.

"I think love is loosening you up just a little bit!"

"Oh, love! Loosening me up!" Anna said. Now, it was her turn for pink cheeks.

"So? When is the wedding?" Miriam asked as her eyes twinkled with mischief.

"If there's to be a wedding, it won't be for another year-and-a-half, at least," Anna said loftily. "We want to get to know each other well."

"Well, of course. I'm just glad that John and I have been able to get together with each other, even though the harvesting season made that difficult."

"At least we know what every harvest season will be like, won't we?" Anna asked

"Not to mention planting season," added Miriam, shivering suddenly.

"Are you all right? You shivered." Anna asked.

"Ya. I'm fine. It's just . . . every time I pass that intersection, I remember Lance Newman nearly striking my horse," Miriam muttered.

"Do you still get memories?"

"Ya, and I suppose I always will. He could have destroyed my life."

"Ya. I'm glad you see that now."

"Anna, I think he was just as crazy as Esther Zook is. If he was, I don't know what his diagnosis would be. When he tried to get to me after the jury said he was guilty . . ." Miriam broke off.

"Miriam, it wasn't your fault. Like you said, he was insane. How is Esther?"

"I haven't seen her. Her doctor doesn't want her to see me or John because she's still getting back to normal. I pray for her and her family. Schizophrenia sounds . . .”

“Scary, is what it sounds. Having a disease in your brain that affects how you think . . . ya, I pray for her and her family as well. She couldn’t help it – even though she did try to kill you. How is your daed’s arm?”

“Thank God mamm and Mrs. Fisher are both nurses! He didn’t have to visit the doctor. Mamm and Mrs. Fisher cleaned his wound and dressed it. When we got home that night, mamm started taking care of it so it wouldn’t get infected. He’s back to normal now. The only thing that still bothers him is his old injury when it’s cold and damp,” Miriam said.

“I wonder if she knows about your engagement,” Anna mused as she drove down the snowy road.

“Nee, because we haven’t announced or published it yet. We won’t do that until several weeks before this year’s wedding season. You, mamm, daed, John’s mamm and daed and our brothers and sisters are the only ones who know. And, as far as Esther Zook goes, I think that’s the safest thing. I don’t want her to have another one of those scary attacks,” Miriam said, shivering as she remembered the scene in the Zook kitchen.

“Oh, Miriam, you are so brave! I would have fallen apart,” Anna said.

“No, you would not have, Anna. You are a very strong woman – a very strong Amish woman and your faith in God would have pulled you through, just as it did me.”

By this time, Anna was pulling up to Miriam's front gate.

"I'll see you at meeting this Sunday. You do know that it was moved from the Zook's farm to ours? Bishop Stoltzfus doesn't believe Esther is ready for the stress of all the crowds," she said, reminding Miriam of the location.

"Ya. I know. We will be there and we will sit together. Let's see if we can get John and Ephraim to sit at the same bench. Then, we can sit together," Miriam said, hopping to the ground. "Denki for the ride!"

"OK! When Ephraim comes by, I'll ask him about sitting with you and John. I think he'll agree," Anna said, waving to Miriam.

As February wore on, with two heavy snow storms, Miriam worked hard on her quilting orders. Because these were smaller orders, she was able to help Sarah around the house before beginning to work.

John and his brothers planned what would be planted on the acreage his father had given to him. Because John would now be busy with his own land, Samuel hired an Amish youth to help him with monitoring the crops once they were planted.

John plotted out what he wanted to plant. Buying the seed, he came home. Samuel looked at the plans he had drawn out, approving them.

"This is good. You'll make good use of the land and your crops will be profitable," Samuel said.

John and Samuel planted their crops and began tending them, weeding the fields so the crops would get all the water they needed. John's brothers helped him keep up with the work in his fields.

It was late March when John looked up from his crops one afternoon. Seeing a buggy passing down the road, he did a double-take when he saw that Esther was the passenger. Remembering the fearful scene in the Zook living room, he turned his back to the buggy and, dropping to his knees, began to pull weeds. As he worked, he prayed that the foot-high crops would shield him. Several minutes later, he dared to look up. Seeing the buggy in the distance, he realized that Esther hadn't seen him or she hadn't recognized him. Sitting next to her daed, she was facing forward.

John slumped to the fertile soil, letting out a huge sigh of relief.

That evening, he went to see Miriam.

"I was working on my crops this afternoon and saw Mr. Zook and Esther coming down the road," he told Miriam. Pacing back and forth, he continued. "I didn't want her to see me, so I got onto my knees and weeded that way. Miriam, I was praying so hard. I don't want anything ever to happen to you! After several minutes, I looked up – I don't think she saw me."

"She's back! John, I hope she takes her medicine every day! Mamm was telling me that, if she doesn't she can slip back into that delusional thinking again. I think we should tell mamm – and pray for Esther and her family," Miriam said, standing up.

Moving to the kitchen, they found Sarah reading her Bible.

"Mamm, I'm sorry to disturb you. John has some news that I think you should hear," Miriam said.

"I think I know what that news is," Sarah said, looking at Miriam. "Esther Zook has returned to Ephrata from the hospital. I'm going to speak with her mamm tomorrow. She wants to know what she should do and what she shouldn't do. I thought you knew she was coming back!"

"Well, ya, I did. I mean, Anna and I were talking how the last meeting was moved from the Zook farm to Anna's parents' farm. They want to give her every opportunity to heal and get better. I just . . . mamm, if she takes her medicine like she's supposed to, she won't, well, fall apart if she sees me?"

"Nee, she shouldn't. But, given what happened when she had her breakdown, it's probably not a good idea to seek her out. Did you have any kind of friendship with her before?"

"Ya. Remember I was giving her quilting lessons?"

"Oh, yes, I do! And those ended because she started . . ." Sarah flapped her hand, indicating that Esther had begun getting fixated on John at about that time.

"Ya. She started liking John and wouldn't leave him alone. Mamm, we haven't published our engagement and we won't

WINTER OF FAITH COLLECTION

for some months. Should we invite Esther to the wedding?"

"Let's talk to the bishop about that. Why are you asking?" asked Sarah with a crease between her eyebrows.

"Because I don't want to put any stress on Esther. It wasn't her fault she fell apart and got sick. But at the same time, I don't want her doing the same things," Miriam said.

"Ahh. Let's talk to the bishop. It may be that he'll give her mamm and daed a warning and they'll try to get her out of town, just to protect her and the two of you," Sarah predicted.

"I think that would be best," John said as he thought.

# CHAPTER THIRTEEN

March came with wind, rain and warming temperatures. John planted more crops and soon found himself busy six days a week with them.

Miriam finished one quilt and, after delivering it to her customer, started on the next order. Anna came to the Beiler farm to work with her one day.

"Have any of your customers ever asked you to cross stitch anything on their quilts?" Anna asked as she stitched.

"Ya, in fact I just took an order the other day. I was going to ask if you could help me with that. Is it better to stitch the design on the fabric before I sew the layers together?" Miriam asked.

"Oh, ya! Stitch the pieces together. Before you attach the quilting, I'll cross stitch the design they want – have they told you what they want?" Anna asked.

"It's going to be a baby quilt and they want . . . let me get my notes. I can't remember," Miriam said, leafing through her pages. "Okay, they want a baby bottle stitched in blue, then a rattle stitched in pink. It's going to be a quilt made of squares, so the bottle and rattle should both fit on individual squares, on diagonal ends of the blanket. If you know what I mean!" Miriam giggled as she spoke.

"I think I do know what you mean," Anna said, turning to a clean page in the notebook. Grabbing a pencil, she drew a quick square with smaller squares inside. She sketched a small bottle in one square on one side of the blanket then, moving to a square on the diagonal opposite, she sketched out a baby rattle. "Is this what you're talking about?"

"Yes, exactly! Can you do that?"

"Oh, ya. Just get me the pieces when you have them and I'll do them for you," Anna promised.

"Oh, denki! I'll pay you for your materials and work," Miriam promised.

"OK, but I'm giving you a discount because we're friends," Anna said as she handed the notebook back to Miriam.

"Nee! I'll pay you the full amount that you'd charge your customers. You have to buy new supplies and it wouldn't be fair," Miriam said, resuming her sewing.

\*\*\*

WINTER OF FAITH COLLECTION

The next Sunday was a meeting Sunday. It was held at the farm of one of the deacons. Miriam came out looking for Anna. Seeing the Zooks, she slowed for a second, then realized that Esther was not with them.

*Oh, they must be hurting!* She walked up to the Zooks and, holding out her hand, greeted both of them.

"How are you? How is Esther doing?"

"We are fine, denki for asking. Esther is doing much better. We think she recognizes just how sick she truly was and she doesn't want to get that sick again. For now, she is taking her medication exactly as ordered," said Micah.

Miriam noticed that his eyes were sad and tired.

"I will pray for her continued recovery, Mr. and Mrs. Zook."

"Denki. You are a very sweet girl," Rebekah said.

The meeting started. Three hours later, the men moved the benches, rearranging them inside the barn so everyone could eat. Outside, the wind freshened and storm clouds began to roll over the community.

Once the lunch had ended, fat raindrops began to splat onto the ground. The Amish youth stayed inside the barn, taking their seats at the long benches for the singing. At ten, when the singing ended, so had the early-spring rainstorm. Established courting couples and those who had not yet paired off climbed into their buggies, going home.

\*\*\*

The year moved into summer, with heat, buzzing insects and welcome storms that helped the district's crops grow. John looked with satisfaction at his crops. By now, they were almost waist-high and thriving. He and his brothers worked on them every week, weeding and pruning.

Miriam continued taking new quilting orders and working six days a week on her orders. The money she earned went into savings, to help her parents with the bills and to help buy the material for her wedding dress.

"Miriam, have you thought about the color you want for your wedding dress?" Sarah asked, coming into the quilting room.

"I was thinking of a sky-blue, mamm. Something I can wear to meeting Sundays," responded Miriam, cutting the threads on her quilt.

"Ya, that's a good choice. Sky-blue will serve you well and, with a white apron and new prayer kapp, you'll be very presentable," Sarah said, sitting next to Miriam. "Let's measure you this weekend and buy the material and thread next weekend," Sarah suggested thinking of the next few days.

"Ya! My wedding dress! Mamm, I am getting excited! Oh. Does Esther still stay at home all the time?"

"That is my understanding. I was talking with her mamm.

She's afraid of coming into town too much. I think she's afraid of getting sick again."

"What are they going to do when John and I get married?"

"Daughter, we'll cross that bridge when we arrive at it. We haven't even published your banns yet. I'm thinking that her parents will have her go stay with a family member in another district. I have been trying to find out what Esther thinks of John. That's another very important question, you know," Sarah said, giving Miriam a significant look.

"Ya, I know. I would hate to wake up one morning and find that she is still . . . obsessed . . . with him, posing a threat to him, me, you, daed or John's parents," Miriam said with a slight frown.

"Keep praying for them, Miriam. We know it isn't her fault that she has this condition. But if she stops taking her medication, she is responsible for anything that happens."

Miriam looked at her mother, unable to say anything after that pronouncement. Her throat had closed in fear. After swallowing several times, trying to dislodge the hard ball of fear inside, she opened her mouth, then closed it.

"Mamm . . . we're always going to have to be watchful, aren't we?"

"You mean for Esther? Ya, we are. Thankfully we know about her schizophrenia. Even more thankfully, she knows what could happen if she stops taking her medication and she's staying on it. I will pray for her continued good health," Sarah said with a firm nod as she stood up.

# EPILOGUE

It was now Wedding Season in Ephrata. All the district's crops had been harvested, stored and made ready for sale to stores and other farmers. Miriam, her mother, sisters, aunts and grandmothers had been busy for several weeks, making Miriam's wedding dress, apron and prayer kapp. The stove and oven had been going all day, six days a week as they baked and cooked the foods that would be served at the wedding festivities.

Families began making plans to attend, with family members coming in from other cities and districts. Miriam and Sarah were busy cleaning every room in the house, preparing for family to come and stay for several days.

Joseph came in, stamping mud from his boots and carrying several bags of food.

"Miriam and Sarah, you might want to hear this. I just ran into Micah Zook. He and Rebekah sent Esther to stay with a relative outside of Philadelphia in another district. She'll be staying there for the next few weeks until Wedding Season is over. And . . . he told me that Esther realizes that she was obsessed with John. She is the one who made the decision to be away from Ephrata when you marry John, Miriam. It appears that she has enough self-awareness that she thinks it's best to be away. For that, I am thanking God!"

Sarah and Miriam looked at each other, open-mouthed.

"Daed, did you ask him this?"

"Nee. He volunteered it," Joseph said, helping Sarah put the food away.

***

The morning of Miriam's and John's wedding day dawned bright and cold. Miriam, unable to sleep, threw her covers back and got out of bed. Looking around her room, she realized she and John would share her room tonight.

Getting carefully dressed, she put on her wedding dress, the crisp apron and black prayer kapp. Going downstairs, she was greeted by her sisters, brothers, in-laws, nieces, nephews, grandmothers and parents.

"Let's eat! We have to get ready for all our guests," Sam, her brother-in-law said.

Miriam, battling nerves and butterflies, smiled as she sipped her coffee.

"Ya! It is! I have already moved my things into the grossmudderhaus," she said, giving a happy, twinkling smile.

By 8:30, everyone was in their places. Guests were on the long prayer benches; John's and Miriam's newehockers were ready. After singing several hymns, the minister counseled John and Miriam on their marital responsibilities in a separate room. Returning to the main room, prayer, Scripture and a sermon took place.

After the sermon had finally ended, the minister asked John and Miriam about their pending marriage. After hearing their answers, he blessed them. Other deacons, Joseph and Samuel gave testimonies about marriage, then, the final prayer marked the end of the marriage ceremony.

All family members and guests, feeling excited and celebratory, moved to the kitchen, where the women got the food ready to serve. While they were taking the food out of the oven, the men were rearranging the tables and benches for the dinner. Miriam and John were escorted to the honorary Eck, where they sat down.

Miriam, seated at John's left, saw her friends seated all around her. Both families were seated in the kitchen, where they ate of the wedding feast.

After dinner, the festivities continued, with matchmaking and games. Miriam had been looking forward to this part of the day. Taking her girlfriends' hands, she walked them to the young, unmatched men and paired them with each other.

The festivities didn't end here – at five, supper was served, with the older guests, Joseph, Sarah, Samuel and Emily sitting to eat first.

By 10:30, Miriam's eyes were drooping. The festivities had just ended and she and John went upstairs to her bedroom.

The next morning, everyone arose early – they needed to help get the Beiler house back into order, and everyone was pressed into service, including John and Miriam.

Beginning that Friday evening, John and Miriam Fisher began their honeymoon, visiting their relatives to share the happiness of their marriage. Because of the sizes of their families, this process would take most, if not all winter.

When they arrived at a relative's home, they stayed overnight, visiting, eating and celebrating. The next afternoon, they left that relative's home and traveled to another relative's home, staying overnight until the next day's noon meal. Miriam counted – they visited six relatives every weekend, staying at their homes, celebrating and getting to know each other better.

One morning, Miriam woke up and helped her mother get breakfast for her, John, Sarah and Joseph. In the quilting room, she felt unusually sleepy and struggled to stay awake as she worked on her newest quilt. Her sleepiness, combined with a sour stomach, continued for several weeks. One morning, Sarah looked at her.

"When did you have your last cycle?"

Miriam stopped sewing, thinking.

"It's been about two months, mamm. Do you think . . ." Miriam asked her eyes growing wide.

"I don't think. I know. Certain foods, you avoid. You're sleepy all the time. Miriam, you are going to have a boppli!"

Miriam dropped the quilt in excitement, standing up.

"Mamm! You're going to be a grossmudder!"

"When will you tell John?"

"As soon as possible. He's noticed my sleepiness, too and he's worried about me. He needs to know it's for the happiest reason of all – that he's going to be a daed!"

"Have you felt nauseated?"

"Only when I smell greasy foods. Otherwise, my stomach is just . . . sour. Do you know what might help?"

"Ginger tea. Keep food on your stomach at all times, daughter. Try to eat breads, crackers, gingersnap cookies. If a food is highly spiced, you will feel sick. If it's greasy, you'll feel sick, so try to eat more fresh fruits and vegetables. When you cook meats, drain the fat off. Drink milk. Your baby needs milk to develop," Sarah said, ticking off the advice on her fingers.

"Denki. I have so much to learn!"

"Ya, and maternity dresses to make. I will show you some patterns and help you alter them. You'll need to buy fabric in town so you can make a few."

"What about my aprons?" Miriam asked, feeling the ties at the back of her still-trim waist.

"I will help you with that, too. You will need to cut and sew the ties longer to accommodate your belly as it grows."

That night, when they were cuddling under the covers, Miriam yawned widely.

"That reminds me, wife. You have been so tired lately. Are you sick?" John asked, leaning on one elbow and looking at Miriam, lying on her pillow.

"N-n-not in the usual sense," Miriam said, feeling her heart thumping hard.

"What do you mean?"

"John, we are going to have our first boppli!"

"What? When?" John asked in in excitement, placing his hand protectively over Miriam's abdomen.

"In about seven months – so, July or August," Miriam said nervously, peering at John in the dark.

John threw the covers back and landed on the floor with a thump.

"Woo-hoo, I'm going to be a daed! Is your stomach upset or

anything?"

"No, not now, but when I smell a strong smell, it gets upset. Mamm and I were talking this afternoon and she was giving me some good advice," Miriam said.

"I'm glad you told her," John said seriously.

"Actually, she figured it out before I did. She asked me how it had been since my last course. That's when I realized what my symptoms are."

"From now on, Miriam, you do not lift anything heavy. I am serious. You allow one of us to pick anything up that is too heavy for you. If you need to take a nap, do so. I'll ask mamm for advice, too," John promised.

"Yes, John," Miriam said, grateful for his help even as she was feeling a bit overwhelmed by his obvious nervousness. "I'll call you or someone else to help me lift anything. My bolts of fabric are not too heavy. Besides, I just move them from the chest to the cutting table and back," Miriam said.

"Nee. Not the new ones, at least. You let me lift those. Tell me that morning, when you need them and I'll take them down for you. I don't want anything happening to this precious little boppli," John said, nuzzling his head on Miriam's stomach. "You are too precious to me, Miriam. I love you. Seeing what you went through with Lance Newman . . . nearly being stabbed by Esther Zook . . . made me realize just how much you mean to me. We married because we love each other and I want us to be together until we are both gray-haired," John said seriously. As he spoke, his hand replaced his head on Miriam's stomach.

Once the news of Miriam's pregnancy became known, her symptoms eased somewhat. Following her mother's and mother-in-law's instructions, she was able to keep her nausea down. She, Sarah and Emily sewed new dresses to fit over her growing belly. At one of the meetings, she ran into Esther Zook. John, standing protectively close to Miriam, watched their interaction closely.

"Congratulations, Miriam. You must be very happy . . . I . . . want to apologize for what I did last year. It was unforgivable. I could have killed you, but now I know it's because I have an illness," Esther said quietly.

"Denki," Miriam said, watching Esther closely. "I . . . we . . . are very happy. And I know you'll meet someone when the Lord wills it."

"Ya. I already have. When mamm and daed took me to my relative's district, I met someone up there. We began courting a few months ago. It seems he's the right man for me, after all. And I won't be bothering you and John. The Lord brought you together," Esther said with a smile

"Esther, you don't know how happy I am for you!" Miriam said, smiling broadly. "Get to know your beau well, because he will be your life-partner, if God wills it."

At home that evening, John looked at Miriam.

"Miriam, you have such a big capacity for forgiveness. When I saw you and Esther Zook talking, I admit, I felt some fear. I didn't know what to expect and, now that your pregnancy is obvious, she could have chosen to do some real harm to you and our boppli," John said with a serious look in his eyes. "I do want you to do one thing. Whenever you see her, get me. If I'm talking to someone, just get me. I don't know if it's me being protective, but . . . I want to be near whenever she's around you. Today, we had no warning, but, in the future . . ."

"Ya, husband. I will. I was a little nervous, but I didn't feel anything, any ill intent coming from her," Miriam said.

Miriam continued sewing her quilts, but as her due date came closer, she slowed down on their production.

"Mamm, I think I'm going to have to slow down to maybe four quilts a year, once I have my boppli. I won't have the time to work all day long like I did before," she said.

"Ya. Pick your projects carefully. Let your customers know that you're a mamm and that you need time with your family, so what used to take four months might take six, if not longer," Sarah advised. "When will you finish this one?"

"I am thinking about one month before I have my little one. Then, I'm going to have to slow down a bit until the baby is older," Miriam said, closing up her sewing machine and putting her notions away. "But I'm going to keep going with it. I'll be a better quilter for being a mamm, and a better mamm for being a quilter."

Sarah nodded. "I'm so proud of you, Miriam." Her voice caught. "So proud."

In the Beiler living room that evening, Miriam and John sat quietly, reading their Bibles and enjoying their evening together.

"Mrs. Fisher," he said, putting an arm around his wife. "I am so grateful to God for bringing us together."

"Me too, Mr. Fisher. You have made me incredibly happy, and I love you."

Their lips came together in a gentle kiss, and after, when Miriam relaxed into her husband's embrace, a feeling of light and happiness flowed through her. Like threads of light, she felt the connection between herself, her husband, and the new life growing inside her.

THE END.

## THANK YOU FOR READING!

And thank you for supporting me as an independent author. I hope you enjoyed reading this as much as I loved writing it! If so, I hope you also enjoy the sample in the next chapter of my other work.

Lastly, if you enjoyed this book and want to continue to support my writing, please leave me a review to let everyone know what you thought of my work. It's the best thing you can do to keep indie authors like me writing. (And if you find something in the book that – YIKES – makes you think it deserves less than 5-stars, drop me a line at Rachel.stoltzfus@globagrafxpress.com, and I'll fix it if I can.)

All the best,

Rachel

# FALSE WORSHIP – BOOK 1

**When Beth Zook's *daed* starts courting a widow with a mysterious past, will Beth uncover this new family's secrets before she loses everything?**

Sixteen-year-old Beth Zook has already lost so much -- first her sister in a tragic accident and then her *mamm* a year later to cancer. As Beth and her *daed* Marcus struggle to rebuild their lives in the Amish community of Indianasburg, Marcus finds love awakening in his heart when a new family -- a widow and her two sons -- move into their quiet community. But things are not as they seem, and the more Beth learns about this new family, the more reason she has to fear. Will Beth uncover this new family's secrets before she loses everything? Find out in Rachel Stoltzfus' False Worship series.

# CHAPTER ONE

I'm running, my heart pounding in my chest, veins swollen with rushing blood. The faster I run, the faster it courses through me, threatening to rupture my arteries and leave me to a slow bleed-out, before I have the chance to escape.

I look back, but I can't see who (or what) is chasing me.

I turn just in time to avoid running face-first into the sturdy trunk of a northern red oak, and I twist my ankle on one of its upraised roots as I run past. I trip, hands reaching out to protect me as I fall into the thorny ground, a thick carpet of mulch and broken twigs, little rocks and littler bugs.

Feet and hands scrambling, I'm back up and running, after missing only a beat.

But I'm afraid it's enough to make all the difference; just a quick moment, a second or two, is all the margin my pursuer needs to gain the ground that separates us. I can imagine myself in the predator's sight: his feeble prey, bent forward and awkwardly pushing through this maze of fallen logs and low-lying branches, prickly shrubs and flittering birds, crying out in panic as I continue my futile flight.

I can feel the heartbeat of my pursuer as the distance between us closes. I can hear the feet pounding the earth behind me, almost as loud as my own strained breath, in the deepest crevices of my ears.

And I know, with the silent inner voice of doom, that I won't make it.

I almost want to stop running, to finally succumb to the cruelty of nature and the casualness of nurture. Nothing could have prepared me for this: only God, and He seems to have deserted me.

I start praying, my mind desperately launching pleas and promises.

Please, God, spare me from the hellfire I can't outrun, from the pain which I know is craving the taste of my soul in its putrid belly. Please, God, don't let me die.

No answer comes, no lightning bolt from On High, no great hand to reach down from the clouds and lift me to safety, high above the bramble and brush.

My nose fills with the stench of wood rot and mold, and my own sweat, dripping down the sides of my face, collecting in the nape of my neck, retreating down the crevice of my spine.

I keep running, even as the predator's panting gets louder behind me. I can almost feel the hot snarl of that churning hatred, frothing over with a desire to end my life, in a way most swift and terrible.

At least, I hope it will be swift.

Something grabs me from behind, but I slip free; fingers or

talons or claws, I can't be sure. But it doesn't matter, because with the second strike, I am captured and knocked to the ground, that murderous weight about to fall upon me from behind, and finish me off.

I bolt up with a start, looking around my quiet, dark bedroom. All is well. I am alone and unhurt, sheltered in the place of my childhood. *Just a dream,* I tell myself, heart pounding in my chest, skin clammy with sweat. *Thank God, it was just a dream.*

***

The quilt slowly takes shape beneath my sure and steady fingers. I've often wondered how many little stitches it takes to create one of these cozy and colorful quilts. *A hundred thousand?* I silently wonder once more. *A million?*

Does it matter?

It doesn't matter to the Englischers who buy them, souvenirs from their weekends among us, ornaments for their homes, gifts for their friends. They don't care how much work these quilts require, but they can certainly appreciate it.

We usually sew in quilting bees, and mine includes Greta and a few older ladies. But I don't always wait for them to collect in our quiet, somber home. There's work to be done, and it helps take my mind off of how quiet the house has become in these last few, terrible years.

When I'm focusing on the intricate diamonds and fine lines of the quilt, I don't have to think about *Mamm*: those awful months she spent in bed, getting weaker and smaller, until, finally, there was nothing left of her at all. When I'm dipping that sharp needle into the cotton, making sure the line is straight and the weaves are even, I'm distracted from thinking about Margaret, struck down by a carriage, just a year before *Mamm* took ill.

I knew then (and I always will be sure of this) that *Mamm* didn't die from cancer, but from a broken heart, over the death of my kid sister. I'm not a doctor, and I have to admit that even those *Englisch*er doctors may have been right about the tumors growing in her stomach, preventing her from eating. But the cancer was only God's way of answering *Mamm*'s own prayers for death. She didn't want to live after what happened to Margaret.

All prayers are heard, I remind myself, even the horrible ones.

I stop and pray that my *daed* won't turn himself over to the same sorrowful resolution. He's always been steady; a calm surface over a deep, still sea. But even the seas themselves can part, even the bowels of the Earth can rip apart and swallow us whole, especially if we ask God to make it so.

So I ask God to prevent it, to give his servant Marcus Zook (and his sole surviving daughter Beth) the strength to endure our losses, and enjoy our blessings. We still have each other,

I remind myself, and our friends here in Indianasburg, and Aunt Sarah in Clarion, just a few counties away.

Maybe it's time we brought Aunt Sarah here to live with us, it occurs to me. She can't be very happy since her own husband died, and that was years before our family tragedy turned its attention to our own household.

What did this family ever do to invite such heartache? I ask God, not for the first time. *Daed* is a good man, even-tempered, and reasonable. Doesn't he deserve to be happy? Won't you turn your loving light upon him, Lord? I don't care for myself; but for his happiness, I'd offer any sacrifice.

No answer, at least not in the form of a lightning bolt or a burning bush; just silence, thick and cold and heavy.

All prayers are heard, and they are answered.

But not all answers are what they appear to be…

## THANK YOU FOR READING!

And thank you for supporting me as an independent author. I hope you enjoyed reading this as much as I loved writing it!

If so, look for this book in eBook or Paperback format at your favorite online book distributors. Also, when a series is complete, we usually put out a discounted collection. If you'd rather read the entire series at once and save a few bucks doing it, we recommend looking for the collection.

Lastly, if you enjoyed this book and want to continue to support my writing, please leave me a review to let everyone know what you thought of my work. It's the best thing you can do to keep indie authors like me writing. (And if you find something in the book that – YIKES – makes you think it deserves less than 5-stars, drop me a line at Rachel.stoltzfus@globagrafxpress.com, and I'll fix it if I can.)

All the best,

Rachel

# ABOUT THE AUTHOR

Rachel was born and raised in Lancaster, Pennsylvania. Being a neighbor of the Mennonite community, she started writing Amish romance fiction as a way of looking at the Amish community. She wanted to present a fair and honest representation of a love that is both romantic and sweet. She hopes her readers enjoy her efforts.

Made in the USA
Middletown, DE
09 November 2019